THE SHAME OF MOTLEY

BEING THE MEMOIR OF CERTAIN TRANS-ACTIONS IN THE LIFE OF LAZZARO BIAN-COMONTE, OF BIANCOMONTE, SOMETIME FOOL OF THE COURT OF PESARO

BY

RAFAEL SABATINI

BOSTON AND NEW YORK

HOUGHTON MIFFLIN COMPANY

The Riverside Press Cambridge

The Riverside Press
CAMBRIDGE · MASSACHUSETTS
PRINTED IN THE U.S.A.

CONTENTS

PART I

FLOWER OF THE QUINCE

PART II

THE OGRE OF CESENA

THE SHAME OF MOTLEY

. .

PART I
FLOWER OF THE QUINCE

THE SHAME OF MOTLEY

.∙.

PART I
FLOWER OF THE QUINCE

CHAPTER I
THE CARDINAL OF VALENCIA

FOR three days I had been cooling my heels about the Vatican, vexed by suspense. It fretted me that I should have been so lightly dealt with after I had discharged the mission that had brought me all the way from Pesaro, and I wondered how long it might be ere His Most Illustrious Excellency the Cardinal of Valencia might see fit to offer me the honourable employment with which Madonna Lucrezia had promised me that he would reward the service I had rendered the House of Borgia by my journey.

Three days were sped, yet nought had happened to signify that things would shape the course by me so ardently desired; that the means would be afforded me of mending my miserable ways, and repairing the wreck my life had suffered on the shoals of Fate. True, I had been housed and fed, and the comforts of indolence had been mine; but, for the rest, I was still clothed in the livery of folly which I had worn on my arrival, and, wherever I might roam, there followed ever at my heels a crowd of underlings, seeking to have their tedium lightened by jests and capers, and

voting me — when their hopes proved barren — the
sorriest Fool that had ever worn the motley.

On that third day I speak of, my patience tried to
its last strand, I had beaten a lacquey with my hands,
and fled from the cursed gibes his fellows aimed at me,
out into the misty gardens and the chill January air,
whose sting I could, perhaps, the better disregard by
virtue of the heat of indignation that consumed me.
Was it ever to be so with me? Could nothing lift the
curse of folly from me, that I must ever be a Fool, and
worse, the sport of other fools?

It was there on one of the terraces crowning the
splendid heights above immortal Rome that Messer
Gianluca found me. He greeted me courteously; I
answered with a snarl, deeming him come to pursue
the plaguing from which I had fled.

'His Most Illustrious Excellency the Cardinal of
Valencia is asking for you, Messer Boccadoro,' he
announced. And so despairing had been my mood of
ever hearing such a summons that, for a moment, I
accounted it some fresh jest of theirs. But the gravity
of his fat countenance reassured me.

'Let us go, then,' I answered with alacrity, and so
confident was I that the interview to which he bade
me was the first step along the road to better fortune,
that I permitted myself a momentary return of the
Fool's estate from which I thought myself on the
point of being for ever freed.

'I shall use the interview to induce His Excellency
to submit a tenth beatitude to the approval of our
Holy Father: Blessed are the bearers of good tidings.
Come on, Messer the seneschal.'

I led the way, in my impatience forgetful of his great
paunch and little legs, so that he was sorely tried to

keep pace with me. Yet who would not have been in haste, urged by such a spur as had I? Here, then, was the end of my shameful travesty. To-morrow a soldier's harness should replace the motley of a jester; the name by which I should be known again to men would be that of Lazzaro Biancomonte, and no longer Boccadoro — the Fool of the Golden Mouth.

Thus much had Madonna Lucrezia's promises led me to expect, and it was with a soul full of joyous expectation that I entered the great man's closet.

He received me in a manner calculated to set me at my ease, and yet there was about him a something that overawed me. Cesare Borgia, Cardinal of Valencia, was then in his twenty-third year, for all that there hung about him the semblance of a greater age, just as his cardinalitial robes lent him the appearance of a height far above the middle stature that was his own. His face was pale and framed in a silky auburn beard; his nose was aquiline and strong; his eyes the keenest that I have ever seen; his forehead lofty and intelligent. He seemed pervaded by an air of feverish restlessness, something surpassing the *vivida vis animi*, something that marked him to discerning eyes for a man of incessant action of body and of mind.

'My sister tells me,' he said in greeting, 'that you are willing to take service under me, Messer Biancomonte.'

'Such was the hope that guided me to Rome, Most Excellent,' I answered him.

Surprise flashed into his eyes, and was gone as quickly as it had come. His thin lips parted in a smile, whose meaning was inscrutable.

'As some reward for the safe delivery of the letter you brought me from her?' he questioned mildly.

'Precisely, Illustrious,' I answered in all frankness.
His open hand smote the table of wood-mosaics at
which he sat.

'Praised be Heaven!' he cried. 'You seem to promise that I shall have in you a follower who deals in
truth.'

'Could Your Excellency, to whom my real name
is known, expect aught else of one who bears it —
however unworthily?'

There was amusement in his glance.

'Can you still swagger it, after having worn that
livery for three years?' he asked, and his lean forefinger pointed at my hideous motley of red and black
and yellow.

I flushed and hung my head, and — as if to mock
that very expression of my shame — the bells on my
cap gave forth a silvery tinkle at the movement.

'Excellency, spare me,' I murmured. 'Did you
know all my miserable story you would be merciful.
Did you know with what joy I turned my back on
the Court of Pesaro —'

'Aye,' he broke in mockingly, 'when Giovanni
Sforza threatened to have you hanged for the over-
boldness of your tongue. Not until then did it occur
to you to turn from the shameful life in which the
best years of your manhood were being wasted.
There! Just now I commended your truthfulness;
but the truth that dwells in you is no more, it seems,
than the truth we may look for in the mouth of Folly.
At heart, I fear, you are a hypocrite, Messer Biancomonte; the worst form of hypocrite — a hypocrite
to your own self.'

'Did Your Excellency know all!' I cried.

'I know enough,' he answered, with stern sorrow;

'enough to make me marvel that the son of Ettore Biancomonte of Biancomonte should play the Fool to Costanzo Sforza, Lord of Pesaro. Oh! you will tell me that you went there for revenge, to seek to right the wrong his father did your father.'

'It was, it was!' I cried, with heated vehemence. 'Be flames everlasting the dwelling of my soul if any other motive drove me to this shameful trade.'

There was a pause. His beautiful eyes flamed with a sudden light as they rested on me. Then the lids drooped demurely, and he drew a deep breath. But when he spoke there was scorn in his voice.

'And, no doubt, it was that same motive kept you there, at peace for three whole years, in slothful ease, the motleyed Fool, jesting and capering for his enemy's delectation — you, a man with the knightly memory of your foully wronged parent to cry hourly shame upon you. No doubt you lacked the opportunity to bring the tyrant to account. Or was it that you were content to let him make a mock of you so long as he housed and fed you and clothed you in your garish livery of shame?'

'Spare me, Excellency,' I cried again. 'Of your charity let my past be done with. When he drove me forth with threats of hanging, from which your gracious sister saved me, I turned my steps to Rome at her bidding to —'

'To find honourable employment at my hands,' he interrupted quietly. Then, suddenly rising, and speaking in a voice of thunder — 'And what, then, of your revenge?' he cried.

'It has been frustrated,' I answered lamely. 'Sufficient do I account the ruin that already I have wrought in my life by the pursuit of that phantom.

I was trained to arms, my lord. Let me discard for good these tawdry rags, and strap a soldier's harness to my back.'

'How came you to journey hither thus?' he asked, suddenly turning the subject.

'It was Madonna Lucrezia's wish. She held that my errand would be safer so, for a Fool may travel unmolested.'

He nodded that he understood, and paced the chamber with bowed head. For a spell there was silence, broken only by the soft fall of his slippered feet and the swish of his silken purple. At last he paused before me and looked up into my face — for I was a good head taller than he was. His fingers combed his auburn beard, and his beautiful eyes were full on mine.

'That was a wise precaution of my sister's,' he approved. 'I will take a lesson from her in the matter. I have employment for you, Messer Biancomonte.'

I bowed my head in token of my gratitude.

'You shall find me diligent and faithful, my lord,' I promised him.

'I know it,' he smiled, 'else should I not employ you.'

He turned from me, and stepped back to his table. He took up a package, fingered it a moment, then dropped it again, and shot me one of his quiet glances.

'That is my answer to Madonna Lucrezia's letter,' he said slowly, his voice as smooth as silk, 'and I desire that you shall carry it to Pesaro for me, and deliver it safely and secretly into her hands.'

I could do no more than stare at him. It seemed as if my mind were stricken numb.

'Well?' he asked at last; and in his voice there was now a suggestion of steel beneath the silk. 'Do you hesitate?'

'And if I do,' I answered, suddenly finding my voice, 'I do no more than might a bolder man. How can I, who am banned by punishment of death, contrive to penetrate again into the Court of Pesaro and reach the Lady Lucrezia?'

'That is a matter that I shall leave to the shrewd wit which all Italy says is the heritage of Boccadoro, the Prince of Fools. Does the task daunt you?' His glance and voice were alike harsh.

In very truth it did, and I told him so, but in the terms which the shrewd wit he said was mine dictated.

'I hesitate, my lord, indeed; but more because I fear the frustration of your own ends — whatever they may be — than because I dread to earn a broken neck by again adventuring into Pesaro. Would not some other messenger — unknown at the Court of Giovanni Sforza — be in better case to acquit himself of such a task?'

'Yes, if I had one I could trust,' he answered frankly. 'I will be open with you, Biancomonte. There are such grave matters at issue, there are such secrets confided to that paper, that I would not for a kingdom, not for our Holy Father's triple crown, that they should fall into alien hands.' He approached me again, and his slender hand, upon which the sacred amethyst was glowing, fell lightly on my shoulder. He lowered his voice. 'You are the man, the one man in Italy, whose interests are bound up with mine in this; therefore are you the one man to whom I can entrust that package.'

'I?' I gasped in amazement — as well I might, for what interests had Boccadoro the Fool in common with Cesare Borgia, Cardinal of Valencia?

'You,' he answered vehemently, 'you, Lazzaro Biancomonte of Biancomonte, whose father Costanzo of Pesaro stripped of his domains. The matters in those papers mean the ruin of the Lord of Pesaro. We are all but ripe to strike at him from Rome, but when we strike he shall be so disfigured by the blow that all Italy shall hold its sides to laugh at the sorry figure he will cut. I would not say so much to any other living man but you, and if I tell it you it is because I need your aid.'

'The lion and mouse,' I murmured.

'Why, yes, if you will.'

'And this man is the husband of your sister!' I exclaimed, almost involuntarily.

'Does that imply a doubt of what I have said?' he flashed, his head thrown back, his brows drawn suddenly together.

'No, no,' I hastened to assure him. He smiled softly.

'Madonna Lucrezia knows all — or nearly all. Of what else she may need to learn, that letter will inform her. It is the last thread, the last knot needed, before we can complete the net in which we are to hold that tyrant. Now, will you bear the letter?'

Would I bear it? Dear God! To achieve the end in view I would have spent my remaining days in motley, making sport for grooms and kitchen wenches. Some such answer did I make him, and he smiled his satisfaction.

'You shall journey as you are,' he bade me. 'I am guided by my sister, assured that the coat of a

Fool is stouter protection than the best hauberk ever tempered. When you have done your errand, come you back to me, and you shall have employment better suited to one who bears the name of Biancomonte.'

'You may depend upon me in this, my lord,' I promised gravely. 'I shall not fail you.'

'It is well,' said he; and those wondrous eyes of his rested again upon my face. 'How soon can you set out?'

'At once, my lord. Does not the by-word say that a fool makes little preparation for a journey?'

He nodded, and moved to a coffer, a beautiful piece of Venetian work in ultramarine and gold. From this he took a heavy bag.

'There,' said he, 'you will find the best of all travelling companions.' I thanked him, and set the bag on the crook of my left arm, and by its weight I knew how true he was to the notorious splendour of his race. 'And this,' said he, 'is a talisman that may serve to help you out of any evil plight, and open many a door that you may find locked.' And he handed me a signet ring on which was graven the steer that is the emblem of the House of Borgia.

He raised aloft the hand on which was glistening the sacred amethyst — two fingers crooked and two erect. Wondering what this should mean, I stared inquiry.

'Kneel,' he bade me. And realising what he would be about, I sank onto my knees, whilst he murmured the Apostolic benediction over my bowed head. The rushes of the floor were the only witnesses of the smile that crept to my lips at this sudden assumption of his churchly office by that most worldly prince.

CHAPTER II

THE LIVERIES OF SANTAFIOR

SUCH preparations as I had to make were soon complete. Although it was agreed that I was to travel in the motley, yet, in my lately born shame of that apparel, I decided that I would conceal it as best might be, revealing it only should the need arise. Moreover, it was incumbent that I should afford myself more protection against the inclement January night than that of my foliated cape, my crested cap, and silken hose. So, a black cloak, heavy and ample, a broad-brimmed hat, and a pair of riding-boots of untanned leather were my further equipment. In the lining of one of those boots I concealed the Lord Cesare's package; his money — some twenty ducats — I carried in a belt about my waist, and his ring I set boldly on my finger.

Few moments did it need me to make ready, yet fewer, it seems, would the Borgia impatience have had me employ; for scarce was I booted when someone knocked at my door. I opened, and there entered a very mountain of a man, whose corselet flashed back the yellow light of my tapers, as might have done a mirror, and whose harsh voice barked out to ask if I was ready.

I had had some former acquaintance with this fellow, having first met him during the previous year, on the occasion of the Court of Pesaro's sojourn at Rome. His name was Ramiro del' Orca, and throughout the Papal army it stood synonymous for masterfulness and grim brutality. He was, as I have said, an enormous man, of prodigious bodily strength, heavy, yet of good proportions. Of his face one gathered the impression of a blazing furnace. His cheeks and nose were of a vivid red, and still more fiery was the hair, now hidden 'neath his morion, and the beard that tapered to a dagger's point. His very eyes kept tune with the red harmony of his ferocious countenance, for the whites were ever bloodshot as a drunkard's — which, with no want of truth, men said he was.

'Come,' grunted that fiery, self-sufficient vassal, 'be stirring, Sir Fool. I have orders to see you to the gates. There is a horse ready saddled for you. It is the Lord Cardinal's parting gift. Resolve me now, which will be the greater ass — the one that rides, or the one that is ridden?'

'O monstrous riddle!' I exclaimed, as I took up my cloak and hat. 'Who am I that I should solve it?'

'It baffles you, Sir Fool?' quoth he.

'In very truth it does.' I ruefully wagged my head so that my bells set up a jangle. 'For the rider is a man and the ridden a horse. But,' I pursued, in that back-biting strain, which is the very essence of the jester's wit, 'were you to make a trio of us, including Messer Ramiro del' Orca, Captain in the army of His Holiness, no doubt would then afflict me. I should never hesitate which of the three to pronounce the ass.'

'What shall that mean?' he asked, with darkening brows.

'That its meaning proves obscure to you confirms the verdict I was hinting at,' I taunted him. 'For asses are notoriously of dull perceptions.' Then stepping forward briskly: 'Come, sir,' I sharply urged him, 'whilst we engage upon this pretty play of wit, His Excellency's business waits, which is an ill thing. Where is this horse you spoke of?'

He showed me his strong, white teeth in a very evil smile.

'Were it not for that same business —' he began.

'You would do fine things, I am assured,' I interrupted him.

'Would I not?' he snarled. 'By the Host! I should be wringing your pert neck, or laying bare your bones with a thong of bullock-hide, you ill-conditioned Fool!'

I looked at him with pleasant, smiling eyes.

'You confirm the opinion that is popularly held of you,' said I.

'What may that be?' quoth he, his eyes very evil.

'In Rome, I'm told, they call you hangman.'

He growled in his throat like an angered cur, and his hands were jerked to the level of his breast, the fingers bending talon-wise.

'Body of God!' he muttered fiercely, 'I'll teach one fool, at least —'

'Let us cease these pleasantries, I entreat you,' I laughed. 'Saints defend me! If your mood incline to raillery you'll find your match in some lad of the stables. As for me, I have not the time, had I the will, to engage you further. Let me remind you that I would be gone.'

The reminder was well-timed. He bethought him of the journey I must go, on which he was charged to see me safely started.

'Come on, then,' he growled, in a white heat of passion that was only curbed by the consideration of that slender, pale young cardinal, his master.

Still, some of his rage he vented in roughly taking
me by the collar of my doublet, and dragging me almost headlong from the room, and so adown a flight
of steps out into the courtyard. Meet treatment for
a Fool — a treatment to which time might have
enured me; for had I not for three years already been
exposed to rough usage of this kind at the hands of
every man above the rank of groom? And had I once
rebelled in act as I did in soul, and used the strength
wherewith God had endowed me to punish my ill-
users, a whip would have reminded me into what sorry
slavery had I sold myself when I put on the motley.

It had been snowing for the past hour, and the
ground was white in the courtyard when we descended.

At our appearance there was a movement of serv-
ing-men and a fall of hoofs, muffled by the snow.
Some held torches that cast a ruddy glare upon the
all-encompassing whiteness, and a groom was leading
forward the horse that was destined to bear me. I
donned my broad-brimmed hat, and wrapped my
cloak about me. Some murmurs of farewell caught
my ears, from those minions with whom I had herded
during my three days at the Vatican. Then Messer
del' Orca thrust me forward.

'Mount, Fool, and be off,' he rasped.

I mounted, and turned to him. He was a surly
dog, if ever surly dog wore human shape, and the shape
was the only human thing about Captain Ramiro.

'Brother, farewell,' I simpered.

'No brother of yours, Fool,' snarled he.

'True — my cousin only. The fool of art is no
brother to the fool of nature.'

'A whip!' he roared to his grooms. 'Fetch me a
whip.'

I left him calling for it, as I urged my nag across the snow and over the narrow drawbridge. Beyond, I stayed a moment to look over my shoulder. They stood gazing after me, a group of some half-dozen men, looking black against the whiteness of the ground. Behind them rose the brown walls of the rocca illumined by the flare of torches, from which the smell of rosin reached my nostrils as I paused. I waved my hat to them in token of farewell, and digging my spurless heels into the flanks of my horse, I ambled down, through the biting wind and drifting snow, into the town.

The streets were deserted and dark save for the ray that here fell from a window, and there stole through the chink of a door to glow upon the snow in earnest of the snug warmth within. Silence reigned, broken only by the moan of the wind under the eaves, for although it was no more than approaching the second hour of night, yet who but the wight whom necessity compelled would be abroad in such weather?

All night I rode despite that weather's foulness — a foulness that might have given pause to one whose haste to bear a letter was less attuned to his own supreme desires.

Betimes next morning I paused at a small *locanda* on the road to Magliano, and there I broke my fast and took some rest. My horse had suffered by the journey more than had I, and I would have taken a fresh one at Magliano, but there was none to be had — so they told me — this side of Narni, wherefore I was forced to set out once more upon that poor jaded beast that had carried me all night.

It was high noon when I came, at last, to Narni, the last league of the journey accomplished at a walk, for

my nag could go no faster. Here I paused to dine,
but here, again, they told me that no horses might be
had. And so, leading by the bridle the animal I dared
no longer ride, lest I should kill it outright, I entered
the territory of Urbino on foot, and trudged wearily
amain through the snow that was some inches deep
by now. In this miserable fashion I covered the
seven leagues, or so, to Spoleto, where I arrived ex-
hausted as night was falling.

There, at the Osteria del Sole, I supped and lay. I
found a company of gentlemen in the common-room,
who upon espying my motley — when I had thrown
off my sodden cloak and hat — pressed me, willy-
nilly, into amusing them. And so I spent the night at
my Fool's trade, giving them drolleries from the
works of Boccaccio and Sacchetti — the horn-books
of all jesters.

I obtained a fresh horse next morning, and I set
out betimes, intending to travel with a better speed.
The snow was thick and soft at first, but as I approached the hills it grew more crisp. Overhead the
sky was of an unbroken blue, and for all that the air
was sharp there was warmth in the sunshine. All day
I rode hard, and never rested until towards nightfall
I found myself on the spurs of the Apennines in the
neighbourhood of Gualdo, the better half of my journey well accomplished. The weather had changed
again at sunset. It was snowing anew, and the north
wind was howling like a choir of the damned.

Before me gleamed the lights of a little wayside
tavern, and since it might suit me better to lie there
than to journey on to Gualdo, I drew rein before that
humble door, and got down from my wearied horse.
Despite the early hour the door was already barred,

for the bedding of travellers formed no part of the traffic of so lowly a house as this nameless, wayside wine-shop. Theirs was a trade that ended with the daylight. Nevertheless I was assured they could be made to find me a rag of straw to lie on, and so I knocked boldly with my whip.

The taverner who opened for me, and stood a moment surveying me by the light of the torch he held aloft, was a slim, mild-mannered man, not over-clean. Behind him surged the figure of his wife; just such a woman as you might look to find the mate of such a man; broad and tall of frame and most scurvily cross-grained of face. It may well be that had he bidden me welcome, she had driven me back into the night; but since he made some demur when I asked for lodging, and protested that in his house was but accommodation too rude to offer my magnificence, the woman thrust him aside, and loudly bade me enter.

I obeyed her readily, hat on head and cloak about me, lest my interests should suffer were my trade disclosed. I bade the man see to my horse, and then, escorted by the woman, I made my way to the single room above, which, in obedience to my demand, she made haste to set at my convenience.

It was an evil-smelling, squalid hole; a bed of wattles in a corner, and in the centre a greasy table with a three-legged stool and a crazy chair beside it. The floor was black with age and filth, and broken everywhere by rat-holes.

She set her noisome, smoking oil lamp on the table, and with some apology for the rudeness of the chamber she asked in tones almost defiant if my excellency would be content.

'Perforce,' said I ungraciously, perceiving surliness to be the key to the respect of such a creature; 'a king might thank Heaven for a kennel on such a night as this.'

She bent her back in a clumsy bow, and with a growing humility wondered had I supped. I had not but sooner would I have starved than have been poisoned by such foulnesses as they might have set before me. So I answered her that all I needed was a cup of wine.

When she had brought me that, and at last I was alone, I closed the door. It had no lock, nor any sort of fastening, so I set the'three-legged stool against it that it might give me warning of intrusion. Next I threw off my cloak and hat and boots, and all dressed as I was I flung myself upon my miserable couch. But jaded though I might be, it was not yet my intent to sleep. Now that the half of my journey was accomplished, I found myself beset by doubts, which had not assailed me before, touching the manner in which this mission of mine was to be accomplished. It would prove no easy thing for me to penetrate unnoticed into the town of Pesaro, much less into the Sforza Court, where for three years I had pursued my Fool's trade. There was scarce a man, a woman, or a child in the entire domains of Giovanni Sforza to whom Boccadoro the Fool was not known; and many a *villano*, who had never noticed the features of the Lord of Pesaro, could have told you the very colour of his jester's eyes; which, after all, is no strange thing, for — sad reflection! — in a world in which Wisdom may be overlooked, Folly goes never disregarded.

The garments I wore might be well enough to

journey in; but if I would gain the presence of Lucrezia Borgia I must see that I arrived in others. And then my thoughts wandered into speculation. What might be this momentous letter that I carried? What was this secret traffic 'twixt Cesare Borgia and his sister? Since Cesare had said that it meant the ruin of Giovanni Sforza — a ruin so utter, so complete and humiliating that it must provoke the scornful mirth of all Italy — the knowledge of it must soon be mine. Meanwhile I was an agent of that ruin. Dear God! how that reflection warmed me! What joy I took in the thought that, though he knew it not, nor could come to know it, I — Lazzaro Biancomonte, whom he had abused and whose spirit he had broken — was become a tool to expedite the work of abasement and destruction that was ripening for him. And realising all this, that letter I vowed to Heaven I would carry, suffering no obstacle to daunt me, suffering nothing to turn me from my path.

And then another voice seemed to arise within me, to cry out impatiently: 'Yes, yes; but how?'

I rose, and, approaching the table, I took up the jug of wine and poured myself a draught. I drank it off, and cast the dregs at an inquisitive rat that had thrust its head above the boards. Then I quenched the light, and flung myself once more upon my bed, in the hope that darkness would prove a stimulant to thought and bring me to the solution I was seeking. It brought me sleep instead. Unconsciously I sank to it, my riddle all unsolved.

I did not wake until the pale sun of that January morning was drawing the pattern of my lattice on the ceiling. The stormy night had been succeeded by a calm and sunlit day. And by its light the place wore a more loathsome look than it had done last night, so that at the very sight of it I leapt from my couch and grew eager to be gone. I set a ducat on the table, and going to the door I called my hostess. The stairs creaked presently 'neath her portentous weight, and, panting slightly, she stood before me.

At sight of me, for I was without my cloak, and my motley was revealed in the cold morning light, she cried out — in amazement first, and then in rage — deeming me one of those parasites who tramp the world in the garb of folly, seeking here a dinner, there a bed, in exchange for some scurvy tumbling or some witless jests.

'Ossa di Cristo!' was her cry. 'Have I housed a Fool?'

'If I am the first you have housed, your tumbling ruin of a tavern has been a singularly choice resort. Woman —'

'Would you "woman" me?' she stormed.

'Why, no,' said I politely. 'I was at fault. I'll keep the title for your husband — God help him!'

She smiled grimly.

'And are these,' she asked, with a ferocious sarcasm, 'the jests with which you pay the score?'

'Jests?' quoth I. 'Score? Pish! More eyes, less tongue would more befit a hostess who has never housed a fool.' And with a splendid gesture I pointed to the ducat gleaming on the table. At sight of the gold her eyes grew big with greed.

'My master —' she began, and coming forward took the piece in her hand, to assure herself that she was not the dupe of magic. 'A fool with gold!' she marvelled.

'Is a shame to his calling,' I acknowledged. Then

— 'Get me a needle and a length of thread,' said I. She scuttled off to do my bidding, like nothing so much as one of the rats that tenanted her unclean sty. She was back in a moment, all servility, and wondering whether there was a rent about me she might make bold to stitch. What a key to courtesy is gold, my masters! I drove her out, and, eager to conciliate me, she went at once.

With my own hands I effected in my doublet the slight repair of which it stood in need. Then I donned my hat, and, cloak on shoulder, made my way below, calling for my horse as I descended.

I scorned the wine they proffered me ere I departed. That last night's draught had quenched my thirst for ever of such grape-juice as it was theirs to tender. I urged the taverner to hasten with my horse, and stood waiting in the squalid common-room, my mind divided 'twixt impatience to resume the road to Pesaro and fresh speculations upon the means I was to adopt to enter it and yet save my neck — for this was now become an obsessing problem.

As I stood waiting, there broke upon my ears the sound of an approaching cavalcade: the noise of voices and the soft fall of hoofs upon the thick snow carpet. The company halted at the door, and a loud, gruff voice was raised to cry:

'Locandiere! Afoot, sluggard!'

I stepped to the door, with very natural curiosity, to behold a company of four mounted men escorting a mule-litter, the curtains of which were drawn so that nothing might be seen of him or her that rode within. Grooms were those four, as all the world might see at the first glance, and the livery they wore was that of

the noble House of Santafior — the holy white flower
of the quince being embroidered on the breast of their
gabardines.

They bore upon them such signs of hard and hasty
travelling that it was soon guessed they had spent the
night in the saddle. Their horses were in a foam of
sweat, and the men themselves were splashed with
mud from foot to cap.

Even as I was going forward to regard them the
taverner appeared, leading my horse by the bridle.
Now at an inn the traveller that arrives is ever of
more importance than he that departs. At sight of
those horsemen, the taverner forgot my impatience,
for he paused to bow in welcome to the one that
seemed the leader.

'Most Magnificent,' said he to that liveried hind,
'command me.'

'We need a guide,' the fellow answered with an ill
grace.

'A guide, Illustrious?' quoth the host. 'A guide?'

'I said a guide, fool,' answered him the groom.
'Heard you never of such animals? We need a man
who knows the hills, to lead us by the shortest road to
Cagli.'

The taverner shook his grey head stupidly. He
bowed again until I fancied I could hear the creak of
his old joints.

'Here be no guides, Magnificent,' he deplored.
'Perhaps at Gualdo —'

'Animal,' was the retort — for true courtesy commend me to a lacquey! — 'it is not our wish to pursue
the road as far as Gualdo, else had we not stopped at
this kennel of yours.'

I scarce know what it can have been that moved me

to act as I then did, for, in the truth, the manner of that rascal of a groom was little prepossessing, and his master, I doubted, could be little better that he left the fellow to hector it thus over that wretched tavern oaf. But I stepped forward.

'Did you say that you were journeying to Cagli?' questioned I.

He eyed me sourly, suspicion writ athwart his round, ill-favored face. But my motley was hidden from his sight. My cloak, my hat and boots allowed naught of my true condition to appear, and might as well have covered a lordling as a jester. Yet his inveterate surliness the rascal could not wholly conquer.

'What may be the purpose of your question?' he growled.

'To serve your master, whoever he may be,' I answered him serenely, 'although it is a service I do not press upon him. I, too, am journeying to Cagli, and, like yourselves, I am in haste and go the shorter way across the hills, with which I am well acquainted. If it so please you to follow me your need of a guide may be thus satisfied.'

It was the tone to take if I would be respected. Had I proposed that we should journey in company I should not have earned me half of the deference which was accorded to my haughtily granted leave that they might follow me if they so chose.

With marked submission did he give me thanks in his master's name.

I mounted and set out, and at my heels came now the litter and its escort. Thus did we quit the plain and breast the slopes, where the snow grew deeper and firmer underfoot as we advanced. And as I went, still plaguing my mind to devise a means by which I might penetrate to the Court of Pesaro, little did I dream that the matter was being solved for me — the solution having begun with my offer to guide that company across the hills.

CHAPTER III

MADONNA PAOLA

WE gained the heights in the forenoon, and there we dismounted and paused awhile to breathe our horses ere we took the path that was to lead us down to Cagli. The air was sharp and cold, for all that overhead was spread a cloudless, cobalt dome of sky, and the sun poured down its light upon the wide expanse of snow-clad earth, of a whiteness so dazzling as to be hurtful to the sight.

Hitherto I had ridden stolidly ahead, as unheeding of that following company as if I had been unconscious of its existence. But now that we paused, their fat, white-faced leader, whose name was Giacopo, approached me and sought to draw me into conversation. I yielded readily enough, for I scented a mystery about that closely curtained litter, and mysteries are ever provoking to such a mind as mine. For all that it might profit me naught to learn who rode there, and why with all this haste, yet these were matters, I confess, on which my curiosity was aroused.

'Are you journeying beyond Cagli?' I asked him presently, in an idle tone.

He cocked his head, and eyed me aslant, the suspicion in his eyes confirming the existence of the mystery I scented.

'Yes,' he answered, after a pause. 'We hope to reach Urbino before night. And you? Are you journeying far?'

'That far, at least,' I answered him, emulating the caution he had shown.

And then, ere more might pass between us, the leather curtains of the litter were sharply drawn aside. At the sound I turned my head, and so far was the vision different from that which — for no reason that I can give — I had expected, that I was stricken with surprise and wonder. A lady — a very child, indeed — had leapt nimbly to the ground ere any of those grooms could offer her assistance.

She was, I thought, the most beautiful woman that I had ever seen, and to one who had read the famous work of Messer Firenzuola on feminine beauty it might seem, at first, that here stood the incarnation of that writer's catalogue of womanly perfections. She was of a good shape and stature, despite her tender years; her face was oval, delicately featured and of an ivory pallor. Her eyes — blue as the heavens overhead — were not of the colour most approved by Firenzuola, nor was her hair of the golden brown which that arbiter commends. Had Firenzuola seen her, it may well be that he had altered or modified his views. She was sumptuously arrayed in a loose-sleeved *camorra* of grey velvet that was heavy with costly furs; above the *lenza* of fine linen on her head gleamed the gold thread of a jewelled net, and at her waist a girdle of surpassing richness, all set with gems, glowed like a thing of fire in the bright sunshine.

She took a deep breath of the sharp, invigorating air, then looked about her, and espying me in conversation with Giacopo she approached us across the gleaming snow.

'Is this,' she inquired, and her sweet, melodious

voice was a perfect match to the graceful charm of her whole presence, 'the traveller who so kindly consented to fill for us the office of a guide?'

Giacopo answered briefly that I was that man.

'I am in your debt, sir,' she protested, with an odd earnestness. 'You do not know how great a service you have rendered me. But if at any time Paola Sforza di Santafior may be able to discharge this obligation, you shall find me very willing.'

White-faced, black-browed Giacopo scowled at this proclamation of her identity.

I made her a low bow, and answered coldly, almost brusquely, for I hated the very name of Sforza, and every living thing that bore it.

'Madonna, you overrate my service. It so chanced that I was travelling this way.'

She looked more closely at me, as if she would have sought the reason of my churlish tone, and I was strangely thankful that she could not see the motley worn by the muffled stranger who confronted her. No doubt she accounted me a clown, whose nature inclined to surliness, and so she turned away, telling Giacopo that as soon as the horses were breathed they might push on.

'We must rest them yet awhile, Madonna,' answered he, 'if they are to carry us as far as Cagli. Heaven send that we may obtain fresh cattle there, else is all lost.'

Her frown proclaimed how much his words displeased her.

'You forget that if there are no horses for us, neither are there any for those others.' And she waved her hand towards the valley below and the road by which we had come. From this and from what was

said I gathered that they were a party of fugitives
with pursuers at their heels.

'They have a warrant which we have not,' was
Giacopo's answer, gloomily delivered, 'and they will
seize cattle where they can find them.'

With a little gesture of impatience, more at his
fears than at the peril that aroused them, she moved
away towards her litter.

'Your horse would be better for the loan of your
cloak, sir stranger,' said Giacopo to me.

I knew him to be right, but I shrugged my shoulders.

'Better the horse should die of cold than I,' I
answered gruffly, and turning from him I set myself
to pace the snow and stir the blood that was chilling
in my veins.

There was a beauty in the white, sunlit landscape
spread before me that compelled my glance. To some
it might compare but ill with the luxuriant splendour that is of the vernal season; but to me there was
a wondrously impressive charm about that solemn,
silent, virginal expanse of snow, expressionless as
the Sphinx, and imposing and majestic by virtue of
that very lack of expression. From Fabriano at our
feet was spread to the east the broad plain that lies
twixt the Esino and the Masone as far as Mount
Comero, which, in the distance, lifted its round shoulder from the haze of sea. To the west the country
lay under the same winding-sheet of snow as far
as eye might range, to the towers of distant Perugia, to the Lake Trasimeno — a silver sheen that
broke the white monotony — to Etruscan Cortona,
perched like an eyrie on its mountain-top, and to the
line of Tuscan hills, like heavy, low-lying clouds upon
the blue horizon.

Lost was I in the contemplation of that scene when a cry, succeeded by a volley of horrid blasphemy, drew my attention of a sudden to my companions. They stood grouped together, and their eyes were on the road by which we had scaled those heights. Their first expression of loud astonishment had been succeeded by an utter silence. I stepped forward to command a better view of what they contemplated, and in the plain below, midway between Narni and the slopes, a mile or so behind us, I caught a glitter as of a hundred mirrors in the sunshine. A company of some dozen men-at-arms it was, riding briskly along the tracks we had left behind us in the snow. Could these be the pursuers?

Even as I formed the question in my mind, the lady's silvery voice, behind me, put it into words. She had drawn aside the curtains of her litter and she was leaning out, her eyes upon those dancing points of brilliance.

'Madonna,' cried one of her grooms, in a quaver of alarm, 'they are Borgia soldiers.'

'Your fear is father to that opinion,' she answered scornfully. 'How can you descry it at this distance?'

Now, either God had given that knave an eagle's sight, or else, as she suggested, fear spurred his imagination and begot his certainty of what he thought he saw.

'The leader's bannerol bears the device of a red bull,' he answered promptly.

I thought she paled a little, and her brows contracted.

'In God's name, let us get forward, then!' cried Giacopo. 'Orsù! To horse, knaves!'

No second bidding did they need. In the twinkling

of an eye they were in the saddle, and one of them had
caught the bridle of the leading mule of the litter.
Giacopo called to me to lead the way with him, with
no more ceremony than if I had been one of themselves. But I made no ado. A chase is an interesting
business, whatever your point of view, and if a
greater safety lies with the hunter, there is a keener
excitement with the hunted.

Down that steep and slippery hillside we blundered,
making for Cagli at a pace in which there lay a
myriad-fold more danger than could menace us from
any party of pursuers. But fear was spur and whip
to the unreasoning minds of those poltroons, and so
from the danger behind us we fled, and courted a more
deadly and certain peril in the fleeing. At first I
sought to remonstrate with Giacopo; but he was deaf
to the wisdom that I spoke. He turned upon me a
face which terror had rendered whiter than its natural
habit, white as the egg of a duck, with a hint of blue
or green behind it. I had, besides, an ugly impression
of teeth and eyeballs.

'Death is behind us, sir,' he snarled. 'Let us get
on.'

'Death is more assuredly before you,' I answered
grimly. 'If you will court it, go your way. As for
me, I am over-young to break my neck and be left on
the mountain-side to fatten crows. I shall follow at
my leisure.'

'Gesù!' he cried, through chattering teeth. 'Are
you a coward, then?'

The taunt would have angered me had his condition been other than it was; but coming from one so
possessed of the devil of terror, it did no more than
provoke my mirth.

'Come on, then, valiant runagate,' I laughed at him.

And on we went, our horses now plunging, now sliding down yard upon yard of moving snow, snorting and trembling, more reasoning far than these rational animals that bestrode them. Twice did it chance that a man was flung from his saddle, yet I know not what prayers Madonna may have been uttering in her litter, to obtain for us the miracle of reaching the plain with never so much as a broken bone.

Thus far had we come, but no farther, it seemed, was it possible to go. The horses, which by dint of slipping and sliding had encompassed the descent at a good pace, were so winded that we could get no more than an amble out of them, saving mine, which was tolerably fresh.

At this a new terror assailed the timorous Giacopo. His head was ever turned to look behind — unfailing index of a frightened spirit; his eyes were ever on the crest of the hills, expecting at every moment to behold the flash of the pursuers' steel. The end soon followed. He drew rein and called a halt, sullenly sitting his horse like a man deprived of wit — which is to pay him the compliment of supposing that he ever had wit to be deprived of.

Instantly the curtain-rings rasped, and Madonna Paola's head appeared, her voice inquiring the reason of this fresh delay.

Sullenly Giacopo moved his horse nearer, and sullenly he answered her.

'Madonna, our horses are done. It is useless to go farther.'

'Useless?' she cried, and I had an instance of how

sharply could ring the voice that I had heard so
gentle. 'Of what do you talk, you knave? Ride on
at once.'

'It is vain to ride on,' he answered obdurately, insolence rising in his voice. 'Another half-league —
another league at most, and we are taken.'

'Cagli is less than a league distant,' she reminded
him. 'Once there, we can obtain fresh horses. You
will not fail me now, Giacopo!'

'There will be delays, perforce, at Cagli,' he reminded her, 'and, meanwhile, there are these to
guide the Borgia *sbirri.*' And he pointed to the
tracks we were leaving in the snow.

She turned from him, and addressed herself to the
other three.

'You will stand by me, my friends,' she cried.
'Giacopo, here, is a coward; but you are better men.'

They stirred, and one of them was momentarily
moved into a faint semblance of valour.

'We will go with you, Madonna,' he exclaimed.
'Let Giacopo remain behind, if so he will.'

But Giacopo was a very ill-conditioned rogue;
neither true himself, nor tolerant, it seemed, of truth
in others.

'You will be hanged for your pains when you are
caught!' he exclaimed, 'as caught you will be, and
within the hour. If you would save your necks, stay
here and make surrender.'

His speech was not without effect upon them, beholding which Madonna leapt from the litter, the
better to confront them. The corners of her sensitive
little mouth were quivering now with the emotion
that possessed her, and on her eyes there was a film
of tears.

'You cowards!' she blazed at them, 'you hinds, that lack the spirit even to run! Were I asking you to stand and fight in defence of me, you could not show yourselves more palsied. I was a fool,' she sobbed, stamping her foot so that the snow squelched under it. 'I was a fool to entrust myself to you.'

'Madonna,' answered one of them, 'if flight could still avail us, you should not find us stubborn. But it were useless. I tell you again, Madonna, that when I spied them from the hilltop yonder, they were but a half-league behind. Soon we shall have them over the mountain, and we shall be seen.'

'Fool!' she cried, 'a half-league behind, you say; and you forget that we were on the summit, and they had yet to scale it. If you but press on we shall treble that distance, at least, ere they begin the descent. Besides, Giacopo,' she added, turning again to the leader, 'you may be at fault; you may be scared by a shadow; you may be wrong in accounting them our pursuers.'

The man shrugged his shoulders, shook his head and grunted.

'Arnaldo, there, made no mistake. He told us what he saw.'

'Now Heaven help a poor, deserted maid, who set her trust in curs!' she exclaimed, between grief and anger.

I had been no better than those hinds of hers had I remained unmoved. I have said that I hated the very name of Sforza; but what had this tender child to do with my wrongs that she should be brought within the compass of that hatred? I had inferred that her pursuers were of the House of Borgia, and in a flash it came to me that were I so inclined I might prove,

by virtue of the ring I carried, the one man in Italy
to serve her in this extremity. And to be of service to
her, her winsome beauty had already inflamed me.
For there was I know not what about this child that
seemed to take me in its toils, and so wrought upon
me that there and then I would have risked my life in
her good service. Oh, you may laugh who read.
Indeed, deep down in my heart I laughed myself, I
think, at the heroics to which I was yielding — I,
the Fool, most base of lacqueys — over a damsel of
the noble House of Santafior. It was shame of my
motley, maybe, that caused me to draw my cloak
more tightly about me as I urged forward my horse,
until I had come into their midst.

'Lady,' said I bluntly and without preamble, 'can
I assist you? I have inferred your case from what I
have overheard.'

All eyes were on me, gaping with surprise — hers
no less than her grooms'.

'What can you do alone, sir?' she asked, her gentle
glance upraised to mine.

'If, as I gather, your pursuers are servants of the
House of Borgia, I may do something.'

'They are,' she answered, without hesitation, some
eagerness, even, investing her tones.

It may seem an odd thing that this lady should so
readily have taken a stranger into her confidence.
Yet reflect upon the parlous condition in which she
found herself. Deserted by her dispirited grooms, her
enemies hot upon her heels, she was in no case to
trifle with assistance, or to despise an offer of services,
however frail it might seem. With both hands she
clutched at the slender hope I brought her in the hour
of her despair.

'Sir,' she cried, 'if indeed it lies in your power to help me, you could not find it in your heart to be sparing of that power did you but know the details of my sorry circumstance.'

'That power, Madonna, it may be that I have,' said I, and at those words of mine her servants seemed to honour me with a greater interest. They leaned forward on their horses and eyed me with eyes grown of a sudden hopeful. 'And,' I continued, 'if you will have utter faith in me, I see a way to render doubly certain your escape.'

She looked up into my face, and what she saw there may have reassured her that I promised no more than I could accomplish. For the rest she had to choose between trusting me and suffering capture.

'Sir,' she said, 'I do not know you, nor why you should interest yourself in the concerns of a desolated woman. But, Heaven knows, I am in no case to stand pondering the aid you offer, nor, indeed, do I doubt the good faith that moves you. Let me hear, sir, how you would propose to serve me.'

'Whence are you?' I inquired.

'From Rome,' she informed me without hesitation, 'to seek at my cousin's Court of Pesaro shelter from a persecution to which the Borgia family is submitting me.'

At her cousin's Court of Pesaro! An odd coincidence, this — and while I was pondering it, it flashed into my mind that by helping her I might assist myself. Had aught been needed to strengthen my purpose to serve her, I had it now.

'Yet,' said I, surprise investing my voice, 'at Pesaro there is Madonna Lucrezia of that same House of Borgia.'

She smiled away the doubt my words implied.

'Madonna Lucrezia is my friend,' she said; 'as sweet and gentle a friend as ever woman had, and she will stand by me even against her own family.'

Since she was satisfied of that, I waived the point, and returned to what was of more immediate interest.

'And you fled,' said I, 'with these?' And I indicated her attendants. 'Not content to leave the clearest of tracks behind you in the snow, you have had yourself attended by four grooms in the livery of Santafior. So that by asking a few questions any that were so inclined might follow you with ease.'

She opened wide her eyes at that. Oftentimes have I observed that it needs a fool to teach some elementary wisdom to the wise ones of this world. I leapt from my saddle and stood in the road beside her, the bridle on my arm.

'Listen now, Madonna. If you would make good your escape it first imports that you should rid yourself of this valiant escort. Separate from it for a little while. Take you my horse — it is a very gentle beast, and it will carry you with safety — and ride on, alone, to Cagli.'

'Alone?' quoth she, in some surprise.

'Why, yes,' I answered gruffly. 'What of that? At the Inn of The Full Moon ask for the hostess, and tell her that you are to await an escort there, begging her, meanwhile, to place you under her protection. She is a worthy soul, or else I do not know one, and she will befriend you readily. But see to it that you tell her nothing of your affairs.'

'And then?' she inquired eagerly.

'Then, wait you there until to-night, or even until

to-morrow morning, for these knaves to rejoin you to the end that you may resume your journey.'

'But we —' began Giacopo.

Scenting his protest, I cut him short.

'You four,' said I, 'shall escort me — for I shall replace Madonna in the litter — you shall escort me towards Fabriano. Thus shall we draw the pursuit upon ourselves, and assure your lady a clear road of escape.'

They swore most roundly and with great circumstance of oaths that they would lend themselves to no such madness, and it took me some moments to persuade them that I was possessed of a talisman that should keep us all from harm.

'Were it otherwise, dolts, do you think I should be eager to go with you? Would any chance wayfarer so wantonly imperil his neck for the sake of a lady with whom he can scarce be called acquainted?'

It was an argument that had weight with them, as indeed, it must have had with the dullest. I flashed my ring before their eyes.

'This escutcheon,' said I, 'is the shield that shall stand between us and danger from any of the house that bears these arms.'

Thus I convinced and wrought upon them until they were ready to obey me — the more ready since any alternative was really to be preferred to their present situation. In danger they already stood from those that followed as they well knew; and now it seemed to them that by obeying one who was armed with such credentials, it might be theirs to escape that danger. But even as I was convincing them, by the same arguments was I sowing doubts in the lady's subtler mind.

'You are attached to that house?' quoth she, in
accents of mistrust. She wanted to say more. I saw
it in her eyes that she was wondering was there
treachery underlying an action so singularly disinterested as to justify suspicion.

'Madonna,' said I, 'if you would save yourself I
implore that you will trust me. Very soon your pursuers will be appearing on those heights, and then
your chance of flight will be lost to you. I will ask you
but this: Did I propose to betray you into their hands,
could I have done better than to have left you with
your grooms?'

Her face lighted. A sunny smile broke on me from
her heavenly eyes.

'I should have thought of that,' said she. And
what more she would have added I put off by urging
her to mount.

Sitting the man's saddle as best she might — well
enough, indeed, to fill us all with surprise and admiration — she took her leave of me with pretty words of
thanks, which again I interrupted.

'You have but to follow the road,' said I, 'and it
will bring you straight to Cagli. The distance is a
short league, and you should come there safely.
Farewell, Madonna!'

'May I not know,' she asked at parting, 'the name
of him that has so generously befriended me?'

I hesitated a second. Then —

'They call me Boccadoro,' answered I.

'If your mouth be as truly golden as your heart,
then are you well named,' said she. Then, gathering
her mantle about her, and waving me farewell, she
rode off without so much as a glance at the cowardly
hinds who had failed her in the hour of her need.

A moment I stood watching her as she cantered away in the sunshine; then stepping to the litter, I vaulted in.

'Now, rogues,' said I to the escort, 'strike me that road to Fabriano.'

'I know you not, sir,' protested Giacopo. 'But this I know — that if you intend us treachery you shall have my knife in your gullet for your pains.'

'Fool!' I scorned him, 'since when has it been worth the while of any man to betray such creatures as are you? Plague me no more! Be moving, else I leave you to your coward's fate.'

It was the tone best understood by hinds of their lily-livered quality. It quelled their faint spark of mutiny, and a moment later one of those knaves had caught the bridle of the leading mule and the litter moved forward, whilst Giacopo and the others came on behind at as brisk a pace as their weary horses would yield. In this guise we took the road south, in the direction opposite to that travelled by the lady. As we rode, I summoned Giacopo to my side.

'Take your daggers,' I bade him, 'and rip me that blazon from your coats. See that you leave no sign about you to proclaim you of the House of Santafior, or all is lost. It is a precaution you would have taken earlier if God had given you the wit of a grasshopper.'

He nodded that he understood my order, and scowled his disapproval of my comment on his wit. For the rest, they did my bidding there and then.

Having satisfied myself that no betraying sign remained about them, I drew the curtains of my litter, and reclining there I gave myself up to pondering the manner in which I should greet the Borgia *sbirri* when they overtook me. From that I passed on to the con-

templation of the position in which I found myself,
and the thing that I had done. And the proportions
of the jest that I was perpetrating afforded me no
little amusement. It was a *burla* not unworthy the
peerless gifts of Boccadoro, and a fitting one on which
to close his wild career of folly. For had I not vowed
that Boccadoro I would be no more once the errand
on which I travelled was accomplished? By Cesare
Borgia's grace I looked to —

A sudden jolt brought me back to the immediate
present, and the realisation that in the last few moments we had increased our pace. I put out my head.

'Giacopo!' I shouted. He was at my side in an
instant. 'Why are we galloping?'

'They are behind,' he answered, and fear was again
overspreading his fat face. 'We caught a glimpse of
them as we mounted the last hill.'

'You caught a glimpse of whom?' quoth I.

'Why, of the Borgia soldiers.'

'Animal,' I answered him, 'what have we to do
with them? They may have mistaken us for some
party of which they are in pursuit. But since we
are not that party, let your jaded beasts travel at a
more reasonable speed. We do not wish to have the
air of fugitives.'

He understood me, and I was obeyed. For a half-
hour we rode at a more gentle pace. That was about
the time they took to come up with us, still a league or
so from Fabriano. We heard their cantering hoofs
crushing the snow, and then a loud, imperious voice
shouting to us a command to stay. Instantly we
brought up in unconcerned obedience, and they
thundered alongside with cries of triumph at having
run their prey to earth.

I cast aside my hat, and thrust my motleyed head through the curtains with a jangle of bells, to inquire into the reason of this halt. Whom my appearance astounded the more — whether the lacqueys of Santafior or the Borgia men-at-arms that now encircled us — I cannot guess. But in the crowd of faces that confronted me there was not one but wore a look of deep amazement.

CHAPTER IV

THE COZENING OF RAMIRO

THE cavalcade that had overtaken us proved to number some twenty men-at-arms, whose leader was no less a person than Ramiro del' Orca — that same mountain of a man who had attended my departure from the Vatican three nights ago. From the circumstance that so important a personage should have been charged with the pursuit of the Lady of Santafior, I inferred that great issues were at stake.

He was clad in mail and leather, and from his lance fluttered the bannerol bearing the Borgia arms, which had announced his quality to Madonna's servants.

At sight of me his bloodshot eyes grew round with wonder, and for a little season a deathly calm preceded the thunder of his voice.

'Sainted Host!' he roared at last. 'What trickery may this be?' And sidling his horse nearer he tore aside the curtains of my litter.

Out of faces pale as death the craven grooms looked on, to behold me reclining there, my cloak flung down across my legs to hide my boots, and my motley garb of red and black and yellow all revealed. I believe their astonishment by far surpassed the Captain's own.

'You are choicely met, Ser Ramiro,' I greeted him. Then, seeing that he only stared, and made no shift to speak: 'Maybe,' quoth I, 'you'll explain why you detain me. I am in haste.'

'Explain?' he thundered. 'Sangue di Cristo! The burden of explaining lies with you. What make you here?'

'Why,' answered I, in tones of deep astonishment, 'I am about the business of the Lord Cardinal of Valencia, our master.'

'Davvero?' he jeered. He stretched out a mighty paw, and took me by the collar of my doublet. 'Now, bethink you how you answer me, or there will be a fool the less in the world.'

'Indeed, the world might spare more.'

He scowled at my pleasantry. To him, apparently, the situation afforded no scope for philosophical reflections.

'Where is the girl?' he asked abruptly.

'Girl?' quoth I. 'What girl? Am I a mother-abbess, that you should set me such a question?'

Two dark lines showed between his brows. His voice quivered with passion.

'I ask you again! — where is the girl?'

I laughed like one who is a little wearied by the entertainment provided for him.

'Here be no girls, Messer del' Orca,' I answered him in the same tone. 'Nor can I think what this babble of girls portends.'

My seeming innocence, and the assurance with which I maintained the expression of it, whispered a doubt into his mind. He released me, and turned upon his men, a baffled look in his eyes.

'Was not this the party?' he inquired ferociously. 'Have you misled me, beasts?'

'It seemed the party, Illustrious,' answered one of them.

'Do you dare tell me that "it seemed"?' he roared,

seeking to father upon them the blunder he was
beginning to fear that he had made. 'But — What is
the livery of these knaves?'

'They wear none,' someone answered him, and at
that answer he seemed to turn limp and lose his fierce
assurance.

Then he bridled afresh.

'Yet the party, I'll swear, is this!' he insisted;
and turning once more to me: 'Explain, animal!'
he bade me in terrifying tones. 'Explain, or, by the
Host! be you ignorant or not, I'll have you hanged.'

I accounted it high time to take another tone with
him. Hanging was a discomfort I was never less
minded to suffer.

'Draw nearer, fool,' said I contemptuously, and
at the epithet, so greatly did my audacity amaze him,
he mildly did my bidding.

'I know not what doubts are battling in your thick
head, Sir Captain,' I pursued. 'But this I know —
that if you persist in hindering me, or commit the
egregious folly of offering me violence, you will
answer for it, hereafter, to the Lord Cardinal of
Valencia.

'I am going upon a secret mission' — and here I
sank my voice to a whisper for his ears alone — 'in
the service of the house that hires you, as for yourself
you might easily have inferred. Behold.' And I
revealed my ring. 'Detain me longer at your peril.'

He must have had some notion of the fact that I
was journeying in Cesare Borgia's service, and this
coupled with the sight of that talisman effected in his
manner a swift and wholesome change. Had I,
arrayed in the panoply of Mother Church, defied the
Devil, my victory could not have been more complete.

He looked about him like a man whose wits have been scattered suddenly to the four winds of Heaven.

'But this litter,' he mumbled, riveting his dazed eyes upon me, 'and these four knaves —?'

'Tell me,' I questioned, with sudden earnestness, 'are you in quest of just such a party?'

'Aye, that I am,' he answered sharply, intelligence returning to his glance, inquiry burning in it.

'And would the men, peradventure, be wearing the livery of the House of Santafior?'

His quick assent came almost choked in a company of oaths.

'Why, then, if that be your quarry, you are but wasting time. Such a party passed us at the gallop about an hour ago. It would be an hour, would it not, Giacopo?'

'I should say an hour,' answered the lacquey dully.

'In what direction?' came Ramiro's frenzied question. He doubted me no longer.

'In the direction of Fabriano I should say,' I answered. 'Although it may well be that they were making for Sinigaglia. The road branches farther on.'

He waited for no more. Without a word of thanks for the priceless information I had given him, he wheeled his horse, and shouted a hoarse command to his followers. A moment later and they were cantering past us, the snow flying beneath their hoofs; within five minutes the last of them had vanished round an angle of the road, and the only indication of the halt they had made was the broad path of dirty brown where their horses had crushed the snow.

I have been an actor in few more entertaining comedies than the cozening of Ser Ramiro, and a witness of nothing that afforded me at once so much relief and relish as his abrupt departure. I sank back on the cushions of my litter, and gave myself over to a burst of full-souled laughter which was interrupted ere it was half done by Giacopo, who had dismounted and approached me.

'You have fooled us finely,' said he, with venom.

I quenched my laughter to regard him. Of what did he babble? Was he, and were his fellows, too, so ungrateful as to bear a grudge against the man who had saved them?

'You have fooled us finely,' he insisted in a louder voice.

'That, knave, is my trade,' said I. 'But it rather seems to me that it was Messer Ramiro del' Orca whom I fooled.'

'Aye,' he answered querulously. 'But what when he discerns how you have played upon him? What when he discovers the trick by which you have thrown him off the scent? What when he returns?'

'Spare me,' I begged, 'I am but indifferently skilful at conjecture.'

'Nay, but you shall answer me,' he cried, livid with a passion that my bantering tone had quickened.

'Can it be that you are indeed curious to know what will befall when he returns?' I questioned meekly.

'I am,' he snorted, with an angry twist of the lips.

'It should be easy to gratify the morbid spirit of curiosity that actuates you. Remain here, and await his return. Thus shall you learn.'

'That will not I,' he vowed.

'Nor I, nor I, nor I!' chorused his followers.

'Then, why plague me with unprofitable questions? What concern is it of ours how Messer del' Orca shall

vent his wrath when he is disillusioned? Your duty
now is to rejoin your mistress. Ride hard for Cagli.
Seek her at the sign of The Full Moon, and then away
for Pesaro. If you are brisk you will gain the shelter
of the Lord Giovanni Sforza's fortress long before
Messer del' Orca again picks up the scent, if, indeed,
he ever does so.'

Giacopo laughed derisively till his fat body shook
with the scornful mirth of him.

'By my faith, I'm done with the business,' he cried,
and the other three expressed a very hearty agree-
ment with that attitude.

'How done with it?' I asked.

'I shall make my way back across the hills and so
retrace my steps to Rome. I'll risk my head no more
for any lady or any Fool.'

'If you should ever chance to risk it for yourself,'
said I, with unmeasured scorn, 'you'll risk it for the
greatest fool and the cowardliest rogue that ever
shamed the name of man. And your mistress? Is
she to wait at Cagli until doomsday? If anywhere
within the bulk of that elephant's body there lurks
the heart of a rabbit, you'll get you to horse and ride
to the help of that poor lady.'

They resented my tone, and showed their resentment plainly. Messer Giacopo went the length
of raising his hand to me. But I am a man of amazing
strength — amazing inasmuch as being slender of
shape I do not have the air of it. Leaping suddenly
from the litter, I caught that miserable vassal by
the breast of his doublet, shook him once or twice,
then tossed him headlong into a drift of snow by the
roadside.

At that they bared their knives and made shift to

attack me. But I flung myself on to one of the mules
of the litter, and showing them the stout Pistoja
dagger that I carried, I presented with it a bold and
truculent front, no whit intimidated by their numbers. Four to one though they were, they thought
better of it. A moment they stood off, consulting
among themselves; then Giacopo mounted, and with
some mocking counsel as to how I should dispose of
the litter and the mules, they made off, no doubt, to
find their way back to Rome. Giacopo, as I was afterwards to discover, was Madonna Paola's purse-
bearer, so that they would not lack for means.

Awhile I stayed there, cursing them for the white-
livered cravens that they were, and thinking of that
poor child who had ridden on to Cagli, and who
would await them in vain. There, on the mule, I sat
in the noontide sunlight, and pondered this, so
absorbed in her affairs as to have grown forgetful of
my own. At last I resolved to ride on to Cagli alone,
and inform her that her men were fled.

There was no time to lose, for as that rogue Giacopo
had said, Ramiro del' Orca might discover at any
moment how he had been tricked, and return hot-
foot to find me and extort the truth from me by such
means as I had no stomach for enduring.

First, then, it was of moment thoroughly to efface
our tracks, leaving no sign that might guide Messer
Ramiro to repair the error into which I had tricked
him. Slowly, says the proverb, one journeys far and
safely. Slowly, then, did I consider! The escort was,
no doubt, on its way back to Rome, and if I could but
rid myself of that cumbrous litter, Ser Ramiro would
find himself mightily hard put to it again to pick up
the trail. I remembered a ravine a little way behind,

and I rode my mule back to that as fast as it would travel with the litter and the other mule attached to it. Arrived there, I unharnessed the beasts on the very edge of that shallow precipice. Then exerting all my strength, I contrived to roll the litter over. Down that steep incline it went, over and over, gathering more snow to itself at every revolution, and sinking at last into the drift at the bottom. There were signs enough to show its presence, but those signs would hardly be read by any but the sharpest eyes, or by such as might be looking for it in precisely such a position. I must trust to luck that it escape the notice of Messer Ramiro. But even if he did discover it, I did not think that it would tell him overmuch.

That done, I resumed my hat and cloak — which I had retained — mounted once more, and urging the other mule along, I proceeded thus as fast as might be for a half-league or so in the direction of Cagli. That distance covered, again I halted. There was not a soul in sight. I stripped one of the mules of all its harness, which I buried in the snow, behind a hedge, then I drove the beast loose into a field. The peasant-owner of that land might conclude upon the morrow that it had rained asses in the night.

And now I was able to travel at a brisker pace, and in an hour or so I had passed the point where the road diverged, and I caught a glimpse of the four grooms, already high up in the hills which they were crossing. Whether they saw me or not I do not know, but with a last curse at their cowardice I put them from my mind, and cantered briskly on towards Cagli. It was a short league farther, and in little more than half an hour, my mule half-dead, I halted at the door of The Full Moon.

Flinging my reins to the ostler, I strode into the inn, swaddled in my cloak, and called for the hostess. The place was empty, as indeed all Cagli had seemed when I rode up. She came forward — a woman with a brown, full face, and large kindly eyes — and I asked her whether a lady had arrived there in safety that morning. At first she seemed mistrustful, but when I had assured her that I was in that lady's service, she frankly owned that Madonna was safe in her own room. Thither I allowed her to lead me, at once eager and reluctant. Eager with my own eyes to assure myself of her perfect safety; reluctant that, since a man may not penetrate to a lady's chamber hat on head, by uncovering I must disclose my shameful trade. Yet there was nothing for it but a bold face, and as I mounted the stairs in the woman's wake, I told myself that I was doubly a fool to be tormented by qualms of such a nature.

Hat in hand I followed the hostess into Madonna's room. The lady rose from the window-seat to greet me, her face pale and her gentle eyes wearing an anxious look. At sight of my head crowned with the crested, horned hood of folly, a frown of bewilderment drew her brows together, and she looked more closely to see whether I was indeed the man who had befriended her that morning in her extremity. In the eyes of the hostess I caught a gleam of recognition. She knew me for the merry loon who had entertained her guests one night a fortnight since, when on my way from Pesaro to Rome. But before she could give expression to this discovery of hers, the lady spoke.

'Leave us awhile, my woman,' she commanded. But I stayed the hostess as she was withdrawing.

'This lady,' said I, 'will need an escort of three or

four stout knaves upon a journey that she is going. She will be setting out as soon as may be.'

'But what of my grooms?' cried the lady.

'Madonna,' I informed her, 'they have deserted you. That is the reason of my presence here. You shall hear the story of it presently. Meanwhile, we must arrange to replace them.' And I turned again to the hostess.

She was standing in thought, a doubtful expression on her face. But as I looked at her she shook her head.

'There is no such escort to be found to-day in Cagli,' she made answer. 'The town is all but empty, and every lusty man is either gone on the pilgrimage to the Holy House of Loretto, or else is at Pesaro for the Feast of the Epiphany.'

It was in vain that I protested that a couple of knaves might surely be found. She answered me that such as were in Cagli were there because they would not be elsewhere.

The lady's face grew clouded as she listened, for from my insistence she shrewdly inferred that it imported to be gone.

'There is your ostler,' quoth I at last. 'He will do for one.'

'He is the only man I have. My husband and my sons are gone to Pesaro.'

'Yet spare us this one, and you shall be well paid his services.'

But no bribe could tempt her to give way, and no doubt she was well advised, for she contended that there was work to be done such as was beyond her years and strength, and that if she sent her ostler off, as well might she close her inn — a thing that was impossible.

Here, then, was an obstacle with which I had not reckoned. It was impossible to send the lady off alone, to travel a distance of some ten leagues, and the most of it by night — for if she would make sure of escaping, she must journey now without pause until she came to Pesaro.

And then, in a flash, it occurred to me that here lay the means, ready to my hand, by avail of which I might boldly reënter Pesaro despite my banishment, and discharge my errand to Lucrezia Borgia. For, surely, considering the mission on which ostensibly I should be returning — as the saviour and protector of his kinswoman — Giovanni Sforza could not enforce that ban against me. Next I bethought me of the other aspect that the business wore. In fooling Ramiro I had thwarted the Borgia ends; in rescuing Madonna Paola I had perhaps set at naught the Cardinal of Valencia's aims. If so, what then? It would seem that because the lady's eyes were mild and sweet, and because her beauty had so deeply wrought upon me, I had indeed fooled away my chance of salvation from the life and trade that were grown hateful to me. For back to Rome and Cesare Borgia I should dare go no more. Clearly I had burned my boats, and I had done it almost unthinkingly, acting upon the good impulse to befriend this lady, and never reckoning the cost down to its total. For all that the thing I had done, and what I might yet do, should offer me the means I needed to enter Pesaro without danger to my neck, I did not see that I was to derive great profit in the end — unless my profit lay in knowing that I had advanced the ruin of Giovanni Sforza by delivering my letter to Lucrezia. That, at any rate, was enough incentive clearly to define for me the line that I should take through this tangle into which the ever-jesting Fates had thrust me.

I was still at my thoughts, still pondering this most perplexing situation, the hostess standing silent by the door, when suddenly Madonna Paola spoke.

'Sir,' said she, in faltering accents, 'I — I have not the right to ask you, and I stand already so deeply in your debt. Not a doubt of it but it will have inconvenienced you to have journeyed thus far to inform me of the flight of my grooms. Yet if you could —' She paused, timid of proceeding, and her glance fell.

The hostess was all ears, struck by the respectful manner in which this very evidently noble lady addressed a Fool. I opened the door for her.

'You may leave us now,' said I. 'I will come to you presently.'

When she was gone I turned once more to the lady, my course resolved upon. My hate had conquered my last doubt. What first imported was that I should get to Pesaro and to Madonna Lucrezia.

'You were about to ask me,' said I, 'that I should accompany you to Pesaro.'

'I hesitated, sir,' she murmured.

I bowed respectfully. 'There was not the need, Madonna,' I assured her. 'I am at your service.'

'But, Messer Boccadoro, I have no claim upon you.'

'Surely,' said I, 'the claim that every distressed lady has upon a man of heart. Let us say no more. It were best not to delay in setting out, although I can scarcely think that there is any imminent danger from Ramiro del' Orca now.'

'Who is he?' she inquired. I told her, whereupon

— 'Did they come up with you?' she asked. 'What passed between you?'

Succinctly I related what had chanced, and how I had sent Ramiro on a fool's errand, adding the particulars of the flight of her grooms, and of how I had rid myself of the litter and the second mule. She heard me, her eyes sparkling, and at times she clapped her hands in a glee that was almost childish, vowing that this was splendid, that was brave. I allayed what little fears remained her by pointing out how effectively we had effaced our tracks, and how vainly now Messer del' Orca might beat the country in quest of a lady in a litter, escorted by four grooms.

And now she beset me with fresh thanks and fresh expressions of wonder at my generous readiness to befriend her — a wonder all devoid of suspicion touching the single-mindedness of my purpose. But I reminded her that we had little leisure to stand talking, and left her to make her preparations for the journey, whilst I went below to see that my mule and her horse were saddled. I made bold to pay the reckoning, and when presently she spoke of it, with flaming cheeks, and would have pledged me a jewel, I bade her look upon it as a loan which anon she might repay me when I had brought her safely to her kinsman's Court of Pesaro.

Thus, at last, we left Cagli, and took the road north, riding side by side and talking pleasantly the while, ever concerning the matter of her flight and of her hopes of shelter at Pesaro, which, being nearest to her heart, found readiest expression. I went wrapped in my cloak once more, my head-dress hidden 'neath my broad-brimmed hat, so that the few wayfarers we chanced on need not marvel to see a lady in such

friendly intercourse with a Fool. And so dull was I
that day as not to marvel, myself, at such a state of
things.

The sun was declining, a red ball of fire, towards the
mountains on our left, casting a blood-red glow upon
the snow that everywhere encompassed us, as we
cantered briskly on towards Fossombrone.

In that hour I fell to pondering, and I even caught
myself hoping that Messer Ramiro del' Orca might
not chance upon the discovery of how egregiously I
had fooled him. He was dull-witted and slow at
inference, and upon that I built the hope that he
might fail to associate me with Madonna Paola's
elusion of his pursuit. Thus the chance might yet
be mine of returning to Rome and the honourable
employment Cesare Borgia had promised me. If
only that were so to fall out, I might yet contrive to
mend the wreckage of my life. I was returned, it
seems, to the ways of early youth, when we build our
hopes of future greatness upon untenable foundations!

Great hopes and great ambitions rose within my
breast that January evening, fired by the gentle child
that rode beside me. Fate had sent me to her aid that
day, and I seemed to have acquired, by virtue of that
circumstance, a certain right in her. Had Fate no
other favours for me in her lap! I bethought me of
the very House of Sforza, to which I had been so
shamefully attached, and of its humble source in that
peasant, Giacomuzza Attendolo, surnamed Sforza for
his abnormal strength of body, who rose to great and
princely heights.

Assuredly I had the advantage of such an one, and
were the chance but given me —

I went no further. Down in my heart I laughed to

scorn my own wild musings. Cesare Borgia would
come to know — he must, whether Ramiro told him,
or whether he inferred it for himself from the account
Ramiro must give him of our meeting — how I had
thwarted him in one thing, whilst I had served him in
another. Fate was against me. I had fallen too low
to ever rise again, and no dreams indulged in a sunset
hour, and inspired, perhaps, by a child who was beautiful as one of the saints of God, would ever come to
be realised by poor Boccadoro.

Night was falling as we clattered through the
slippery streets of Fossombrone.

CHAPTER V

MADONNA'S INGRATITUDE

WE stayed in Fossombrone little more than a half-hour, and having made a hasty supper we resumed our way, giving out that we wished to reach Fano ere we slept. And so by the first hour of night Fossombrone was a league or so behind us, and we were advancing briskly towards the sea. Overhead a moon rode at the full in a clear sky, and its light was reflected by the snow, so that we were not discomforted by any darkness. We fell, presently, into a gentler pace, for, after all, there could be no advantage in reaching Pesaro before morning, and as we rode we talked, and I made bold to ask her the cause of her flight from Rome.

She told me then that she was Madonna Paola Sforza di Santafior, and that Pope Alexander, in his nepotism and his desire to make rich and powerful alliances for his family, had settled upon her as the wife for his nephew, Ignacio Borgia. He had been emboldened to this step by the fact that her only protector was her brother, Filippo di Santafior, whom they had sought to coerce. It was her brother, who, seeing himself in a dangerous and unenviable position, had secretly suggested flight to her, urging her to repair to her kinsman Giovanni Sforza at Pesaro. Her flight, however, must have been speedily discovered and the Borgias, who saw in that act a defiance of their supreme authority, had ordered her pursuit.

But for me, she concluded, that pursuit must have resulted in her capture, and once they had her back in Rome, willing or unwilling, they would have driven her into the alliance by means of which they sought to bring her fortune into their own house. This drew her into fresh protestations of the undying gratitude she entertained towards me, protestations which I would have stemmed but that she persisted in them.

'It is a good and noble thing that you have done,' said she, 'and I think that Heaven must have directed you to my aid, for it is scarce likely that in all Italy I should have found another man who would have done so much.'

'Why, what, after all, is this much that I have done?' I cried. 'It is no less than my manhood bade me do; no less than any other would have done seeing you so beset.'

'Nay, that is more than I can ever think,' she answered. 'Who for the sake of an unknown would have suffered such inconveniences as have you? Who would have returned as you have returned to advise me of the defection of my grooms? Who, when other escort failed, would have gone the length of journeying all this way to render a service that is beyond repayment? And, above all, who for the sake of an unknown maid would have submitted to this travesty of yours?'

'Travesty?' quoth I, so struck by that as to interrupt her at last. 'What travesty, Madonna?'

'Why, this garb of motley that you donned the better to fool my pursuers and that you still wear in my poor service.'

I turned in the saddle to stare at her, and in the moonlight I clearly saw her eyes meet mine. So!

that was the reason of her kindness and of the easy
familiarity of her speech with me! She deemed me
some knight-errant who caracoled through Italy in
quest of imperilled maidens needing aid. Of a certainty she had gathered her knowledge of the world
from the works of Messer Bojardo, or perhaps from
the 'Amadis of Gaul' of Messer Bernardo Tasso.
And, no doubt, she thought that suits of motley grew
on bushes by the roadside, whence those who had a
fancy for disguise might cull them.

Well, well, it were better she should know the truth
at once, and choose such a demeanour as she considered fitting towards a Fool. I had no stomach for
the courtesies that were meant for such a man as I
was not.

'Madonna, you are in error,' I informed her,
speaking slowly. 'This garb is no travesty. It is my
usual raiment.'

There was a pause and I saw the slackening of her
reins. No doubt, had we been afoot she would have
halted, the better to confront me.

'How?' she asked, and a new note, imperious and
chill, was sounding already in her voice. 'You would
not have me understand that you are by trade a Fool?'

'Allowing that I am not a Fool by birth, under
what other circumstances, think you, I should be
likely to wear the garments of a Fool?'

'But this morning,' she protested, after a brief
pause, 'when first I met you, you were not so arrayed.'

'I was arrayed even as I am now, in a cloak and
hat and boots that hid my motley from such undis-
cerning eyes as were yours and your grooms' — all
taken up with your own fears as you then were.'

There was in the tail of that a sting, as I meant there should be, for the sudden haughtiness of her tone was cutting into me. Was I less worthy of thanks because I was a Fool? Had I on that account done less to serve and save her? Or was it that the action which, in a spurred and armoured knight, had been accounted noble was deemed unworthy of thanks in a crested, motleyed jester? It seemed, indeed, that some such reasoning she followed, for after that we spoke no more until we were approaching Fano.

A many times before had I felt the shame of my ignoble trade, but never so acutely as at that moment. It had seared my soul when Giovanni Sforza had told my story to his Court, ere he had driven me from Pesaro with threats of hanging, and it had burned even deeper when later, Madonna Lucrezia, upon entrusting me with her letter to her brother, had upbraided me with the supineness that so long had held me in that vile bondage. But deepest of all went now the burning iron of that disgrace. For my companion's silence seemed to argue that had she known my quality she would have scorned the aid of which she had availed herself to such good purpose. If any doubt of this had mercifully remained me, her next words would have served to have resolved it. It was when the lights of Fano gleamed ahead; we were coming to a cross-roads, and I urged the turning to the left.

'But Fano is in front,' she remonstrated coldly.

'This way we can avoid the town and gain the Pesaro road beyond it,' answered I, my tone as cool as hers.

'Yet may it not be that at Fano I might find an escort?'

I could have cried out at her cruelty, for in her words I could but read my dismissal from her service. There had been no more talk of an escort other than that which I afforded, and with which at first she had been well content.

I sat my mule in silence for a moment. She had been very justly served had I been the vassal that she deemed me, and had I borne myself in that character without consideration of her sex, her station or her years. She had been very justly served had I wheeled about and left her there to make her way to Fano, and thence to Pesaro, as best she might. She was without money, as I knew, and she would have found in Fano such a reception as would have brought the bitter tears of late repentance to her pretty eyes.

But I was soft-hearted, and so I reasoned with her; yet in a manner that was to leave her no doubt of the true nature of her situation, and the need to use me with a little courtesy for the sake of what I might yet do, if she lacked the grace to treat me with gratitude for the sake of that which I had done already.

'Madonna,' said I, 'it were wiser to choose the by-road and forgo the escort, since we have dispensed with it so far. There are many reasons why a lady should not seek to enter Fano at this hour of night.'

'I know of none,' she interrupted me.

'That may well be. Nevertheless they exist.'

'This night-riding in so lonely a fashion is little to my taste,' she told me sullenly. 'I am for Fano.'

She had the mercy to spare me the actual words, yet her tone told me as plainly as if she had uttered them that I could go with her or not, as I should

choose. In silence, very sore at heart, I turned my
mule's head once more towards the lights of the town.

'Since you are resolved, so be it,' was all my
answer; and we proceeded.

No word did we exchange until we had entered the
main street, when she curtly asked me which was the
best inn.

'The Golden Fish,' said I, as curtly, and to The
Golden Fish we went.

Arrived there, Madonna Paola took affairs into her
own hands. She dismounted, leaving the reins with
a groom, and entering the common-room she proclaimed her needs to those that occupied it by loudly
calling upon the landlord to find her an escort of three
or four knaves to accompany her at once to Pesaro,
where they should be well rewarded by the Lord
Giovanni, her cousin.

I had followed her in, and I ground my teeth at
such an egregious piece of folly. Her hood was
thrown back, displaying the lenza of fine linen on her
sable hair, and over this a net of purest gold all set
with jewels. Her camorra, too, was open, and in her
girdle there were gems for all to see. There were but
a half-dozen men in the room. Two of these had a
venerable air — they may have been traders journeying to Milan — whilst a third, who sat apart, was a
slender, effeminate-looking youth. The remaining
three were fellows of rough aspect, and when one of
them — a black-browed ruffian — raised his eyes and
fastened them upon the riches that Madonna Paola
with such indifference displayed, I knew what was to
follow.

He rose upon the instant, and stepping forward, he
made her a low bow.

'Illustrious lady,' said he, 'if these two friends of mine and I find favour with you, here is an escort ready found. We are stout fellows, and very faithful.' Faithful to their cut-throat trade, I made no doubt he meant.

His fellows now rose also, and she looked them over, giving herself the airs of having spent her virgin life in judging men by their appearance. It was in vain I tugged her cloak, in vain I murmured the word 'wait' under cover of my hand. She there and then engaged them, and bade them make ready to set out at once. One more attempt I made to induce her to alter her resolve.

'Madonna,' said I, 'it is an unwise thing to go a-journeying by night with three unknown men, and of such villainous appearance. To me they seem no better than bandits.'

We were standing apart from the others, and she was sipping a cup of spiced wine that the host had mulled for her. She looked at me with a tolerant smile.

'They are poor men,' said she. 'Would you have them robed in velvet?'

'My quarrel is with their looks, Madonna, not their garments,' I answered patiently.

She laughed lightly, carelessly; even, I thought, a trifle scornfully.

'You are very fanciful,' said she, then added — 'but if so be that you are afraid to trust yourself in their company, why, then, sir, I need bring you no farther out of the road that you were following when first we met.'

Did the child think that some jealousy actuated me, and prompted me to inspire her with mistrust of my supplanters? She angered me. Yet now, more than ever was I resolved to journey with her. Leave her at the mercy of those ruffians, whom in her ignorance she was mad enough to trust, I could not — not even had she whipped me. She was so young, so frail and slight, that none but a craven could have found it in his heart to have deserted her just then.

'If it please you, Madonna,' I answered smoothly, 'I will make bold to travel on with you.'

It may be that my even accents stung her; perhaps she read in them some measure of reproof of the ingratitude that lay in her altered bearing towards me. Her eyes met mine across the table, and seemed to harden as she looked. Her answer came in a vastly altered tone.

'Why, if you are bent that way, I shall be glad to have you avail yourself of my escort, Boccadoro.'

I had suffered the scorn now of her speech, now of her silence, for some hours, but never was I so near to turning on her as at that moment; never so near to consigning her to the fate to which her headstrong folly was compelling her. That she should take that tone with me!

The violence of the sudden choler I suppressed turned me pale under her steady glance. So that, seeing it, her own cheeks flamed crimson, and her eyes fell, as if in token that she realised the meanness of her bearing. To some natures there can be nothing more odious than such a realisation, and of those, I think, was she; for she stamped her foot in a sudden pet, and curtly asked the host why there was such delay with the horses.

'They are at the door, Madonna,' he protested,

bowing as he spoke. 'And your escort is already wait-ing in the saddle.'

She turned and strode abruptly towards the threshold. Over her shoulder she called to me:

'If you come with us, Boccadoro, you had best be brisk.'

'I follow, Madonna,' said I, with a grim relish, 'so soon as I have paid the reckoning.'

She halted and half turned, and I thought I saw a slight droop at the corners of her mouth.

'You are keeping count of what I owe you?' she muttered.

'Aye, Madonna,' I answered, more grimly still, 'I am keeping count.' And I thought that my wits were vastly at fault if that account were not to be greatly swelled ere Pesaro was reached. Haply, in-deed, my own life might go to swell it. I almost took a relish in that thought. Perhaps then, when I was stiff and cold — done to death in her service — this handsome, ungrateful child would come to see how much discomfort I had suffered for her sake.

My thoughts still ran in that channel as we rode out of Pesaro, for I misliked the way in which those knaves disposed themselves about us. In front went Madonna Paola; and immediately behind her, so that their horses' heads were on a level with her saddle-bow, one on each side, went two of those ruffians. The third, whom I had heard them call Stefano, and who was the one who had made her the offer of their services, ambled at my side, a few paces in the rear, and sought to draw me into conversation, haply by way of throwing me off my guard.

Mistrust is a fine thing at times. 'Forewarned is forearmed,' says the proverb, and of all forewarnings there is none we are more likely to heed than our own mistrust; for whereas we may leave unheeded the warnings of a friend, we seldom leave unheeded the warnings of our spirit.

And so, while my amiable and garrulous Ser Stefano engaged me in pleasant conversation — addressing me ever as Messer the Fool, since he knew me not by name — I wrapped my cloak about me, and under cover of it kept my fingers on the hilt of my stout Pistoja dagger, ready to draw and use it at the first sign of mischief. For that sign I was all eyes, and had I been Argus himself I could have kept no better watch. Meanwhile I plied my tongue and maintained as merry a conversation with Ser Stefano as you could wish to hear, for he seemed a ready-witted knave of a most humorous turn of fancy — God rest his rascally soul! And so it came to pass that I did by him the very thing he sought to do by me; I lulled him into a careless confidence.

At last the sign I had been waiting for was given. I saw it as plainly as if it had been meant for me; I believe I saw it before the man for whom it was intended, and but for my fears concerning Madonna Paola, I could have laughed outright at their clumsy assurance. The man who rode on Madonna's right turned in his saddle and put up his hand as if to beckon Stefano. I was regaling him with one of the choicest of Messer Sacchetti's paradoxes, gurgling, myself, at the humour of the thing I told. I paid no heed to the sign. I continued to expound my quip, as though we had the night before us in which to make its elusive humour clear. But out of the tail of my eye I watched my good friend Stefano, and I saw his right hand steal round to the region of his back where

I knew his dagger to be slung. Yet I was patient.
There should be no blundering through an excessive
precipitancy. I talked on until I saw that my suspicions were amply realised. I caught the cold gleam
of steel in the hand that he brought back as stealthily
as he had carried it to his poniard. Sant' Iddio!
What a coward he was for all his bulk, to go so slyly
about the business of stabbing a poor, helpless,
defenceless Fool.

'But Sacchetti makes his point clear,' I babbled
on, most blandly; 'almost as clear, as comprehensive
and as penetrating as should be to you the point of
this.' And with a swift movement I swung half-
round in my saddle, and sank my dagger to the hilt
in his side even as he was in the act of raising his.

He made no sound beyond the faintest gurgle —
the first vowel of a suddenly choked word of wonder
and surprise. He rocked a second in his saddle, then
crashed over, and lay with arms flung wide, like a
huge black crucifix, upon the white ground. At the
same moment a piercing scream broke from Madonna Paola.

I tremble still to think what might have been her
fate had not those ruffians who had laid hands on her
fallen into the sorry error of holding their single adversary too lightly. They heard the thud of the gallant Stefano's fall, and they never doubted that mine
was the body that had gone down. They heard the
rapid hoof-beats of my approach, yet they never
turned their heads to ascertain whether they might
not be mistaken in their firm conviction that it was
Messer Stefano who was joining them.

I kissed my blade for luck, and drove it straight and
full into the back of the fellow on Madonna Paola's

right. He cried out, essayed to turn in his saddle that
he might deal with this unlooked-for assailant, then,
overcome, he lurched forward on to the withers of his
horse and thence rolled over, and was dragged away
at the gallop, his foot caught in a stirrup, by the suddenly startled brute he rode.

So far things had gone with an amazing and
delightful ease. If only the last of them had had the
amiability to be intimidated by my prowess and to
have taken to his heels, I might have issued from that
contest with the unscathed glory of a very Mars. But
from his throat there came, in answer to his comrade's
cry, a roar of rage. He fell back from Madonna,
and wheeled his horse to come at me, drawing his
sword as he advanced.

'Ride on, Madonna,' I shouted. 'I will rejoin you
presently.'

The fellow laughed, a mighty ugly and discompos-
ing laugh, which may or may not have shaken her
faith in my promise to rejoin her. It certainly went
near to shaking mine. However, she displayed a
presence of mind full worthy of the haughtiness and
ingratitude of which she had showed herself capable.
She urged her mule forward, and so left him a clear
road to attack me. I made a mistake then that went
mighty near to costing me my life. I paused to twist
my cloak about my left arm intending to use it as a
buckler. Had I but risked the arm itself, all un-
protected, in that task, it may well be that it had
served me better. As it was, my preparations were
far from complete when already he was upon me,
with the result that the waving slack of my cloak was
in my way to hamper and retard the movements of
my arm.

His sword leapt at me, a murderous blue-white flash of moonlit steel. I put up my half-swaddled arm to divert the thrust, holding my dagger ready in my right, and gripping my mule with all the strength of my two knees. I caught the blade, it is true, and turned aside the stroke intended for my heart. But the slack of the cloak clung to the neck of my mule, so that I could not carry my arm far enough to send his point clear of my body. It took me in the shoulder, stinging me, first icy cold then burning hot, as it went tearing its way through. For just a second was I daunted, more at knowing myself touched than by the actual pain. Then I flung my whole body forward to reach him at the close quarters to which he had come, and I buried my dagger in his breast, high up at the base of his dirty throat.

The force of the blow carried me forward, even as it bore him backward; and so, with his sword-blade in my shoulder, and my dagger where I had planted it, we hurtled over together and lay a second amidst what seemed a forest of equine legs. Then something smote me across the head, and I was knocked senseless.

Conceive me, if you can, a sorrier, or more useless thing. A senseless Fool!

CHAPTER VI

FOOL'S LUCK

MY return to consciousness seemed to afford me such sensations as a diver may experience as he rises up and up through the depth of water he has plumbed, or as a disembodied soul may know in its gentle ascent towards Heaven. Indeed the latter parallel may be more apt. For through the mist that suffused my senses there penetrated from overhead a voice that seemed to invoke every saint in the calendar on the behalf of some poor mortal. A very litany of intercession was it, not quite, it would appear, devoid of self-seeking.

'Sainted Virgin, restore him! Good Saint Paul, who wert done to death with a sword, let him not perish, else am I lost indeed!' came the voice.

I took a deep breath, and opened my eyes, whereat the voice cried out gladly that its intercessions had been heard, and I knew that it was on my behalf that the saints of Heaven had been disturbed in their beatific peace. My head was pillowed in a woman's lap, and it took me a moment or two to realise that that lap was Madonna Paola's, as was hers the voice that had reached my awakening senses, the voice that now welcomed me back to life in terms that were very different from the last that I could remember her having used towards me.

'Thank God, Messer Boccadoro!' she exclaimed, as she bent over me.

Her face was black with shadow, but in her voice

I caught a hint of tears, and I wondered whether they were shed on my behalf or on her own.

'I do,' I answered fervently. 'Have you any notion of what hour it is?'

'None,' she sighed. 'You have been so long unconscious that I was losing hope of ever hearing your voice again.'

I became aware of a dull ache on the right side of my head. I put up my hand, and withdrew it moist. She saw the action.

'One of the horses must have struck you with its hoof after you fell,' she explained. 'But I was more concerned for your other wound. I withdrew the sword with my own hands.'

That other wound she spoke of was now making itself felt as well. It was a gnawing, stinging pain in the region of my left shoulder, which seemed to turn me numb to the waist of that side of my body, and render powerless my arm. I questioned her touching my three adversaries, and she silently pointed to three black masses that lay some little distance from us in the snow.

'Not all dead?' I cried.

'I do not know,' she answered, with a sob. 'I have not dared go near them. They frighten me. Mother of Heaven, what a night of horror it has been! Oh, that I had taken your advice, Messer Boccadoro!' she exclaimed in a passion of self-reproach.

I laughed, seeking to soften her distress.

'To me it seems, that whether you would or not, you have been compelled to take it, after all. Those fellows lie there harmless enough, and I am still — as I urged that I should be — your only escort.'

'A nobler protector never woman had,' she assured me, and I felt a hot pearl of moisture fall upon my brow.

'You were wise, at least, to journey with a Fool,' I answered her. 'For fools are proverbially lucky folk, and to-night has proven me of all fools the luckiest. But, Madonna,' I suggested, in a different tone, 'should we not be better advised to attempt to resume this interesting journey of ours? We do not seem to lack for horses?'

A couple of nags were standing by the roadside, together with our mules, and I was afterwards to learn that she, herself, it was had tethered them.

'It must be yet some three leagues to Pesaro,' I added, 'and if we journey slowly, as I fear me that we must, we should arrive there soon after daybreak.'

'Do you think that you can stand?' she asked, a hopeful ring in her voice.

'I might essay it,' answered I, and I would have done so, there and then, but that she detained me.

'First let me see to this hurt in your head,' said she. 'I have been bathing it with snow while you were unconscious.'

She gathered a fresh handful as she spoke, and very tenderly she wiped away the blood. Then from her own head she took the fine linen lenza that she wore, and made a bandage — a bandage sweet with the faint fragrance of marshmallow — and bound it about my battered skull. When that was done she turned her attention to my shoulder. This was a more difficult matter, and all that we could do was to attempt to stanch the blood, which already had drenched my doublet on that side. To this end she passed a long scarf under my arm, and wound it several times about my shoulder.

At last, her gentle ministrations ended, I sought to rise. A dizziness assailed me scarce was I on my feet, and it is odds I had fallen back, but that she caught and steadied me.

'Mother in Heaven! You are too weak to ride,' she exclaimed. 'You must not attempt it.'

'Nay, but I will,' I answered, with more stoutness of tone than I felt of body; and notwithstanding that my knees were loosening under my weight. 'It is a faintness that will pass.'

If ever man willed himself to conquer weakness, that did I then, and with some measure of success — or else it was that my faintness passed of itself. I drew away from her support, and, straightening myself, I crossed to where the animals were tethered, staggering at first, but presently with a surer foot. She followed me, watching my steps with as much apprehension as a mother may feel when her first-born makes his earliest attempts at walking, and as ready to spring to my aid did I show signs of stumbling. But I kept up, and presently my senses seemed to clear, and I stepped out more surely.

Awhile we stood discussing which of the animals we should take. It was my suggestion that we should ride the horses, but she wisely contended that the mules would prove the more convenient if the slower. I agreed with her, and then, ere we set out, I went to see to my late opponents. One of them — Ser Stefano — was cold and stiff; the other two still lived, and from the nature of their wounds seemed likely to survive, if only they were not frozen to 'death before some good Samaritan came upon them.

I knelt a moment to offer up a prayer for the repose of the soul of him that was dead, and I bound

up the wounds of the living as best I could, to save
them greater loss of blood. Indeed, had it lain in my
power, I would have done more for them. But in
what case was I to render further aid? After all,
they had brought their fate upon themselves, and I
doubt not they were paying a score that they had
heaped up heavily in the past.

I went back to the mules, and, despite my remon-
strances, Madonna Paola insisted upon aiding me to
mount, urging me to have care of my wound, and
to make no violent movement that should set it
bleeding again. Then she mounted too, nimble as
any boy that ever robbed an orchard, and we set out
once more. And now it was a very contrite and
humbled lady that rode with me, and one that was
at no pains to dissemble her contrition, but, rather,
could speak of nothing else.

It moved me strangely to have her suing pardon
from me, as though I had been her equal instead of
the sometime Jester of the Court of Pesaro, dismissed
for an excessive pertness towards one with whom his
master curried favour.

And presently, as was perhaps but natural after all
that she had witnessed, she fell to questioning me as
to how it came to pass that one of such wit, resource,
and courage should follow the mean calling to which I
had owned. In answer I told her without reservation
the full story of my shame. It was a thing that I had
ever most zealously kept hidden, as already I have
shown.

To be a Fool was evil enough in all truth; but to
let men know that under my motley was buried the
identity of a man patrician-born was something infinitely worse. For, however vile the trade of a Fool

may be, it is not half so vile for a low-born clod who is too indolent or too sickly to do honest work as for one who has accepted it out of a half-cowardice and persevered in it through very sloth.

Yet on that night and after all that had chanced, no matter how my cheeks might burn in the gloom as I rode beside her, I was glad for once to tell that ignominious story, glad that she should know what weight of circumstance had driven me to wear my hideous livery.

But since my story dealt oddly with that Lord of Pesaro, the kinsman whose shelter she was now upon her way to seek, I must first assure myself that the candour to which I was disposed would not offend.

'Does it happen, Madonna,' I inquired, 'that you are well acquainted with the Lord of Pesaro?'

'Nay; I have never seen him,' answered she. 'When he was at Rome, a year ago, in the service of the Pope, I was at my studies in the convent. His father was my father's cousin, so that my kinship is none so near. Why do you ask?'

'Because my story deals with him, Madonna, and it is no pretty tale. Not such a narrative as I should choose wherewith to entertain you. Still, since you have asked for it, you shall hear it.

'It was in the year that Giovanni Sforza, Lord of Pesaro, celebrated his nuptials with the Lady Lucrezia Borgia — three years ago, therefore — that one morning there rode into the courtyard of his Castle of Pesaro a tall and lean young man on a tall and lean old horse. He was garbed and harnessed after a fashion that proclaimed him half-knight, half-peasant, and caused the castle lacqueys to eye him with amusement and greet him with derision. Lacqueys are great arbiters of fashion.

'In a loud, imperious voice this cockerel called for Giovanni, Lord of Pesaro, whereupon, resenting the insolence of his manner, the men-at-arms would have driven him out without more ado. But it chanced that from one of the windows of his stronghold the tyrant espied his odd visitor. He was in a mood that craved amusement, and marvelling what madman might this be, he made his way below and bade them stand back and let me speak — for I, Madonna, was that lean young man.

'"Are you," quoth I, "the Lord of Pesaro?"

'He answered me courteously that he was, whereupon I did my errand to him. I flung my gauntlet of buffalo-hide at his feet in gage of battle.

'"Your father," said I, "Costanzo of Pesaro, was a foul brigand, who robbed my father of his castle and lands of Biancomonte, leaving him to a needy and poverty-stricken old age. I am here to avenge upon your father's son my father's wrongs; I am here to redeem my castle and my lands. If so be that you are a true knight, you will take up the challenge that I fling you, and you will do battle with me, on horse or foot, and with whatsoever arms you shall decree, God defending him that has justice on his side."

'Knowing the world as I know it now, Madonna,' I interpolated, 'I realise the folly of that act of mine. But in those days my views belonged to a long-departed age of chivalry, of which I had learnt from such books as came my way at Biancomonte, and which I believed was the life of to-day in the world of men. It was a thing for which some tyrants would have had me broken on the wheel. But Giovanni

Sforza never so much as manifested anger. There was a complacent smile on his white face and his fingers toyed carelessly with his beard.

'I waited patiently, very haughty of mien and very fierce of heart, and when the amusement began to fade from his eyes, I begged that he would deliver me his answer.

'"My answer," quoth he, "is that you get you back to the place from whence you came, and render thanks to God on your knees every morning of the life I am sparing you that Giovanni Sforza is more entertained than affronted by your frenzy."

At his words I went crimson from chin to brow.

'"Do you disdain me?" I questioned, choking with rage.

'He turned with a shrug and a laugh, and bade one of his men give this cavalier his glove, and conduct him from the castle. Several that had stood at hand made shift to obey him, whereat I fell into such a blind, unreasoning fury that incontinently I drew my sword, and laid about me. They were many, I was but one; and they were not long in overpowering me and dragging me from my horse.

'They bound me fast, and Giovanni bade them let me have a priest, then get me hanged without delay. Had he done that, the world being as it is, perhaps none could blame him. But he elected to spare my life, yet on such terms as I could never have accepted had it not been for the consideration of my poor widowed mother, whom I had left in the hills of Biancomonte whilst I went forth to seek my fortune — such was the tale I had told her. I was her sole support, her only hope in life; and my death must have been her own, if not from grief, why then from very want. The thought of that poor old woman crushed my spirit as I sat in durance waiting for my end, and when the priest came, whom they had sent to shrive me, he found me weeping, which he took to argue a contrite heart. He bore the tale of it to Giovanni, and the Lord of Pesaro came to visit me in consequence, and found me sorely changed from my furious mood of some hours earlier.

'I was a very coward, I own; but it was for my mother's sake. If I feared death, it was because I bethought me of what it must mean to her.

'At sight of Giovanni I cast myself at his feet, and with tears in my eyes and in heartrending tones, bespeaking a humility as great as had been my erstwhile arrogance, I begged my life of him. I told him the truth — that for myself I was not afraid to die, but that I had a mother in the hills who was dependent on me, and who must starve if I were thus cut off.

'He watched me with his moody eyes, a saturnine smile about his lips. Then of a sudden he shook with a silent mirth, whose evil, malicious depth I was far indeed from suspecting. He asked me would I take solemn oath that if he spared my life I would never again raise my hand against him. That oath I took with a greediness born of my fear of the death that was impending.

'"You have been wise," said he, "and you shall have your life on one condition — that you devote it to my service."

'"Even that will I do," I answered readily.

'He turned to an attendant, and ordered him to go fetch a suit of motley. No word passed between us until that man returned with those garish garments.

Then Giovanni smiled on me in his mocking, infernal way.

'"Not that," I cried, guessing his purpose.

'"Aye, that," he answered me; "that or the hangman's noose. A man who could devise so monstrous a jest as was your challenge to the Tyrant of Pesaro should be a merry fellow if he would. I need such a one. There are two Fools at my Court, but they are mere tumblers, deformed vermin that excite as much disgust as mirth. I need a sprightlier man, a man of some learning and more drollery; such a man, in short, as you would seem to be."

'I recoiled in horror and disgust. Was this his clemency — this sparing of my life that he might submit it to an eternal shame? For a moment my mother was forgotten. I thought only of myself, and I grew resolved to hang.

'"When you spoke of service," said I, "I thought of service of an honourable sort."

'"The service that I offer you is honourable," he said, with cold amusement. "Indeed, remembering that your life was forfeit, you should account yourself most fortunate. You shall be well housed and well fed, you shall wear silk and lie in fine linen, on condition that you are merry. If you prove dull, our castellan shall have you whipped — for such a one as you could not be dull save out of sullenness, of which we shall seek to cure you if you show signs of it."

'"I will not do it," I cried, "it were too base."

'"My friend," he answered me, "the choice is yours. You shall have an hour in which to resolve what you will do. When they open this door for you at sunset, come forth clad as you are, and you shall hang. If you prefer to live, then don me that robe and cap of motley, and, on condition that you are merry, life is yours."'

I paused a moment. Our horses were moving slowly, for the tale engrossed us both, me in the telling, her in the hearing. Presently —

'I need not harass you with the reflections that were mine during that hour, Madonna. Rather let me ask you: How should a man so placed make choice to be full worthy of the office proffered him?'

There was a moment's silence while she pondered.

'Why,' she answered me, at last, 'a fool I take it would have chosen death: the wise man life, since it must hold the hope of better days.'

'And since it asked a man of wit to play the fool to such a tune as the Lord Giovanni piped, that wise young man chose life and folly. But was that choice indeed so wise? The story ends not there. That young man whose early life had been one of hardships found himself, indeed, well-housed and fed as the Lord Giovanni had promised him, and so he fell into a slothful spirit, and was content to play the Fool for bed and board.

'There were times when conscience knocked loudly at my heart, and I was tortured with shame to see myself in the garb of Fools, the sport of all, from prince to scullion. But in the three years that I had dwelt at Pesaro my identity had been forgotten by the few who had ever been aware of it. Moreover, a court is a place of changes, and in three years there had been such comings and goings at the Court of Giovanni Sforza, that not more than one or two remained of those that had inhabited it when first I entered on my existence there. Thus had my position grown steadily more bearable. I was just a jester

and no more, and so, in a measure — though I blush
to say it — I grew content. I gathered consolation
from the fact that there were not any who now
remembered the story of my coming to Pesaro, or
who knew of the cowardliness I had been guilty of
when I consented to mask myself in the motley and
assume the name of Boccadoro. I counted on the
Lord Giovanni's generosity to let things continue
thus, and, meanwhile, I provided for my mother out
of the vails that were earned me by my shame. But
there came a day when Giovanni in evil wantonness
of spirit chose to make merry at the Fool's expense.

'To be held up to scorn and ridicule is a part of the
trade of such as I, and had it been just Boccadoro
whom Giovanni had exposed to the derision of his
Court, haply I had been his jester still. But such
poor sport as that would have satisfied but ill the
deep-seated malice of his soul. The man whom his
cruel mockery crucified for their entertainment was
Lazzaro Biancomonte, whom he revealed to them,
relating in his own fashion the tale I have told you.

'At that I rebelled, and I said such things to him
in that hour, before all his Court, as a man may not
say to a prince and live. Passion surged up in him,
and he ordered his castellan to flog me to the bone —
in short, to slay me with a whip.

'From that punishment I was saved by the intercessions of Madonna Lucrezia, but I was driven out
of Pesaro that very night, and so it happens that I am
a wanderer now.'

At that I left it. I had no mind to tell her what
motives had impelled Lucrezia Borgia to rescue me,
nor on what errand I had gone to Rome and was
from Rome returning.

She had heard me in silence, and now that I had done, she heaved a sigh, for which gentle expression of pity out of my heart I thanked her. We were silent, thereafter, for a little while. At length she turned her head to regard me in the light of the now declining moon.

'Messer Biancomonte,' said she — and the sound of the old name, falling from her lips, thrilled me with a joy unspeakable, and seemed already to reinvest me in my old estate — 'Messer Biancomonte, you have done me in these four-and-twenty hours such service as never did knight of old for any lady — and you did it, too, out of the most disinterested and noble of motives, proving thereby how truly knightly is that heart of yours, which, for my sake, has all but beat its last to-night. You must journey on to Pesaro with me despite this banishment of which you have told me. I will be surety that no harm shall come to you. I could not do less, and I shall hope to do far more. Such influence as I may prove to have with my cousin of Pesaro shall be exerted all on your behalf, my friend; and if in the nature of Giovanni Sforza there be a tithe of the gratitude with which you have inspired me, you shall, at least, have justice, and Biancomonte shall be yours again.'

I was silent for a spell, so touched was I by the kindness she manifested me — so touched, indeed, and so unused to it that I forgot how amply I had earned it, and how rudely she had used me ere that was done.

'Alas!' I sighed. 'God knows I am no longer fit to sit in the house of the Biancomonte. I am come too low, Madonna.'

'That Lazzaro, after whom you are named,' she

answered, 'had come yet lower. But he lived again, and resumed his former station. Take your courage from that.'

'He lived not at the mercy of Giovanni of Pesaro,' said I.

There was a fresh pause at that. Then — 'At least,' she urged me, 'you'll come to Pesaro with me?'

'Why, yes,' said I. 'I could not let you go alone.' And in my heart I felt a pang of shame, and called myself a cur for making use of her as I was doing to reach the Court of Giovanni Sforza.

'You need fear no consequences,' she promised me. 'I can be surety for that at least.'

In the east a brighter, yellower light than the moon's began to show. It was the dawn, from which I gathered that it must be approaching the thirteenth hour. Pesaro could not be more than a couple of leagues farther, and, presently, when we had gained the summit of the slight hill we were ascending, we beheld in the distance a blurred mass looming on the edge of the glittering sea. A silver ribbon that un-coiled itself from the western hills disappeared behind it. That silvery streak was the river Foglia; that heap of buildings looking black against the land-scape's virgin white, the town of Pesaro.

Madonna pointed to it with a sudden cry of glad-ness.

'See, Messer Biancomonte, how near we are. Courage, my friend; a little farther, and yonder we have rest and comfort for you.'

She had need, in truth, to cry me 'Courage!' for I was weakening fast once more. It may have been the much that I had talked, or the infernal jolting of my mule, but I was losing blood again, and as we

were on the point of riding forward my senses swam,
so that I cried out; and but for her prompt assistance
I might have rolled headlong from my saddle.

As it was, she caught me about the waist as any
mother might have done her son.

'What ails you?' she inquired, her newly aroused
anxiety contrasting sharply with her joyous cry of a
moment earlier. 'Are you faint, my friend?'

It needed no confession on my part. My condition
was all too plain as I leaned against her frail body for
support.

'It is my wound,' I gasped. Then I set my teeth
in anguish. So near the haven, and to fail now! It
could not be; it must not be. I summoned all my
resolution, all my fortitude; but in vain. Nature
demanded payment for the abuses she had suffered.

'If we proceed thus,' she ventured fearfully, 'you
leaning against me, and going at a slow pace — no
faster than a walk — think you, you can bear it?
Try, good Messer Biancomonte.'

'I will try, Madonna,' I replied. 'Perhaps thus,
and if I am silent, we may yet reach Pesaro together.
If not — if my strength gives out — the town is
yonder and the day is coming. You will find your
way without me.'

'I will not leave you, sir,' she vowed; and it was
good to hear her.

'Indeed, I hope you may not know the need,' I
answered wearily. And thus we started on once more.

Sant' Iddio! What agonies I suffered ere the sun
rose up out of the sea to flood us with his winter
glory! What agonies were mine during those two
hours or so of that last stage of our eventful journey!
'I must bear up until we are at the gates of Pesaro,' I

kept murmuring to myself, and, as if my spirit were inclined to become the servant of my will and hold my battered flesh alive until we got that far, Pesaro's gates I had the joy of entering ere I was constrained to give way.

Dimly I remember — for very dim were my perceptions growing — that as we crossed the bridge and passed beneath the archway of the Porta Romana, the officer turned out to see who came. At sight of me he gaped a moment in astonishment.

'Boccadoro?' he exclaimed, at last. 'So soon returned?'

'Like Perseus from the rescue of Andromeda,' answered I, in a feeble voice, 'saving that Perseus was less bloody than am I. Behold the Madonna Paola Sforza di Santafior, the noble cousin of our High and Mighty Lord.'

And then as if, my task being done, I were free to set my weary brain to rest, my senses grew confused, the officer's voice became a hum that gradually waxed fainter as I sank into what seemed the most luxurious and delicious sleep that ever mortal knew.

Two days later, when I was conscious once more, I learned what excitement those words of mine had sown, with what honours Madonna Paola was escorted to the Castle, and how the citizens of Pesaro turned out upon hearing the news which ran like fire before us. And Madonna, it seems, had loudly proclaimed how gallantly I had served her, for as they bore me along in a cloak carried by four men-at-arms, the cry that was heard in the streets of Pesaro that morning was 'Boccadoro!' They had loved me, had those good citizens of Pesaro, and the news of my departure had cast a gloom upon the town. To have their hero return in a manner so truly heroic provoked that brave display of their affection, and I deeply doubt if ever in the days of greatest loyalty the name of Sforza was as loudly cried in Pesaro as, they tell me, was the name of Sforza's Fool that day.

CHAPTER VII

THE SUMMONS FROM ROME

IF Madonna Paola did not achieve quite all that she had promised me so readily, yet she achieved more than from my acquaintance with the nature of Giovanni Sforza — and my knowledge of the deep malice he entertained for me — I should have dared to hope.

The Tyrant of Pesaro, as I was soon to learn, was greatly taken with this fair cousin of his, whom that morning he had beheld for the first time. And being taken with her, it may be that Giovanni listened the more readily to her intercessions on my poor behalf. Since it was she who begged this thing, he could not wholly refuse. But since he was Giovanni Sforza, he could not wholly grant. He promised her that my life, at least, should be secure, and that not only would he pardon me, but that he would have his own physician see to it that I was made sound again. For the time, that was enough, he thought. First let them bring me back to life. When that was achieved, it would be early enough to consider what course this life should take thereafter.

And she, knowing him not and finding him so kind and gracious, trusted that he would perform that which he tricked her into believing that he promised.

For some ten days I lay abed, feverish at first and later very weak from the great loss of blood I had sustained. But after the second day, when my fever had abated, I had some visitors, among whom was

Madonna Paola, who bore me the news that her intercessions for me with the Lord of Pesaro were likely to
bear fruit, and that I might look for my reinstate-
ment. Yet, if I permitted myself to hope as she bade
me, I did so none too fully.

My situation, bearing in mind how at once I had
served and thwarted the ends of Cesare Borgia, was
perplexing.

Another visitor I had was Messer Magistri — the
pompous seneschal of Pesaro — who, after his own
fashion, seemed to have a liking for me, and a certain
pity. Here was my chance of discharging the true
errand on which I was returned.

'I owe thanks,' said I, 'to many circumstances for
the sparing of my life; but above all people and all
things do I owe thanks to our gracious Lady Lucrezia.
Do you think, Messer Magistri, that she would
consent to see me and permit me again to express the
gratitude that fills my heart?'

Messer Magistri thought that he could promise
this, and consented to bear my message to her.
Within the hour she was at my bedside and divining
that, haply, I had news to give her of the letter I had
borne her brother, she dismissed Magistri who was in
attendance.

Once we were alone her first words were of kindly
concern for my condition, delivered in that sweet,
musical voice that was by no means the least charm
of a princess to whom Nature had been prodigal of
gifts. For without going to that length of exaggerated
praise which some have bestowed — for her own ear,
and with an eye to profit — upon Madonna Lucrezia,
yet were I less than truthful if I sought to belittle her
ample claims to beauty. Some six years later than

the time of which I write, she was met on the occasion
of her entry into Ferrara by a certain clown dressed
in the scanty guise of the shepherd Paris, who
proffered her the apple of beauty, with the mean-
souled flattery that since beholding her he had been
forced to alter his old-time judgment in favour of
Venus.

He lied, like the brazen, self-seeking adulator that
he was, and for which he should have been soundly
whipped. Her nose was a shade too long, her chin a
shade too short to admit, even remotely, of such
comparisons. Still, that she had a certain gracious
beauty, as I have said, it is not mine to deny. There
was an almost childish freshness in her face, an
almost childish innocence in her fine grey eyes, and,
above all, a golden crown of such splendid and
resplendent hair as brought to mind the tresses of
God's angels.

That fair child — for no more than a child was
she — drew a chair to my bedside.

There she sate herself, whilst I thanked her for her
concern on my behalf, and answered that I was doing
well enough, and should be abroad again in a day or
two.

'Brave lad,' she murmured, patting my hand,
which lay upon the coverlet, as though she had been
my sister and I anything but a Fool, 'count me ever
your friend hereafter, for what you have done for
Madonna Paola. For although it was my own family
you thwarted, yet you did so to serve one who is
more to me than any family, more than any sister
could be.'

'What I did, Madonna,' I answered, 'I did with
the better heart since it opened out a way that was

barred me, solved me a riddle which my lord, your
illustrious brother, set me — one that otherwise
might well have overtaxed my wits.'

'Ah?' Her grey eyes fell on me in a swift and
searching glance, a glance that revealed to the full
their matchless beauty. Care seemed of a sudden to
have aged her face. The question of her eyes needed
no translation into words.

'The Lord Cardinal of Valencia entrusted me with
a letter for you, in answer to your own,' I informed
her, and from underneath my pillow I drew the
package, which during Magistri's absence I had
abstracted from my boot that I might have it in readiness when she came.

She sighed as she took it, and a wistful smile invested the corners of her mouth.

'I had hoped he would have found better employment for you,' she said.

'His Excellency promised that he would more
fitly employ me in the future did I discharge this
errand with secrecy and despatch. But by aiding
Madonna Paola I have burned my boats against
returning to claim the redemption of that promise;
though had it not been for Madonna Paola and what
I did, I scarce know how I should have penetrated
here to you.'

She broke the seal, and, rising, crossed to the
window, where she stood reading the letter, her back
towards me. Presently I heard a stifled sob. The
letter was crushed in her hand. Then moments
passed ere she confronted me once more. But her
manner was all changed; she was agitated and pre-
occupied, and for all that she forced herself to talk of
me and my affairs, her mind was clearly elsewhere.

At last she left me, nor did I see her again during the time I was confined to my bed.

On the eleventh day I rose, and the weather being mild and springlike, I was permitted by my grave-faced doctor to take the air a little on the terrace that overlooks the sea. I found no garments but some suits of motley, and so, in despite of my repugnance now to reassume that garb, I had no choice but to array myself in one of these. I selected the least garish one — a suit of black and yellow stripes, with hose that was half black, half yellow, too; and so, leaning upon the crutch they had left me, I crept forth into the sunlight, the very ghost of the man that I had been a fortnight ago.

I found a stone seat in a sheltered corner looking southward towards Ancona, and there I rested me and breathed the strong invigorating air of the Adriatic. The snows were gone, and between me and the wall — some twenty paces off — there was a stretch of soft, green turf.

I had brought with me a book that Madonna Lucrezia had sent me while I was yet abed. It was a manuscript collection of Spanish odes, with the proverbs of one Domenico Lopez — all very proper nourishment for a jester's mind. The odes seemed to possess a certain quaintness, and among the proverbs there were many that were new to me in framing and in substance. Moreover, I was glad of this means of improving my acquaintance with the tongue of Spain, and I was soon absorbed. So absorbed, indeed, as never to hear the footsteps of the Lord Giovanni, when presently he approached me unattended, nor to guess at his presence until his shadow fell athwart my page. I raised my eyes, and seeing who it was I made shift to get on my feet; but he commanded me to remain seated, commenting sympathetically upon my weak condition.

He asked me what I read, and when I had told him, a thin smile fluttered across his white face.

'You choose your reading with rare judgment,' said he. 'Read on, and prime your mind with fresh humour, prepare yourself with new conceits for our amusement against the time when health shall be more fully restored you.'

It was in such words as these that he intimated to me that I was pardoned, and reinstated — as the Fool of the Court of Pesaro. That was to be the sum of his clemency. We were precisely where we had been. Once before had he granted me my life on condition that I should amuse him; he did no more than repeat that mercy now. I stared at him in wonder, open-mouthed, whereat he laughed.

'You are agreeably surprised, my Boccadoro?' said he, his fingers straying to his beard as was his custom. 'My clemency is no more than you deserve in return for the service you have rendered to the House of Sforza.' And he patted my head as though I had been one of his dogs that had borne itself bravely in the chase.

I answered nothing. I sat there as if I had been a part of the stone from which my seat was hewn, for I lacked the strength to rise and strangle him as he deserved — moreover, I was bound by an oath, which it would have damned my soul to break, never to raise my hand against him.

And then, before he could say more, two ladies issued from the doorway on my right. They were Madonna Lucrezia and Madonna Paola. Upon espying me they hastened forward with expressions of pleased surprise at seeing me risen and out, and when I would have got to my feet they stayed me as Giovanni had done. Madonna Paola's words seemed addressed to Heaven rather than to me, for they were words of thanksgiving for this recovery of my strength.

'I have no thanks,' she ended warmly, 'that can match the deeds by which you earned them, Messer Biancomonte.'

My eyes drifting to Giovanni's face surprised its sudden darkening.

'Madonna Paola,' said he, in an icy voice, 'you have uttered a name that must not be heard within my walls of Pesaro, if you would prove yourself the friend of Boccadoro. To remind me of his true identity is to remind me of that which counts not in his favour.'

She turned to regard him, a mild surprise in her blue eyes.

'But, my lord, you promised —' she began.

'I promised,' he interposed, with an easy smile and manner never so deprecatory, 'that I would pardon him, grant him his life and restore him to my favour.'

'But did you not say that if he survived and was restored to strength you would then determine the course his life should take?'

Still smiling, he produced his comfit-box, and raised the lid.

'That is a thing he seems to have determined for himself,' he answered smoothly — he could be smooth as a cat upon occasion, could this bastard of Costanzo Sforza. 'I came upon him here, arrayed as you behold him, and reading a book of Spanish quips. Is it not clear that he has chosen?'

Between thumb and forefinger he balanced a sugar-crusted comfit of coriander seed steeped in marjoram vinegar, and having put his question he bore the sweetmeat to his mouth. The ladies looked at him, and from him to me. Then Madonna Paola spoke, and there seemed a reproachful wonder in her voice.

'Is this indeed your choice?' she asked me.

'It is the choice that was forced on me,' said I, with heat. 'They left me no garments save these of folly. That I was reading this book it pleases my lord to interpret into a further sign of my intentions.'

She turned to him again, and to the appeal she made was joined that of Madonna Lucrezia. He grew serious and put up his hand in a gesture of rare loftiness.

'I am more clement than you think,' said he, 'in having done so much. For the rest, the restoration that you ask for him is one involving political issues you little dream of. What is this?'

He had turned abruptly. A servant was approaching, leading a mud-splashed courier, whom he announced as having just arrived.

'Whence are you?' Giovanni questioned him.

'From the Holy See,' answered the courier, bowing, 'with letters for the High and Mighty Lord Giovanni Sforza, Tyrant of Pesaro, and his noble spouse, Madonna Lucrezia Borgia.'

He proffered his letters as he spoke, and Giovanni, whose brow had grown overcast, took them with a hand that seemed reluctant. Then bidding the servant see to the courier's refreshment, he dismissed them both.

A moment he stood, balancing the parchments as if from their weight he could infer the gravity of their contents; and the affairs of Boccadoro were, there and then, forgotten by us all. For the thought that rose uppermost in our minds — saving always that of Madonna Lucrezia — was that these communications concerned the sheltering of Madonna Paola, and were a command for her immediate return to Rome. At last Giovanni handed his wife the letter intended for her, and, in silence, broke the seal of his own.

He unfolded it with a grim smile, but scarce had he begun to read when his expression softened into one of terror, and his face grew ashen. Next it flared crimson, the veins on his brow stood out like ropes, and his eyes flashed furiously upon Madonna Lucrezia. She was reading, her bosom rising and falling in token of the excitement that possessed her.

'Madonna,' he cried in an awful voice, 'I have here a command from the Holy See to repair at once to Rome, to answer certain charges that are preferred against me relating to my marriage. Madonna, know you aught of this?'

'I know, sir,' she answered steadily, 'that I, too, have here a letter calling me to Rome. But there is no reason given for the summons.'

Intuitively it flashed across my mind that whatever the matter might be, Madonna Lucrezia had full knowledge of it through the letter I had brought her from her brother.

'Can you conjecture, Madonna, what are these charges to which my letter so vaguely alludes?' Giovanni was inquiring.

'Your pardon, but the subject is scarcely of a nature to permit discussion in the Castle courtyard. Its character is intimate.'

He looked at her very searchingly, but for all that

he was a man of almost twice her years, her wits were more than a match for his, and his scrutiny can have told him nothing. She preserved a calm, unruffled front.

'In five minutes, Madonna,' said he, very sternly, 'I shall be honoured if you will receive me in your closet.'

She inclined her head, murmuring an unhesitating assent. Satisfied, he bowed to her and to Madonna Paola — who had been looking on with eyes that wonder had set wide open — and turning on his heel he strode briskly away. As he passed into the castle, Madonna Lucrezia heaved a sigh and rose.

'My poor Boccadoro,' she cried, 'I fear me your affairs must wait a while. But think of me always as your friend, and believe that if I can prevail upon my brother to overlook the ill turn you did him when you entered the service of this child' — and she pointed to Madonna Paola — 'I shall send for you from Rome, for in Pesaro I fear you have little to hope for. But let this be a secret between us.'

From those words of hers I inferred, as perhaps she meant I should, that once she left Pesaro to obey her father's summons, our little northern State was to know her no more. Once again, only, did I see her, on the occasion of her departure, some four days later, and then but for a moment. Back to Pesaro she came no more, as you shall learn anon; but behind her she left a sweet and fragrant memory, which still endures though many years are sped and much calumny has been heaped upon her name.

I might pause here to make some attempt at refuting the base falsehoods that had been bruited by that time-serving vassal Guicciardini, and others of his

kidney, whom the upstart Cardinal Giuliano della
Rovere — sometime pedlar — in his jealous fury at
seeing the coveted pontificate pass into the family of
Borgia, bought and hired to do his loathsome work of
calumny and besmirch the fame of as sweet a lady as
Italy has known. But this poor chronicle of mine is
rather concerned with the history of Madonna Paola
di Santafior, and it were a divergence well-nigh
unpardonable to set my pen at present to that other
task. Moreover, there is scarce the need. If any
there be who doubt me, or if future generations should
fall into the error of lending credence to the lies of
that villain Guicciardini, of that arch-villain Giuliano
della Rovere, or of other smaller fry who have lent
their helot's pens to weave mendacious records of her
life, dubbing her murderess, adulteress, and Heaven
knows what besides — I will but refer them to the
archives of Ferrara, whose Duchess she became at
the age of one-and-twenty, and where she reigned for
eighteen years. There shall it be found recorded that
she was an exemplary, God-fearing woman; a faithful
and honoured wife; a wise, devoted mother; and a
princess, beloved and esteemed by her people for her
piety, her charity and her wisdom. If such records as
are there to be read by earnest seekers after truth be
not sufficient to convince, and to reveal those others
whom I have named in the light of their true base-
ness, then were it idle for me to set up in these pages
a passing refutation of the falsehoods which it has
grieved me so often to hear repeated.

It was two days later that the Lord Giovanni set
out for Rome, obedient to the command he had
received. But before his departure — on the eve of
it, to be precise — there arrived at Pesaro a very

wonderful and handsome gentleman. This was the brother of Madonna Paola, the High and Mighty Lord Filippo di Santafior. He had had a hint in Rome that his connivance at his sister's defiant escape was suspected at the Vatican, and he had wisely determined that his health would thrive better in a northern climate for a while.

A very splendid creature was this Lord Filippo, all shimmering velvet, gleaming jewels, costly furs and glittering gold. His face was effeminate, though finely featured, and resembled, in much, his sister's. He rode a cream-coloured horse, which seemed to have been steeped in musk, so strongly was it scented. But of all his affectations the one with which I was taken most was to see one of his grooms approach him when he dismounted, to dust his wondrous clothes down to his shoes, which he wore in the splayed fashion set by the late King of France who was blessed with twelve toes on each of his deformed feet.

The Lord Giovanni, himself not lacking in effeminacy, was greatly taken by the wondrous raiment, the studied lisp, and the hundred affectations of this peerless gallant. Had he not been overburdened at the time by the Papal business that impended, he might there and then have cemented the intimacy which was later to spring up between them. As it was, he made him very welcome, and placed at his and his sister's disposal the beautiful palace that his father had begun, and he, himself, had completed, which was known as the Palazzo Sforza.

On the morrow Giovanni left Pesaro with but a small retinue, in which I was thankful not to be included. Two days later Madonna Lucrezia followed

her husband, the fact that they journeyed not together seeming to wear an ominous significance. Her
eyes had a swollen look, such as attends much weeping, which afterwards I took as proof that she knew
for what purpose she was going, and was moved to
bitter grief at the act to which her ambitious family
was constraining her.

After their departure things moved sluggishly at
Pesaro. The nobles of the Lord Giovanni's Court
repaired to their several houses in the neighbouring
country, and save for the officers of the household the
place became deserted.

Madonna Paola remained at the Sforza Palace,
but I saw her only once during the two months that
followed, and then it was about the streets, and she
had little more than a greeting for me as she passed.
At her side rode her brother, a splendid blaze of
finery, falcon on wrist.

My days were spent in reading and reflection, for
there was naught else to do. I might have gone my
ways, had I so wished it, but something kept me
there at Pesaro, curious to see the events with which
the time was growing big.

We grew sadly stagnant during Lent, and what
with the uneventful course of things, and the lean
fare prescribed by Mother Church, it was a very
dispirited Boccadoro that wandered aimlessly whither
his dulling fancy took him. But in Holy Week, at
last, we received an abrupt stir, which set a whirlpool
of excitement in the Dead Sea of our lives. It was
the sudden reappearance of the Lord Giovanni.

He came alone, dust-stained and haggard, on a
horse that dropped dead from exhaustion the moment Pesaro was reached, and in his pallid cheek

and hollow eye we read the tale of some great fear and some disaster.

That night we heard the story of how he had performed the feat of riding all the way from Rome in four-and-twenty hours, fleeing for his life from the peril of assassination, of which Madonna Lucrezia had warned him.

He went off to his Castle of Gradara, where he shut himself up with the trouble we could but guess at, and so in Pesaro, that brief excitement spent, we stagnated once again.

I seemed an anomaly in so gloomy a place, and more than once did I think of departing and seeking out my poor old mother in her mountain home, contenting myself hereafter with labouring like any honest *villano* born to the soil. But there ever seemed to be a voice that bade me stay and wait, and the voice bore a suggestion of Madonna Paola. But why dissemble here? Why cast out hints of voices heard, supernatural in their flavour? The voice, I doubt not, was just my own inclination, which bade me hope that once again it might be mine to serve that lady.

An eventful year in the history of the families of Sforza and Borgia was that year of grace 1497.

Spring came, and ere it had quite grown to summer we had news of the assassination of the Duke of Gandia, and the tale that he was done to death by his elder brother, Cesare Borgia; a tale which seemed to lack for reasonable substantiation, and which, despite the many voices that make bold to noise it broadcast, may or may not be true.

In that same month of June messages passed between Rome and Pesaro, and gradually the burden of the messages leaked out in rumours that Pope

Alexander and his family were pressing the Lord Giovanni to consent to a divorce. At last he left Pesaro again; this time to journey to Milan and seek counsel with his powerful cousin, Lodovico, whom they called 'The Moor.' When he returned he was more sulky and downcast than ever, and at Gradara he lived in an isolation that had been worthy of a hermit.

And thus that miserable year wore itself out, and, at last, in December, we heard that the divorce was announced, and that Lucrezia Borgia was the Tyrant of Pesaro's wife no more. The news of it and the reasons that were put forward as having led to it were roared across Italy in a great, derisive burst of laughter, of which the Lord Giovanni was the unfortunate and contemptible butt.

CHAPTER VIII

MENE, MENE, TEKEL, UPHARSIN

AND now, lest I grow tedious and weary you with this narrative of mine, it may be well that I but touch with a fugitive pen upon the events of the next three years of the history of Pesaro.

Early in 1498 the Lord Giovanni showed himself once more abroad, and he seemed again the same weak, cruel, pleasure-loving tyrant he had been before shame overtook him and drove him for a season into hiding. Madonna Paola and her brother, Filippo di Santafior, remained in Pesaro, where they now appeared to have taken up their permanent abode. Madonna Paola — following her inclinations — withdrew to the Convent of Santa Caterina, there to pursue in peace the studies for which she had a taste, whilst her splendid, profligate brother became the ornament — the *arbiter elegantiarum* — of our Court.

Thus were they left undisturbed; for in the cauldron of Borgia politics a stew was simmering that demanded all that family's attention, and of whose import we guessed something when we heard that Cesare Borgia had flung aside his cardinalitial robes to put on armour and give freer rein to the boundless ambition that consumed him.

With me life moved as if that winter excursion and adventure had never been. Even the memory of it must have faded into a haze that scarce left discernible any semblance of reality, for I was once

again Boccadoro, the golden-mouthed Fool, whose
sayings were echoed by every jester throughout
Italy. My shame that for a brief season had risen up
in arms seemed to be laid to rest once more, and I
was content with the burden that was mine. Money
I had in plenty, for when I pleased him the Lord
Giovanni's vails were often handsome, and much of
my earnings went to my poor mother, who would
sooner have died starving than have bought herself
bread with those ducats could she have guessed at
what manner of trade Lazzaro Biancomonte had
earned them.

The Lord Giovanni was a frequent visitor at the
Convent of Santa Caterina, whither he went, ever
attended by Filippo di Santafior, to pay his duty to
his fair cousin. In the summer of 1500, she being
then come to the age of eighteen, and as divinely
beautiful a lady as you could find in Italy, she allowed
herself to be persuaded by her brother — who, I
make no doubt, had been, in his turn, persuaded by
the Lord of Pesaro — to leave her convent and her
studies, and to take up her life at the Sforza Palace,
where Filippo held by now a sort of petty court of
his own.

And now it fell out that the Lord Giovanni was
oftener at the Palace than at the Castle, and during
that summer Pesaro was given over to such merry-
making as it had never known before. There was
endless lute-thrumming and recitation of verses by a
score of parasite poets whom the Lord Giovanni
encouraged, posing now as a patron of letters; there
were balls and masques and comedies beyond number, and we were as gay as though Italy held no
Cesare Borgia, Duke of Valentinois, who was sweep-

ing northward with his all-conquering flood of mercenaries.

But one there was who, though the very centre of
all these merry doings, the very one in whose honour
and for whose delectation they were set afoot, seemed
listless and dispirited in that boisterous crowd. This
was Madonna Paola, to whom, rumour had it, that
her kinsman, the Lord Giovanni, was paying a
most ardent suit.

I saw her daily now, and often would she choose
me for her sole companion; often, sitting apart with
me, would she unburden her heart and tell me much
that I am assured she would have told no other. A
strange thing may it have seemed, this confidence
between the Fool and the noble Lady of Santafior —
my Holy Flower of the Quince, as in my thoughts I
grew to name her. Perhaps it may have been because
she found me ever ready to be sober at her bidding,
when she needed sober company as those other fools
— the greater fools since they accounted themselves
wise — could not afford her.

That winter adventure betwixt Cagli and Pesaro
was a link that bound us together, and caused her to
see under my motley and my masking smile the true
Lazzaro Biancomonte whom for a little season she
had known. And when we were alone it had become
her wont to call me Lazzaro, leaving that other name
that they had given me for use when others were at
hand. Yet never did she refer to my condition, or
wound me by seeking to spur me to the ambition to
become myself again. Haply she was content that I
should be as I was, since had I sought to become different it must have entailed my quitting Pesaro, and
this poor lady was so bereft of friends that she could

not afford to lose even the sympathy of the despised jester.

It was in those days that I first came to love her with as pure a flame as ever burned within the heart of man, for the very hopelessness of it preserved its holy whiteness. What could I do, if I would love her, but love her as the dog may love his mistress? More was surely not for me — and to seek more were surely a madness that must earn me less. And so, I was content to let things be, and keep my heart in check, thanking God for the mercy of her company at times, and for the precious confidences she made me, and praying Heaven — for of my love was I grown devout — that her life might run a smooth and happy course, and ready, in the furtherance of such an object, to lay down my own should the need arise. Indeed, there were times when it seemed to me that it was a good thing to be a Fool to know a love of so rare a purity as that — such a love as I might never have known had I been of her station, and in such case as to have hoped to win her some day for my own.

One evening of late August, when the vines were heavy with ripe fruit, and the scent of roses was permeating the tepid air, she drew me from the throng of courtiers that made merry in the Palace, and led me out into the noble gardens to seek counsel with me, she said, upon a matter of gravest moment. There, under the sky of deepest blue, crimsoning to saffron where the sun had set, we paced awhile in silence, my own senses held in thrall by the beauty of the eventide, the ambient perfumes of the air and the strains of music that faintly reached us from the Palace. Madonna's head was bent, and her eyes were set upon the ground and burdened, so my furtive glance assured me, with a gentle sorrow. At length she spoke, and at the words she uttered my heart seemed for a moment to stand still.

'Lazzaro,' said she, 'they would have me marry.'

For a little spell there was a silence, my wits seeming to have grown too numbed to attempt to seek an answer. I might be content, indeed, to love her from a distance, as the cloistered monk may love and worship some particular saint in Heaven; yet it seems that I was not proof against jealousy for all the abstract quality of my worship.

'Lazzaro,' she repeated presently, 'did you hear me? They would have me marry.'

'I have heard some such talk,' I answered, rousing myself at last; 'and they say that it is the Lord Giovanni who would prove worthy of your hand.'

'They say rightly, then,' she acknowledged. 'The Lord Giovanni it is.'

Again there was a silence, and again it was she who broke it.

'Well, Lazzaro?' she asked. 'Have you naught to say?'

'What would you have me say, Madonna? If this wedding accords with your own wishes, then am I glad.'

'Lazzaro, Lazzaro! You know that it does not.'

'How should I know it, Madonna?'

'Because your wits are shrewd, and because you know me. Think you this petty tyrant is such a man as I should find it in my heart to conceive affection for? Grateful to him am I for the shelter he has afforded us here; but my love — that is a thing I keep, or fain would keep, for some very different man. When I love, I think it will be a valorous knight, a gentleman of lofty mind, of noble virtues and ready address.'

'An excellent principle on which to go in quest of a husband, Madonna mia. But where in this degenerate world do you look to find him?'

'Are there, then, no such men?'

'In the pages of Bojardo and those other poets whom you have read too earnestly there may be.'

'Nay, there speaks your cynicism,' she chided me. 'But even if my ideals be too lofty, would you have me descend from the height of such a pinnacle to the level of the Lord Giovanni — a weak-spirited craven, as witnesses the manner in which he permitted the Borgias to mishandle him; a cruel and unjust tyrant, as witnesses his dealing with you, to seek no further instances; a weak, ignorant, pleasure-loving fool, devoid of wit and barren of ambition? Such is the man they would have me wed. Do not tell me, Lazzaro, that it were difficult to find a better one than this.'

'I do not mean to tell you that. After all, though it be my trade to jest, it is not my way to deal in falsehood. I think, Madonna, that if we were to have you write for us such an appreciation of the High and Mighty Giovanni Sforza, you would leave a very faithful portrait for the enlightenment of posterity.'

'Lazzaro, do not jest!' she cried. 'It is your help I need. That is the reason why I am come to you with the tale of what they seek to force me into doing.'

'To force you?' I cried. 'Would they dare so much?'

'Aye, if I resist them further.'

'Why, then,' I answered, with a ready laugh, 'do not resist them further.'

'Lazzaro!' she cried, her accents telling of a spirit wounded by what she accounted a flippancy.

'Mistake me not,' I hastened to elucidate. 'It is lest they should employ force and compel you at once to enter into this union that I counsel you to offer no resistance. Beg for a little time, vaguely suggesting that you are not indisposed to the Lord Giovanni's suit.'

'That were deceit,' she protested.

'A trusty weapon with which to combat tyranny,' said I.

'Well? And then?' she questioned. 'Such a state of things cannot endure for ever. It must end some day.'

I shook my head, and I smiled down upon her a smile that was very full of confidence.

'That day will never dawn, unless the Lord Giovanni's impatience transcends all bounds.'

She looked at me, a puzzled glance in her eyes, a bewildered expression knitting her fine brows.

'I do not take your meaning, my friend,' she complained.

'Then mark the enucleation. I will expound this meaning of mine through the medium of a parable. In Babylon of old there dwelt a king whose name was Belshazzar, who, having fallen into habits of voluptuousness and luxury, was so enslaved by them as to feast and make merry whilst a certain Darius, King of the Medes, was marching in arms against his capital. At a feast one night the fingers of a man's hand were seen to write upon the wall, and the words they wrote were a belated warning: "Mene, mene, tekel, upharsin."'

She looked at me, her eyes round with inquiry, and a faint smile of uncertainty on her lips.

'Let me confess that your elucidation helps me but little.'

'Ponder it, Madonna,' I urged her. 'Substitute Giovanni Sforza for Belshazzar, Cesare Borgia for King Darius, and you have the key to my parable.'

'But is it indeed so? Does danger threaten Pesaro from that quarter?'

'Aye, does it,' I answered, almost impatiently. 'The tide of war is surging up, and presently will whelm us utterly. Yet here sits the Lord Giovanni making merry with balls and masques and *burle* and banquets, wholly unprepared, wholly unconscious of his peril. There may be no hand to write a warning on his walls — or else, as in the case of Babylon, the hand will write when it is too late to avert the evil — yet there are not wanting other signs for those that have the wit to read them; nor is a wondrous penetration needed.'

'And you think then —' she began.

'I think that if you are obdurate with him, he and your brother may hurry you by force into this union. But if you temporise with half-promises, with suggestions that before Christmas you may grow reconciled to his wishes, he will be patient.'

'But what if Christmas comes and finds us still in this position?'

'It will need a miracle for that; or, at least, the death of Cesare Borgia — an unlikely event, for they say he uses great precautions. Saving the miracle, and providing Cesare lives, I will give the Lord Giovanni's reign in Pesaro at most two months.'

We had halted now, and were confronting each other in the descending gloom.

'Lazzaro, dear friend,' she cried, almost with gaiety, 'I was wise to take counsel with you. You have planted in my heart a very vigorous growth of hope.'

We turned soon after, and started to retrace our steps, for she might be ill-advised to remain absent overlong.

I left her on the terrace in a very different spirit from that in which she had come to me, bearing with me her promise that she would act as I had advised her. No doubt I had taken a load from her gentle soul, and oddly enough I had taken, too, a load from mine.

Things fell out as I said they would in so far as Giovanni Sforza and Filippo were concerned. Madonna's seeming amenability to their wishes stayed their insistence, and they could but respect her wishes to let the betrothal be delayed yet a little while. And during the weeks that followed, it was I scarce know whether more pitiable or more amusing to see the efforts that Giovanni made to win her ardently desired affection.

Love has sharp eyes at times, and a dullard under the influence of the baby god will turn shrewd and exert rare wiles in the conduct of his wooing. Giovanni, by some intuition usually foreign to his dull nature, seemed to divine what manner of man would be Madonna Paola's ideal, and strove to pass himself off as possessed of the attributes of that ideal, with an ardour that was pitiably comical. He became an actor by the side of whom those comedians that played impromptus for his delectation were the merest bunglers with the art. He gathered that Madonna

Paola loved the poets and their stately diction, and so, to please her better, he became a poet for the season.

'Poeta nascitur' the proverb runs, and that proverb's truth was doubtless forced home upon the Lord Giovanni at an early stage of his excursions into the flowery meads of prosody. Fortunately he lacked the supreme vanity that is the attribute of most poetasters, and he was able to see that such things as after hours of midnight-labour he contrived to pen would evoke nothing but her amusement — unless, indeed, it were her scorn — and render him the laughing-stock of all his Court.

So, in the wisdom of despair, he came to me, and with a gentleness that in the past he had rarely manifested for me, he asked me was I skilled in writing verse. There were not wanting others to whom he might have gone, for there was no lack of rhymesters about his Court; but perhaps he thought he could be more certain of my silence than of theirs.

I answered him that were the subject to my taste, I might succeed in throwing off some passable lines upon it. He pressed gold upon me, and bade me there and then set about fashioning an ode to Madonna Paola, and to forget, when it was done, under pain of a whipping to the bone, that I had written it.

I obeyed him with a right good will. For what subject of all subjects possible was there that made so powerful an appeal to my inclinations? Within an hour he had the ode — not perhaps such a poem as might stand comparison with the verses of Messer Petrarca, yet a very passable effusion, chaste of conceit, and palpitating with sincerity and adoration. It was in that that I addressed her as the 'Holy

Flower of the Quince,' which was the symbol of the House of Santafior.

So great an impression made that ode that on the morrow the Lord Giovanni came to me with a second bribe and a second threat of torture. I gave him a sonnet of Petrarchian manner which went near to outshining the merits of the ode. And now, these requests of the Lord Giovanni's assumed an almost daily regularity, until it came to seem that did affairs continue in this manner for yet a little while I should have earned me enough to have repurchased Biancomonte, and so ended my troubles. And good was the value that I gave him for his gold. How good, he never knew; for how was he, the clod, to guess that this despised jester of his Court was pouring out his very soul into the lines he wrote to the tyrant's orders?

It is scant wonder that, at last, Madonna Paola who had begun by smiling, was touched and moved by the ardent worship that sighed from those perfervid verses. So touched, indeed, was she as to believe the Lord Giovanni's love to be the pure and holy thing those lines presented it, and to conclude that this love had wrought in him a wondrous and ennobling transformation. That so she thought I have the best of all reasons to affirm, for I had it from her very lips one day.

'Lazzaro,' she sighed, 'it is occurring to me that I have done the Lord Giovanni an injustice. I have misgauged his character. I held him to be a shallow, unlettered clown, devoid of any finer feelings. Yet his verses have a merit that is far above the common note of these writings, and they breathe such fine and lofty sentiments as could never spring from any but a fine and lofty soul.'

How I came to keep my tongue from wagging out the truth I scarcely know. It may be that I was frightened of the punishment that might overtake me did I betray my master; but I rather think that it was the fear of betraying myself, and so being flung into the outer darkness where there was no such radiant presence as Madonna Paola's. For had I told her it was I had penned those poems that were the marvel of the Court, she must of necessity have guessed my secret, for to such quick wits as hers it must have been plain at once that they were no va-pourings of artistry, but the hot expressions of a burning truth. It was in that — in their supreme sincerity — that their chief virtue lay.

Thus weeks wore on. The vintage season came and went; the roses faded in the gardens of the Palazzo Sforza, and the trees put on their autumn garb of gold. October was upon us, and with it came, at last, the fear that long ago should have spurred us into activity. And now that it came it did not come to stimulate, but to palsy. Terror-stricken at the con-quering advance of Valentino — which was the name they now gave Cesare Borgia; a name derived from his Duchy of Valentinois — Giovanni Sforza abruptly ceased his revelling, and made a hurried appeal for help to Francesco Gonzaga, Lord of Mantua — his brother-in-law, through the Lord of Pesaro's first marriage. The Mantuan Marquis sent him a hundred mercenaries under the command of an Albanian named Giacomo. As well might he have sent him a hundred figs wherewith to pelt the army of Valentino!

Disaster swooped down swiftly upon the Lord of Pesaro. His very people, seeing in what case they were, and how unprepared was their tyrant to defend

them, wisely resolved that they would run no risks
of fire and pillage by aiding to oppose the irresistible
force that was being hurled against us.

It was on the second Sunday in October that the
storm burst over the Lord Giovanni's head. He was
on the point of leaving the Castle to attend Mass at
San Domenico, and in his company were Filippo
Sforza of Santafior and Madonna Paola, besides
courtiers and attendants, amounting in all to perhaps
a score of gallant cavaliers and courtly ladies. The
cavalcade was drawn up in the quadrangle, and Giovanni was on the point of mounting, when, of a
sudden, a rumbling noise, as of distant thunder, but
too continuous for that, arrested him, his foot already in the stirrup.

'What is that?' he asked, an ashen pallor overspreading his effeminate face, as, doubtless, the
thought of the enemy came uppermost in his mind.

Men looked at one another with fear in their eyes,
and some of the ladies raised their voices in querulous
beseeching for reassurance. They had their answer
even as they asked. The Albanian Giacomo, who was
now virtually the provost of the Castle, appeared
suddenly at the gates with half a score of men. He
raised a warning hand, which compelled the Lord
Giovanni to pause; then he rasped out a brisk command to his followers. The winches creaked, and
the drawbridge swung up even as with a clank and
rattle of chains the portcullis fell.

That done, he came forward to impart the ominous
news which one of his riders had brought him at the
gallop from the Porta Romana.

A party of some fifty men, commanded by one of
Cesare's captains, had ridden on in advance of the

main army to call upon Pesaro to yield to the forces
of the Church. And the people, without hesitation, had
butchered the guard and thrown wide the gates, invit-
ing the enemy to enter the town and seize the Castle.
And to the end that this might be the better achieved,
a hundred or so had traitorously taken up arms, and
were pressing forward to support the little company
that came, with such contemptuous daring, to storm
our fortress and prepare the way for Valentino.

It was a pretty situation this for the Lord Giovanni,
and here were fine opportunities for some brave acting
under the eyes of his adored Madonna Paola. How
would he bear himself now? I wondered.

He promised mighty well once the first shock of the
news was overcome.

'By God and His saints!' he roared, 'though it
may be all that it is given me to do, I'll strike a blow
to punish these dastards who have betrayed me, and
to crush the presumption of this captain who attacks
us with fifty men. It is a contempt which he shall
bitterly repent him.'

Then he thundered to Giacomo to marshal his
men, and he called upon those of his courtiers who
were knights to put on their armour that they might
support him. Lastly he bade a page go help him to
arm, that he might lead his little force in person.

I saw Madonna Paola's eyes gleam with a sudden
light of admiration, and I guessed that in the matter
of Giovanni's valour her opinions were undergoing
the same change as the verses had caused them to
undergo in the matter of his intellect.

Myself, I was amazed. For here was a Lord
Giovanni I seemed never to have known, and I was
eager to behold the sequel to so fine a prologue.

CHAPTER IX

THE FOOL-AT-ARMS

THAT valorous bearing that the Lord Giovanni showed whilst, with Madonna Paola's glance upon him, his fear of seeming afraid was greater than his actual fear of our assailants, he cast aside like a mantle once he was within the walls of his Castle, and under the eyes of none save the page and myself, for I followed idly at a respectful distance.

He stood irresolute and livid of countenance, his eagerness to arm and to lead his mercenaries and his knights all departed out of him. It was that curiosity of mine to see the sequel to his stout words that had led me to follow him, and what I saw was, after all, no more than I might have looked for — the proof that his big talk of sallying forth to battle was but so much acting. Yet it must have been acting of such a quality as to have deceived even his very self.

Now, however, by the main steps, he halted in the cool gloom of the gallery, and I saw that fear had caught his heart in an icy grip and was squeezing it empty. In his irresolution he turned about, and his gloomy eye fell upon me loitering in the porch. At that he turned to the page who followed in obedience to his command.

'Begone!' he growled at the lad, 'I will have Boccadoro, there, to help me arm.' And with a poor attempt at mirth — 'The act is a madness,' he muttered, 'and so it is fitting that Folly should put on my armour for it. Come with me, you,' he bade me, and I, obediently, gladly, went forward and up the wide stone staircase after him, leaving the page to speculate as he listed on the matter of his abrupt dismissal.

I read the Lord Giovanni's motives, as clearly as if they had been written for me by his own hand. The opinion in which I might hold him was to him a matter of so small account that he little cared that I should be the witness of the weakness which he feared was about to overcome him — nay, which had overcome him already. Was I not the one man in Pesaro who already knew his true nature, as revealed by that matter of the verses which I had written, and of which he had assumed the authorship? He had no shame before me, for I already knew the very worst of him, and he was confident that I would not talk lest he should destroy me at my first word. And yet, there was more than that in his motive for choosing me to go with him in that hour, as I was to learn once we were closeted in his chamber.

'Boccadoro,' he cried, 'can you not find me some way out of this?' Under his beard I saw the quiver of his lips as he put the question.

'Out of this?' I echoed, scarce understanding him at first.

'Aye, man — out of this Castle, out of Pesaro. Bestir those wits of yours. Is there no way in which it might be done, no disguise under which I might escape?'

'Escape?' quoth I, looking at him, and endeavouring to keep from my eyes the contempt that was in my heart. Dear God! Had revenge been all I sought of him, how I might have gloated over his miserable downfall!

'Do not stand there staring with those hollow eyes!' he cried, anger and fear blending horridly in his voice and rendering shrill its pitch. 'Find me a way! Come, knave, find me a way, or I'll have you broken on the wheel. Set your wits to save that long, lean body from destruction. Think, I bid you.'

He was moving restlessly as he spoke, swayed by the agitation of terror that possessed him like a devil. I looked at him now without dissembling my scorn. Even in such an hour as this the habit of hectoring cruelty remained him.

'What shall it avail me to think?' I asked him in a voice that was as cold and steady as his was hot and quavering. 'Were you a bird I might suggest to you flight across the sea. But you are a man, a very human, a very mortal man, although your father made you Lord of Pesaro.'

Even as I was speaking, the thunder of the besiegers reached our ears — such a dull roar it was as that of a stormy sea in winter time. Maddened by his terror he stood over me now, his eyes flashing wildly in his white face.

'Another word in such a tone,' he rasped, his fingers on his dagger, 'and I'll make an end of you. I need your help, animal!'

I shook my head, my glance meeting his without fear. I was of twice his strength, we were alone, and the hour was one that levelled ranks. Had he made the least attempt to carry out his threat, had he but drawn an inch of the steel he fingered, I think I should have slain him with my hands without fear or thought of consequences.

'I have no help for you such as you need,' I answered him. 'I am but the Fool of Pesaro. Whoever looked to a Fool for miracles?'

'But here is death,' he almost moaned.

'Lord of Pesaro,' I reminded him, 'your mercenaries are under arms by your command, and your knights are joining them. They wait for the fulfilment of your promise to lead them out against the enemy. Shall you fail them in such an hour as this?'

He sank, limp as an empty scabbard, to a chair.

'I dare not go. It is death,' he answered miserably.

'And what but death is it to remain here?' I asked, torturing him with more zest than ever he had experienced over the agonies of some poor victim on the rack. 'In bearing yourself gallantly there lies a slender chance for you. Your people seeing you in arms and ready to defend them may yet be moved to a return of loyalty.'

'A fig for their loyalty,' was his peevish, craven answer. 'What shall it avail me when I'm slain!'

God! was there ever such a coward as this, such a weak-souled, water-hearted dastard?

'But you may not be slain,' I urged him. And then I sounded a fresh note. 'Bethink you of Madonna Paola and of the brave things you promised her.'

He flushed a little, then paled again, then sat very still. Shame had touched him at last, yet its grip was not enough to make a man of him. A moment he remained irresolute, whilst that shame fought a hard battle with his fears.

But those fears proved stronger in the end, and his shame was overthrown by them.

'I dare not,' he gasped, his slender, delicate hands clutching at the arms of his chair. 'Heaven knows I am not skilled in the use of arms.'

'It asks no skill,' I assured him. 'Put on your armour, take a sword and lay about you. The most
ignorant scullion in your kitchens could perform it
given that he had the spirit.'

He moistened his lips with his tongue, and his eyes
looked dead as a snake's. Suddenly he rose and took a
step towards the armour that was piled about a great
leathern chair. Then he paused and turned to me
once more.

'Help me to put it on,' he said in a voice that he
strove to render steady. Yet scarcely had I reached
the pile and taken up the breastplate, when he
recoiled again from the task. He broke into a torrent
of blasphemy.

'I will not sacrifice myself,' he almost screamed.
'Jesus! not I. I will find a way out of this. I will live
to return with an army and regain my throne.'

'A most wise purpose. But, meanwhile, your men
are waiting for you; Madonna Paola di Santafior is
waiting for you, and — hark! — the bellowing crowd
is waiting for you.'

'They wait in vain,' he snarled. 'Who cares for
them? The Lord of Pesaro am I.'

'Care you, then, nothing for them? Will you have
your name written in history as that of a coward who
would not lift his sword to strike one blow for honour's sake ere he was driven out like a beast by the
mere sound of voices?'

That touched him. His vanity rose in arms.

'Take up that corselet,' he commanded hoarsely.

I did his bidding, and, without a word, he raised
his arms that I might fit it to his breast. Yet in the
instant that I turned me to pick up the back-piece,
a crash resounded through the chamber. He had

hurled the breastplate to the ground in a fresh access of terror-rage. He strode towards me, his eyes glittering like a madman's.

'Go you!' he cried, and with outstretched arms he pointed wildly across the courtyard. 'You are very ready with your counsels. Let me behold your deeds. Do you put on the armour and go out to fight those animals.'

He raved, he ranted, he scarce knew what he said or did, and yet the words he uttered sank deep into my heart, and a sudden, wild ambition swelled my bosom.

'Lord of Pesaro,' I cried, in a voice so compelling that it sobered him, 'if I do this thing what shall be my reward?'

He stared at me stupidly for a moment. Then he laughed in a silly, crackling fashion.

'Eh?' he queried. 'Gesù!' And he passed a hand over his damp brow, and threw back the hair that cumbered it. 'What is the thing that you would do, Fool?'

'Why, the thing you bade me,' I answered firmly. 'Put on your armour, and shut down the visor so that all shall think it is the Lord Giovanni, Tyrant of Pesaro, who rides. If I do this thing, and put to rout the rabble and the fifty men that Cesare Borgia has sent, what shall be my reward?'

He watched me with twitching lips, his glance fixed upon me and a faint colour kindling in his face. He saw how easy the thing might be. Perhaps he recalled that he had heard that I was skilled in arms — having spent my youth in the exercise of them, against the time when I might fling the challenge that had brought me to my Fool's estate. Maybe he recalled how I had borne myself against long odds on that adventure with Madonna Paola, years ago. Just such a vanity as had spurred him to have me write him verses that he might pretend were of his own making, moved him now to grasp at my proposal. They would all think that Giovanni's armour contained Giovanni himself. None would ever suspect Boccadoro the Fool within that shell of steel. His honour would be vindicated, and he would not lose the esteem of Madonna Paola. Indeed, if I returned covered with glory, that glory would be his; and if he elected to fly thereafter, he might do so without hurt to his fair name, for he would have amply proved his mettle and his courage.

In some such fashion I doubt not that the High and Mighty Giovanni Sforza reasoned during the seconds that we stood, face to face and eye to eye, in that room, the cries of the impatient ones below almost drowned in the roar of the multitude beyond.

At last he put out his hands to seize mine, and drawing me to the light he scanned my face, Heaven alone knowing what it was he sought there.

'If you do this,' said he, 'Biancomonte shall be yours again, if it remains in my power to bestow it upon you now or at any future time. I swear it by my honour.'

'Swear it by your fear of hell or by your hope of Heaven, and the compact is made,' I answered, and so palsied was he and so fallen in spirit that he showed no resentment at the scorn of his honour my words implied, but there and then took the oath that I demanded.

'And now,' I urged, 'help me to put on this armour of yours.'

Hurriedly I cast off my jester's doublet and my headdress with its jangling bells, and with a wild exultation, a joy so fierce as almost to bring tears to my eyes, I held my arms aloft whilst that poor craven strapped about my body the back and breast plates of his corselet. I, the Fool, stood there as arrogant as any knight, whilst with his noble hands the Lord of Pesaro, kneeling, made secure the greaves upon my legs, the sollerets with golden spurs, the cuissarts and the genouillères. Then he rose up, and with hands that trembled in his eagerness, he put on my brassarts and shoulder-plates, whilst I, myself, drew on my gauntlets. Next he adjusted the gorget, and handed me, last of all, the helm, a splendid headpiece of black and gold, surmounted by the Sforza lion.

I took it from him and passed it over my head. Then ere I snapped down the visor and hid the face of Boccadoro, I bade him, unless he would render futile all this masquerade, to lock the door of his closet, and lie there concealed till my return. At that a sudden doubt assailed him.

'And what,' quoth he, 'if you do not return?'

In the fever that had possessed me this was a thing that had not entered into my calculations, nor should it now. I laughed, and from the hollow of my helmet not a doubt but the sound must have seemed charged with mockery. I pointed to the cap and doublet I had shed.

'Why, then, Illustrious, it will but remain for you to complete the change.'

'Dog!' he cried; 'beast, do you deride me?'

My answer was to point out towards the yard.

'They are clamouring,' said I. 'They wax impatient. I had better go before they come for you.'

As I spoke I selected a heavy mace for only weapon, and swinging it to my shoulder I stepped to the door. On the threshold he would have stayed me, urged by his fear of what might befall him did I not return. But I heeded him not.

'Fare you well, my Lord of Pesaro,' said I. 'See that none penetrates to your closet. Make fast the door.'

'Stay!' he called after me. 'Do you hear me? Stay!'

'Others will hear you if you commit this folly,' I called back to him. 'Get you to cover.' And so I left him.

Below, in the courtyard, my coming was hailed by a great, enthusiastic clamour. They had all but abandoned hope of seeing the Lord Giovanni, so long had he been about his arming. As they brought forward my charger, I sought with my eyes Madonna Paola. I beheld her by her brother — who, it seemed, was not going with us — in the front rank of the spectators. Her cheeks were tinged with a slight flush of excitement, and her eyes glowed at the brave sight of armed men.

I mounted, and as I rode past her to take my place at the head of that company, I lowered my mace and bowed. She detained me a moment, setting her hand upon the glossy neck of my black charger.

'My lord,' she said, in a low voice, intended for my ear alone, 'this is a brave and gallant thing you do, and however slight may be your hope of prevailing, yet your honour will be safeguarded by this act, and men will remember you with respect should it come to pass that a usurper shall possess anon your throne. Bear you that in mind to lend you a glad courage. I shall pray for you, my lord, till you return.'

I bowed, answering never a word lest my voice should betray me; and musing on the matter of the strange roads that lead to a woman's heart, I passed on, to gain the van.

Two months ago, knowing Giovanni as he was, he had been detestable to her, and she contemplated with loathing the danger in which she stood of being allied to him by marriage. Since then he had made good use of a poor jester's mental gifts to incline her by the fervour of some verses to a kindlier frame of mind, and now, making good use of that same jester's courage, he completed her subjection by the display of it. She was prepared to wed the Lord Giovanni with a glad heart and a proud willingness whensoever he should desire it.

But Giacomo was beside me now, and in the quadrangle a silence reigned, all waiting for my command. From without there came such a din as seemed to argue that all hell was at the Castle gates. There were shouts of defiance and screams of abuse, whilst a constant rain of stones beat against the raised drawbridge.

They thought, no doubt, that Giovanni and his followers were at their prayers, cowering with terror. No notion had they of the armed force, some six score strong, that waited to pour down upon them. I briskly issued my command, and four men detached themselves and let down the bridge. It fell with a crash, and ere those without had well grasped the situation we had hurled ourselves across and into them with the force of a wedge, flinging them to right and to left as we crashed through with hideous slaughter. The bridge swung up again when the last of Giacomo's mercenaries was across, and we were shut out, in the midst of that fierce human maelstrom.

For some five minutes there raged such a brief, hot fight as will be remembered as long as Pesaro stands. No longer than that did it take for the crowd of citizens to realise that war was not their trade, and that they had better leave the fighting to Cesare Borgia's men; and so they fell away and left us a clear road to come at the men-at-arms. But already some forty of our saddles were empty, and the fight, though brief, had proved exhausting to many of us.

Before us, like an array of mirrors in the October sun, shone the serried ranks of the steel-cased Borgia soldiers, their lances in rest, waiting to receive us. Their leader, a gigantic man whose head was armed by no more than a pot of burnished steel, from which escaped the long red ringlets of his hair, was that same Ramiro del' Orca who had commanded the party pursuing Madonna Paola three years ago. He was, since, become the most redoubtable of Cesare's captains, and his name was, perhaps, the best hated in Italy for the grim stories that were connected with it.

As we rode on he backed to join the foremost rank of his soldiers, and his voice — a voice that Stentor might have envied — trumpeted a laugh at sight of us.

'Gesù!' he roared, so that I heard him above the thunder of our hoofs. 'What has come to Giovanni Sforza? Has he, perchance, become a man since Madonna Lucrezia divorced him? I will bear her the news of it, my good Giovanni — my living thunderbolt of Jove!'

His men echoed his boisterous mood, infected by it, and this, I argued, boded ill for the courage of those that followed me. Another moment and we had swept into them, and many there were who laughed no more, or went to laugh with those in hell.

For myself I singled out the blustering Ramiro, and I let him know it by a swinging blow of my mace upon his morion. It was a most finely tempered piece of steel, for my stroke made no impression on it, though Ramiro winced and raised his stout sword to return the compliment.

'Body of God!' he croaked, 'you become a very god of war, Giovanni. To me, then, my lusty Mars! We'll make a fight of it that poets shall sing of over winter fires. Look to yourself!'

His sword caught me a cunning, well-aimed blow on the side of my helm, and thence, glanced to my shoulder. But for the quality of Giovanni's head-piece of a truth there had been an end to the warring of a Fool. I smote him back, a mighty blow upon his epaulière that shore the steel plate from his shoulder, and left him a vulnerable spot. At that he swore ferociously, and his bloodshot eyes grew wicked as the fiend's. A second time he essayed that sidelong blow upon my helm, and with such force and ready address that he burst the fastening of my visor on the left, so that it swung down and left my beaver open.

With a cry of triumph he closed with me, and shortened his sword to stab me in the face. And then a second cry escaped him, for the countenance he beheld was not the countenance he had looked to see. Instead of the fair skin, the handsome features and the bearded mouth of the Lord Giovanni, he beheld a shaven face, a hooked nose and a complexion swarthy as the devil's.

'I know you, rogue,' he roared. 'By the Host! your valour seemed too fierce for Giovanni Sforza. You are Bocca—'

Exerting all the strength that I had been gradually collecting, I hurled him back with a force that almost drove him from the saddle, and rising in my stirrups I rained blow after blow upon his morion ere he could recover.

'Dog!' I muttered softly, 'your knowledge shall be the death of you.'

He drew away from me at last, and during the moments that I spent in readjusting my visor he sallied, and charged me again. His blustering was gone and his face grown pale, for such blows as mine could not have been without effect. Not a doubt of it but he was taken with amazement to find such fighting qualities in a Fool — an amazement that must have eclipsed even that of finding Boccadoro in the armour of Giovanni Sforza.

Again he swung his sword in that favourite stroke of his; but this time I caught the edge upon my mace, and ere he could recover I aimed a blow straight at his face. He lowered his head, like a bull on the point of charging, and so my blow descended again upon his morion, but with a force that rolled him, senseless, from the saddle.

Before I could take a breathing space I was beset by at least a dozen of his followers who had stood at hand during the encounter, never doubting that victory must be ultimately with their invincible captain. They drove me back foot by foot, fighting lustily, and performing — it was said afterwards by the anxious ones that watched us from the Castle, among whom was Madonna Paola — such deeds of strength

and prowess as never romancer sang of in his wildest
flight of fancy.

My men had suffered sorely, but the brave Giacomo still held them together, fired by the example
that I set him, until in the end the day was ours.
Discouraged by the disabling of their captain, so
soon as they had gathered him up, our opponents
thought of nothing but retreat; and retreat they did,
hotly pursued by us, and never allowed to pause or
slacken rein until we had hurled them out of the town
of Pesaro, to get them back to Cesare Borgia with
the tale of their ignominious discomfiture.

CHAPTER X

THE FALL OF PESARO

AS we rode back through the town of Pesaro, some fifty men of the six score that had sallied from the Castle a half-hour ago, we found the streets well-nigh deserted, the rebellious citizens having fled back to the shelter of their homes, like rats to their burrows in time of peril.

As we advanced through the shambles that we had left about the Castle gates, it occurred to me that within the courtyard a crowd would be waiting to receive and welcome me, and it became necessary to devise some means of avoiding this reception. I beckoned Giacomo to my side.

'Let it be given out that I will speak to no man until I have rendered thanks to Heaven for this signal victory,' I muttered to the unsuspecting Albanian. 'Do you clear a way for me so soon as we are within.'

He obeyed me so well that when the bridge had been let down, he preceded me with a couple of his men, and gently but firmly pressed back those that would have approached — among the first of whom were Madonna Paola and her brother.

'Way!' he shouted. 'Make way for the High and Mighty Lord of Pesaro!'

Thus I passed through, my half-shattered visor sufficiently closed still to conceal my face, and in this manner I gained the door of the eastern wing and dismounted. Two or three attendants sprang forward, ready to go with me that they might assist me to disarm. But I waved them imperiously back, and mounted the stairs alone. Alone I crossed the ante-chamber, and tapped at the door of the Lord Gio-vanni's closet. Instantly it opened, for he had watched my return and been awaiting me. Hastily he drew me in and closed the door.

He was flushed with excitement and trembling like a leaf. Yet at the sight that I presented he lost some of his high colour, and recoiled to stare at my armour, battered, dinted, and splashed with browning stains, which loudly proclaimed the fray through which I had been.

He fell to praising my valour, to speaking of the great service I had rendered him, and of the gratitude that he would ever entertain for me, all in terms of a fawning, cloying sweetness that disgusted me more than ever his cruelties had done. I took off my hel-met whilst he spoke, and let it fall with a crash. The face I revealed to him was livid with fatigue, and blackened with the dust that had caked upon my sweat. He came forward again and helped hastily to strip off my harness, and when that was done he fetched a great silver basin and a ewer of embossed gold from which he poured me fragrant rosewater that I might wash. Macerated sweet herbs he found me, lupin meal and glasswort, the better that I might cleanse myself; and when, at last, I was refreshed by my ablutions, he poured me a goblet of a full-bodied golden wine that seemed to infuse fresh life into my veins. And all the time he spoke of the prowess I had shown, and lamented that all these years he should have had me at his Court and never guessed my worth.

At length I turned to resume my clothes. And

since it must excite comment and perhaps arouse suspicion were I to appear in any but my jester's garish livery, I once more assumed my foliated cape, my cap and bells.

'Wear it yet for a little while,' he said, 'and thus complete the service you have done me. Presently you may doff it for all time, and resume your true estate. Biancomonte, as I promised you, shall be yours again. The Lord of Pesaro does not betray his word.'

I smiled grimly at the pride of his utterance.

'It is an easy thing,' said I, 'freely to give that which is no longer ours.'

He coloured with the anger that was ever ready.

'What shall that mean?' he asked.

'Why, that in a few days you will have Cesare Borgia here, and you will be Lord of Pesaro no more. I have saved your honour for you. More than that it were idle to attempt.'

'Think not that I shall submit,' he cried. 'I shall find in Italy the help I need to return and drive the usurper out. You must have faith in that, yourself, else had you never bargained with me as you have done for the return of your estates.'

To that I answered nothing, but urged him to go below and show himself; and the better that he might bear himself among his courtiers, I detailed to him the most salient features of that fight.

He went, not without a certain uneasiness which, however, was soon dispelled by the thunder of acclamation with which he was received, not only by his courtiers, but by the soldiers who had fought in that hot skirmish, and who believed that it was he had led them.

Meanwhile I sat above, in the closet he had vacated, and thence I watched him, with such mingling feelings in my heart as baffle now my halting pen. Scorn there was in my mood and a hot contempt of him that he could stand there and accept their acclamation with an air of humility that I am persuaded was assumed; a certain envious anger was there, too, to think that such a weak-kneed, lily-livered craven should receive the plaudits of the deeds that I, his buffoon, had performed for him. Those acclamations were not for him, although those who acclaimed him thought so. They were for the man who had routed Ramiro del' Orca and his followers, and that man assuredly was I. Yet there I crouched above, behind the velvet curtains where none might see me, whilst he stood smiling and toying with his brown beard and listening to the fine words of praise that, I could imagine, were falling from the lips of Madonna Paola, who had drawn near and was speaking to him.

There is in my nature a certain love of effectiveness, a certain taste for theatrical parade and the contriving of odd situations. This bent of mine was whispering to me then to throw wide the window, and, stemming their noisy plaudits, announce to them the truth of what had passed. Yet what if I had done so? They would have accounted it but a new jest of Boccadoro, the Fool, and one so ill-conceived that they might urge the Lord Giovanni to have him whipped for it.

Aye, it would have been a folly, a futile act that would have earned me unbelief, contempt and anger. And yet there was a moment when jealousy urged me almost headlong to that rashness. For in Madonna Paola's eyes there was a new expression as they rested

on the face of Giovanni Sforza—an expression that
told me she had come to love this man whom a little
while ago she had despised.

God! was there ever such an irony? Was there
ever such a paradox? She loved him, and yet it was
not him she loved. The man she loved was the man
who had shown the qualities of his mind in the verses
with which the Court was ringing; the man who had
that morning given proof of his high mettle and
knightly prowess by the deeds of arms he had performed. I was that man—not he at whom so ador-
ingly she looked. And so—I argued, in my warped
way and with the philosophy worthy of a Fool—it
was I whom she loved, and Giovanni was but the
symbol that stood for me. He represented the songs
and the deeds that were mine.

But if I did not throw wide that window and proclaim the fact to ears that would have been deaf to
the truth of them, what think you that I did? I took
a subtler vengeance. I repaired to my own chamber,
procured me pen and ink, and there, with a heart that
was brimming over with gall, I penned an epic
modelled upon the stately lines of Virgil, wherein I
sang the prowess of the Lord Giovanni Sforza, de-
scribing that morning's mighty feat of arms, and
detailing each particular of the combat 'twixt Giovanni and Ramiro del' Orca.

It was a brave thing when it was done; a finer and
worthier poetical achievement than any that I had
yet encompassed, and that night, after they had
supped, as merrily as though Duke Valentino had
never been heard of, and whilst they were still sitting
at their wine, I got me a lute and stole down to the
banqueting-hall.

I announced myself by leaping on a table and loudly twanging the strings of my instrument. There was a hush, succeeded by a burst of acclamation. They were in a high good-humour, and the Fool with a new song was the very thing they craved.

When silence was restored I began, and whilst my fingers moved sluggishly across the strings, striking here and there a chord, I recited the epic I had penned. My voice swelled with a feverish enthusiasm whose colossal irony none there save one could guess. He, at first surprised, grew angry presently, as I could see by the cloud that had settled on his brow. Yet he restrained himself, and the rest of the company were too enthralled by the breathless quality of my poem to bestow their glances on any countenance save mine.

Madonna Paola sat upon the Lord of Pesaro's right, and her blue eyes were round and her lips parted with enthusiasm as I proceeded. And when presently I came to that point in the fight betwixt Giovanni and Ramiro del' Orca, when Ramiro, having broken down the Lord Giovanni's visor, was on the point of driving his sword into his adversary's face, I saw her shrink in a repetition of the morning's alarm, and her bosom heaved more swiftly, as though the issue of that combat hung now upon my lines and she were made anxious again for the life of the man whom she had learnt to love.

I finished on a slow and stately rhythm, my voice rising and falling softly, after the manner of a Gregorian chant, as I dwelt on the piety that had succeeded the Lord of Pesaro's brave exploits, and how upon his return from the stricken field he had repaired straight to his closet, his battered and bloody

harness on his back, that he might kneel ere he disarmed and render thanks to God for the victory vouch-
safed him.

On that 'Te Deum' I finished softly, and as my
voice ceased and the vibration of my last chord
melted away, a thunder of applause was my reward.

Men leapt from their chairs in their enthusiasm,
and crowded round the table on which I was perched,
whilst, when presently I sprang down, one noble
woman kissed me on the lips before them all, saying
that my mouth was indeed a mouth of gold.

Madonna Paola was leaning towards the Lord Giovanni, her eyes shining with excitement and filmed
with tears as they proudly met his glance, and I knew
that my song had but served to endear him the more
to her by causing her to realise more keenly the brave
qualities of the adventure that I sang. The sight of it
almost turned me faint, and I would have eluded
them and got away as I had come but that they lifted
me up and bore me so to the table at which the Lord
Giovanni sat. He smiled, but his face was very pale.
Could it be that I had touched him? Could it be that
I had driven the iron into his soul, and that he could
not bear to confront me, knowing what a dastard I
must deem him?

The splendid Filippo of Santafior had risen to his
feet, and was waving a white, bejewelled hand in an
imperious demand for silence. When at last it came
he spoke, his voice silvery and his accents mincing.

'Lord of Pesaro, I demand a boon. He who for
years has suffered the ignominy of the motley is at
last revealed to us as a poet of such magnitude of soul
and richness of expression that he would not suffer by
comparison with the great Bojardo or the greater

Virgil. Let him be stripped for ever of that hideous garb he wears, and let him be treated, hereafter, with the dignity his high gifts deserve. Thus shall the day come when Pesaro will take honour in calling him her son.'

Loud and long was the applause that succeeded his words, and when at last it had died down, the Lord Giovanni proved equal to the occasion, like the consummate actor that he was.

'I would,' said he, 'that these high gifts, of which to-night he has afforded proof, could have been employed upon a worthier subject. I fear me that since you have heard his epic you will be prone to over-estimate the deed of which it tells the story. I would, too, my friends,' he continued, with a sigh, 'that it were still mine to offer him such encouragement as he deserves. But I am sorely afraid that my days in Pesaro are numbered, that my sands are all but run — at least, for a little while. The conqueror is at our gates, and it would be vain to set against the overwhelming force of his numbers the handful of valiant knights and brave soldiers that to-day opposed and scattered his forerunners. It is my intention to withdraw, now that my honour is safe by what has passed, and that none will dare to say that it was through fear that I fled. Yet my absence, I trust, may be but brief. I go to collect the necessary resources, for I have powerful friends in this Italy whose interests touching the Duca Valentino go hand in hand with mine, and who will, thus, be the readier to lend me assistance. Once I have this, I shall return and then — woe to the vanquished!'

The tide of enthusiasm that had been rising as he spoke, now overflowed. Swords leapt from their

scabbards — mere toy weapons were they, meant
more for ornament than offence, yet were they the
earnest of the stouter arms those gentlemen were
ready to wield when the time came. He quieted
their clamours with a dignified wave of the hand.

'When that day comes I shall see to it that Boccadoro has his deserts. Meanwhile let the suggestion of
my illustrious cousin be acted upon, and let this
gifted poet be arrayed in a manner that shall sort
better with the nobility of his mind that to-night he
has revealed to us.'

Thus was it that I came, at last, to shed the motley and move among men garbed as themselves.
And with my outward trappings I cast off, too, the
name of Boccadoro, and I insisted upon being known
again as Lazzaro Biancomonte.

But in so far as the Court of Pesaro was concerned,
this new life upon which I was embarked was of little
moment, for on the Tuesday that followed that first
Sunday in October of such momentous memory, the
Lord Giovanni's Court passed out of being.

It came about with his flight to Bologna, accompanied by the Albanian captain and his men, as well
as by several of the knights who had joined in Sunday's fray. Ardently, as I came afterwards to learn,
did he urge Madonna Paola and her brother to go
with them, and I believe that the lady would have
done his will in this had not the Lord Filippo opposed
the step. He was no warrior himself, he swore — for
it was a thing he made open boast of, affecting to
despise all who followed the coarse trade of arms —
and, as for his sister, it was not fitting that she should
go with a fugitive party made up of a handful of
knights and some fifty rough mercenaries, and be

exposed to the hardships and perils that must be theirs. Not even when he was reminded that the advancing conqueror was Cesare Borgia did it affect him, for despite his shallow, mincing ways, and his paraded scorn of war and warriors, the Lord Filippo was stout enough at heart. He did not fear the Borgia, he answered serenely, and if he came, he would offer him such hospitality as lay within his power.

He came at last, did the mighty Cesare, although between his coming and Giovanni's flight a full fortnight sped. As for myself, I spent the time at the Sforza Palace, whither the Lord Filippo had carried me as his guest, he being greatly taken with me and determined to become my patron. We had news of Giovanni, first from Bologna and later from Ravenna, whither he was fled. At first he talked of returning to Pesaro with three hundred men he hoped to have from the Marquis of Mantua. But probably this was no more than another piece of that big talk of his, meant to impress the sorrowing and repining Madonna Paola, who suffered more for him, maybe, than he suffered himself.

She would talk with me for hours together of the Lord Giovanni, of his mental gifts, and of his splendid courage and military address, and for all that my gorge rose with jealousy and with the force of this injustice to myself, I held my peace. Indeed, indeed, it was better so. For all that I was no longer Boccadoro the Fool, yet as Lazzaro Biancomonte, the poet, I was not so much better that I could indulge any mad aspirations of my own such as might have led me to betray the dastard who had arrayed his raven self in the peacock feathers of my achievements.

In the course of the confidence with which the Lord

Filippo honoured me I made bold, on the eve of
Cesare's arrival, to suggest to him that he should remove his sister from the Palace and send her to the
Convent of Santa Caterina whilst the Borgia abode
in the town, lest the sight of her should remind Cesare
of the old-time marriage plans which his family had
centred round this lady, and lead to their revival.
Filippo heard me kindly, and thanked me freely for
the solicitude which my counsel argued. For the
rest, however, it was a counsel that he frankly ad-
mitted he saw no need to follow.

'In the three years that are sped since the Holy
Father entertained such plans for the temporal advancement of his nephew Ignacio, the fortunes of the
House of Borgia have so swollen that what was then
a desirable match for one of its members is now scarce
worthy of their attention. I do not think,' he concluded, 'that we have the least reason to fear a re-
newal of that suit.'

It may be that I am by nature suspicious and
quick to see ignoble motives in men's actions, but it
occurred to me then that the Lord Filippo would not
be so greatly put about if indeed the Borgias were to
reopen negotiations for the bestowing of Madonna
Paola's hand upon the Pope's nephew Ignacio. That
swelling of the Borgia fortunes which in the three
years had taken place, and which, he contended,
would render them more ambitious than to seek
alliance with the House of Santafior, rendered them,
nevertheless, in his eyes a more desirable family to
be allied with than in the days when he had counselled his sister's flight from Rome.

And so, I thought, despite what stood between her
and the Lord Giovanni, Filippo would know no scru-

ple now in urging her into an alliance with the House
of Borgia, should they manifest a willingness to have
that old affair reopened.

On the 29th of that same month of October, Cesare
arrived in Pesaro. His entry was a triumphant procession, and the orderliness that prevailed among the
two thousand men-at-arms that he brought with
him was a thing that spoke eloquently for the wondrous discipline enforced by this great condottiero.

The Lord Filippo was among those that met him,
and like the time-server that he was, he placed the
Sforza Palace at his disposal.

The Duca Valentino came with his retinue and the
gentlemen of his household, among whom was ever
conspicuous by his great size and red ugliness the
Captain Ramiro del' Orca, who now seemed to act
in many ways as Cesare's factotum. This captain,
for reasons which it is unnecessary to detail, I most
sedulously avoided.

On the evening of his arrival Cesare supped in
private with Filippo and the members of Filippo's
household — that is to say, with Madonna Paola and
two of her ladies, and three gentlemen attached to
the person of the Lord Filippo. Cesare's only attendants were two cavaliers of his retinue, Bartolomeo
da Capranica, his field-marshal, and Dorio Savelli, a
nobleman of Rome.

Cesare Borgia, this man whose name had so
terrible a sound in the ears of Italy's little princelings,
this man whose power and whose great gifts of
mind had made him the subject of such bitter envy
and fear, until he was the best-hated gentleman in
Italy — and, therefore, the most calumniated — was
little changed from that Cardinal of Valencia, in

whose service I had been for a brief season. The pallor of his face was accentuated by the ill health in which he found himself just then, and the air of feverish restlessness that had always pervaded him was grown more marked in the years that were sped, as was, after all, but natural, considering the nature of the work that had claimed him since he had deposed his priestly vestments. He was splendidly arrayed, and he bore himself with an imperial dignity, a dignity, nevertheless, tempered with graciousness and charm, and as I regarded him then, it was borne in upon me that no fitter name could his godfathers have bestowed on him than that of Cesare.

The Lord Filippo exerted all his powers worthily to entertain his noble and illustrious guest, and by his extreme, almost servile affability it not only would seem that he had forgotten the favour and shelter he had received at the hands of the Lord Giovanni, but it confirmed my suspicions of his willingness to advance his own fortunes by breaking faith with the fallen tyrant in so far as his sister was concerned.

Short of actually making the proposal itself, it would seem that Filippo did all in his power to urge his sister upon the attention of Cesare. But Duke Valentino's mind at that time was too full of the concerns of conquest and administration to find room for a matter to him so trifling as the enriching of his cousin Ignacio by a wealthy alliance. To this alone, I thought, was it due that Madonna Paola escaped the persecution that might then have been hers.

On the morrow Cesare moved on to Rimini, leaving his administrators behind him to set right the affairs of Pesaro, and ensure its proper governing, in his name, hereafter.

And now that, for the present, my hopes of ever seeing my own wrongs redressed and my estates returned to me were too slender to justify my remaining longer in Pesaro, I craved of the Lord Filippo permission to withdraw, telling him frankly that my tardily aroused duty called me to my widowed mother, whom for some six years I had not seen. He threw no difficulty in the way of my going; and I was free to depart. And now came the hidden pain of my leave-taking of Madonna Paola. She seemed to grieve at my departure.

'Lazzaro,' she cried, when I had told her of my intention, 'do you, too, desert me? And I have ever held you my best of friends.'

I told her of the mother and of the duty that I owed her, whereupon she remonstrated no more, nor sought to do other than urge me to go to her. And then I spoke of Madonna's kindness to me, and of the friendship with which she had honoured one so lowly, and in the end I swore, with my hand on my heart and my soul on my lips, that if ever she had work for me, she would not need to call me twice.

'This ring, Madonna,' said I, 'was given me by the Lord Cesare Borgia, and was to have proved a talisman to open wide for me the door to fortune. It did better service than that, Madonna. It was the talisman that saved you from your pursuers that day at Cagli, three years ago.'

'You remind me, Lazzaro,' she cried, 'of how much you have sacrificed in my service. Yours must be a very noble nature that will do so much to serve a helpless lady without any hope of guerdon.'

'Nay, nay,' I answered lightly, 'you must not make so much of it. It would never have sorted with my inclinations to have turned man-at-arms. This ring, Madonna, that once has served you, I beg that you will keep, for it may serve you again.'

'I could not, Lazzaro! I could not!' she exclaimed, recoiling, yet without any show of deeming presumptuous my words or of being offended by them.

'If you would make me the reward that you say I have earned, you will do this for me. It will make me happier, Madonna. Take it' — I thrust it into her unwilling hand — 'and if ever you should need me send it back to me. That ring and the name of the place where you abide by the lips of the messenger you choose, and with a glad heart, as fast as horse can bear me, shall I ride to serve you once again.'

'In such a spirit, yes,' said she, 'I take it willingly, to treasure it as a buckler against danger, since by means of it I can bring you to my aid in time of peril.'

'Madonna, do not overestimate my powers,' I besought her. 'I would have you see in me no more than I am. But it sometimes happens that the mouse may aid the lion.'

'And when I need the lion to aid the mouse, my good Lazzaro, I will send for you.'

There were tears in her voice, and her eyes were very bright.

'Addio, Lazzaro,' she murmured brokenly. 'May God and His saints protect you. I will pray for you, and I shall hope to see you again some day, my friend.'

'Addio, Madonna!' was all that I could trust myself to say ere I fled from her presence that she might not see my deep emotion, nor hear the sobs that were threatening to betray the anguish that was ravaging my soul.

PART II
THE OGRE OF CESENA

CHAPTER XI

MADONNA'S SUMMONS

HOWEVER great the part that my mother —
sainted woman that she was — may have
played in my life, she nowise enters into the affairs
of this chronicle, so that it would be an irrelevance
and an impertinence to introduce her into these
pages. Of the joy with which she welcomed me to the
little home near Biancomonte, in which the earnings
of Boccadoro the Fool had placed her, it could interest you but little to read in detail, nor could it
interest you to know of the gentle patience with which
she cheered and humoured me during that period that
I sojourned there, tilling the little plot she owned,
reaping and garnering like any born *villano*. With a
woman's quick intuition she guessed perhaps the
canker that was eating at my heart, and with a
mother's blessed charity she sought to soothe and
mitigate my pain.

It was during this period of my existence that the
poetic gifts I had discovered myself possessed of
whilst at Pesaro, burst into full bloom; and not a little
relief did I find in the penning of those love-songs —
the true expression of what was in my heart —
which have since been given to the world under the
title of 'Le Rime di Boccadoro.' And what time I
tended my mother's land by day, and wrote by night
of the feverish, despairing love that was consuming
me, I waited for the call that, sooner or later, I knew
must come. What prophetic instinct it was had

rooted that certainty in my heart I do not pretend to say. Perhaps my hope was of such a strength that it assumed the form of certainty to solace the period of my hermitage. But that some day Madonna Paola's messenger would arrive bringing me the Borgia ring, I was as confident as that some day I must die.

Two years went by, and we were in the autumn of 1502, yet my faith knew no abating, my confidence was strong as ever. And, at last, that confidence was justified. One night of early October, as I sat at supper with my mother after the labours of the day, a sound of hoofs disturbed the peace of the silent night. It drew rapidly nearer, and long before the knock fell upon our door, I knew that it was the messenger from my lady.

My mother looked at me across the board, an expression of alarm overspreading her old face. 'Who,' her eyes seemed to ask me, 'was this horseman that rode so late?'

My hound rose from the hearth with a growl, and stood bristling, his eyes upon the door. White-haired old Silvio, the last remaining retainer of the House of Biancomonte, came forth from the kitchen, with inquiry and fear blending on his wrinkled, weather-beaten countenance.

And I, seeing all these signs of alarm, yet knowing what awaited me on the threshold, rose with a laugh, and in a bound had crossed the intervening space. I flung wide the door, and from the gloom without a man's voice greeted me with a question.

'Is this the house of Messer Lazzaro Biancomonte?'

'I am that Lazzaro Biancomonte,' answered I. 'What may your pleasure be?'

The stranger advanced until he came within the

light. He was plainly dressed, and wore a jerkin of
leather and long boots. From his air I judged him a
servant or a courier. He doffed his hat respectfully,
and held out his right hand in which something was
gleaming yellow. It was the Borgia ring.

'Pesaro,' was all he said.

I took the ring and thanked him, then bade him
enter and refresh himself ere he returned, and I called
old Silvio to bring wine.

'I am not returning,' the man informed me. 'I
am a courier riding to Parma, whom Madonna
charged with that message to you in passing.'

Nevertheless he consented to rest him a while and
sip the wine we set before him, and what time he did
so I engaged him in talk, and led him to tell me what
he knew of the trend of things at Pesaro, and what
news there was of the Lord Giovanni. He had little
enough to tell. Pesaro was flourishing and prospering
under the Borgia dominion. Of the Lord Giovanni
there was little news, saving that he was living under
the protection of the Gonzagas in Mantua, and that
so long as he was content to abide there the Borgias
seemed disposed to give him peace.

Next I made him tell me what he knew of Filippo
di Santafior and Madonna Paola. On this subject he
was better informed. Madonna Paola was well and
still with her brother at the Palace of Pesaro. The
Lord Filippo was high in favour with the Borgias,
and Cesare lately had been frequently his guest at
Pesaro, whilst once, for a few days, the Lord Ignacio
de Borgia had accompanied his illustrious cousin.

I flushed and paled at that piece of news, and the
reason of her summons no longer asked conjecture.
It was an easy thing for me, knowing what I knew,

to fill in the details which the courier omitted in ignorance from the story.

The Lord Filippo, seeking his own advancement,
had so urged his sister upon the notice of the Borgia
family — perhaps even approached Cesare — in such
a manner that it was again become a question of
wedding her to Ignacio, who had, meanwhile, remained unmarried. I could read that opportunist's
motives as easily as if he had written them down for
my instruction. Giovanni Sforza he accounted lost
beyond redemption, and I could imagine how he had
plied his wits to aid his sister to forget him, or else to
remember him no longer with affection. Whether he
had succeeded or not I could not say until I had seen
her; but meanwhile, deeming ripe the soil of her
heart for the new attachment that should redound
so much to his own credit — now that the House of
Borgia had risen to such splendid heights — he was
driving her into this alliance with Ignacio.

Faithful to the very letter of the promise I had
made her, I set out that same night, after embracing
my poor, tearful mother, and promising to return as
soon as might be. All night I rode, my soul now tortured with anxiety, now exalted at the supreme joy
of seeing Madonna, which was so soon to be mine.
I was at the gates of Pesaro before matins, and within
the Palazzo Sforza ere its inmates had broken their
fast.

The Lord Filippo welcomed me with a certain effusion, chiding me for my long absence and the ingratitude it had seemed to indicate, and never dreaming
by what summons I was brought back.

'You are well returned,' he told me in conclusion.
'We shall need you soon, to write an epithalamium.'

'You are to be wed, Magnificent?' quoth I at last, at which he laughed consumedly.

'Nay, we shall need the song for my sister's nuptials. She is to wed the Lord Ignacio Borgia, before Christmas.'

'A lofty theme,' I answered with humility, 'and one that may well demand resources nobler than those of my poor pen.'

'Then get you to work at once upon it. I will have your chamber prepared.'

He sent for his seneschal, a person — like most of the servants at the Palace — strange to me, and he gave orders that I should be sumptuously lodged. He was grown more splendid than ever in the prosperity that seemed to surround him here at Pesaro, in this palace that had undergone such changes and been so enriched during the past two years as to go near defying recognition.

When the seneschal had shown me to the quarters he had set apart for me, I made bold to make inquiries concerning Madonna Paola.

'She is in the garden, Illustrious,' answered the seneschal, deeming me, no doubt, a great lord, from the respect which Filippo had indicated should be shown me. 'Madonna has the wisdom to seek the little sunshine the year still holds. Winter will be soon upon us.'

I agreed with the old man, and dismissed him. So soon as he was gone, I quitted my chamber, and all dust-stained as I was I made my way down to the garden. A turn in one of the boxwood-bordered alleys brought me suddenly face to face with Madonna Paola.

A moment we stood looking at each other, my

heart swelling within me until I thought that it must burst. Then I advanced a step and sank on one knee before her.

'You sent for me, Madonna. I am here.'

There was a pause, and when presently I looked up into her blessed face I saw a smile of infinite sorrow on her lips, blending oddly with the gladness that shone from her sweet eyes.

'You faithful one,' she murmured at last. 'Dear Lazzaro, I did not look for you so soon.'

'Within an hour of your messenger's arrival I was in the saddle, nor did I pause until I had reached the gates of Pesaro. I am here to serve you to the utmost of my power, Madonna, and the only doubt that assails me is that my power may be all too small for the service that you need.'

'Is its nature known to you?' she asked in wonder. Then, ere I had answered, she bade me rise, and with her own hand assisted me.

'I have guessed it,' answered I, 'guided by such scraps of information as from your messenger I gleaned. It concerns, unless I err, the Lord Ignacio Borgia.'

'Your wits have lost nothing of their quickness,' she said, with a sad smile, 'and I doubt me you know all.'

'The only thing I did not know your brother has just told me — that you are to be wed before Christmas. He has ordered me to write your epithalamium.'

She drew into step beside me, and we slowly paced the alley side by side, and, as we went, withered leaves overhead, and withered leaves to make a carpet for our feet, she told me in her own way more or less what I have set down, even to her brother's self-seeking share in the transaction that she dubbed hideous and abhorrent.

She was little changed, this winsome lady, in the time that was sped. She was in her twenty-first year, but in reality she seemed to me no older than she had been on that day when first I saw her arguing with her grooms upon the road to Cagli. And from this I reassured myself that she had not been fretted overmuch by the absence of the Lord Giovanni.

Presently she spoke of him and of her plighted word, which her brother and those supple gentlemen of the House of Borgia were inducing her to dishonour.

'Once before, in a case almost identical, when all seemed lost, you came — as if Heaven directed — to my rescue. This it is that gives me confidence in such aid as you might lend me now.'

'Alas! Madonna,' I sighed, 'but the times are sorely changed, and the situations with them. What is there now that I can do?'

'What you did then. Take me beyond their reach.'

'Ah! But whither?'

'Whither but to the Lord Giovanni? Is it not to him that my troth is plighted?'

I shook my head in sorrow, a thrust of jealousy cutting me the while.

'That may not be,' said I. 'It were not seemly, unless the Lord Giovanni were here himself to take you hence.'

'Then I will write to the Lord Giovanni,' she cried. 'I will write, and you shall bear my letter.'

'What think you will the Lord Giovanni do?' I burst out, with a scorn that must have puzzled her.

'Think you his safety does not give him care enough in the hiding-place to which he has crept, that he should draw upon himself the vengeance of the Borgias?'

She stared at me in ineffable surprise. 'But the Lord Giovanni is brave and valiant,' she cried, and down in my heart I laughed in bitter mockery.

'Do you love the Lord Giovanni, Madonna?' I asked bluntly.

My question seemed to awaken fresh astonishment. It may well be that it awakened, too, reflection. She was silent for a little space. Then —

'I honour and respect him for a noble, chivalrous and gifted gentleman,' she answered me, and her answer made me singularly content, spreading a balm upon the wounds my soul had taken. But to her fresh intercessions that I should carry a letter to him, I shook my head again. My mood was stubborn.

'Believe me, Madonna, it were not only unwise, but futile.'

She protested.

'I swear it would be,' I insisted, with a convincing force that left her staring at me and wondering whence I derived so much assurance. 'We must wait. From now till Christmas we have more than two months. In two months much may befall. As a last resource we may consider communication with the Lord Giovanni. But it is a forlorn hope, Madonna, and so we will leave it until all else has failed us.'

She brightened at my promise that at least if other measures proved unavailing, we should adopt that course, and her brightening flattered me, for it bore witness to the supreme confidence she had in me.

'Lazzaro,' said she, 'I know you will not fail me. I trust you more than any living man; more, I think, than even the Lord Giovanni, whom, if God pleases, I shall some day wed.'

'Thanks, Madonna mia,' I answered, gratefully indeed. 'It is a trust that I shall ever strive to justify. Meanwhile have faith and hope, and wait.'

Once before, when, to escape the schemes of her brother who would have wed her to the Lord Giovanni, she had appealed to me, the counsel I had given her had been much the same as that which I gave her now. At the irony of it I could have laughed had any other been in question but Madonna Paola — this tender White Flower of the Quince that was like to be rudely wilted by the ruthless hands of scheming men.

CHAPTER XII

THE GOVERNOR OF CESENA

THAT night I would have supped in my own quarters but that Filippo sent for me and bade me join him and swell the little court he kept. At times I believe he almost thought that he was the true Lord of Pesaro — an opinion that may have been shared by not a few of the citizens themselves. Certainly he kept a greater state and was better housed than the Duke of Valentinois's governor.

It was a jovial company of perhaps a dozen nobles and ladies that met about his board, and Filippo bade his servants lay for me beside him. As we ate he questioned me touching the occupation that I had found during my absence from Pesaro. I used the greatest frankness with him, and answered that my life had been partly a peasant's, partly a poet's.

'Tell me what you wrote,' he bade me, his eyes resting on my face with a new look of interest, for his love of letters was one of the few things about him that was not affected.

'A few *novelle*, dealing with Court life; but chiefly verses,' answered I.

'And with these verses — what have you done?'

'I have them by me, Illustrious,' I answered.

He smiled, seemingly well pleased.

'You must read them to us,' he cried. 'If they rival that epic of yours, which I have never forgotten, they should be worth hearing.'

And presently, supper being done, I went at his

bidding to my chamber for my precious manuscripts, and, returning, I entertained the company with the reading of a portion of what I had written. They heard me with an attention that might have rendered me vain had my ambition really lain in being accounted a great writer; and when I paused, now and again, there was a murmur of applause, and many a pat on the shoulder from Filippo whenever a line, a phrase, or a stanza took his fancy.

I was perhaps too absorbed to pay any great attention to the impression my verses were producing, but presently, in one of my pauses, the Lord Filippo startled me with words that awoke me to a sense of my imprudence.

'Do you know, Lazzaro, of what your lines remind me in an extraordinary measure?'

'Of what, Excellency?' I asked politely, raising my eyes from my manuscript. They chanced to meet the glance of Madonna Paola. It was riveted upon me, and its expression was one I could not understand.

'Of the love-songs of the Lord Giovanni Sforza,' answered he. 'They resemble those poems infinitely more than they resemble the epic you wrote two years ago.'

I stammered something about the similarity being merely one of subject. But he shook his head at that, and took good note of my confusion.

'No,' said he, 'the resemblance goes deeper. There is the same facile beauty of the rhymes, the same freshness of the rhythm — remotely resembling that of Petrarca, yet very different. Conceits similar to those that were the beauty-spots of the Lord Giovanni's verses are ubiquitous in yours, and above all

there is the same fervent earnestness, the same burning tone of sincerity that rendered his *strambotti* so
worthy of admiration.'

'It may be,' I answered him, my confusion growing
under the steady gaze of Madonna Paola, 'it may be
that having heard the verses of the Lord Giovanni, I
may, unconsciously, have modelled my own lines
upon those that made so deep an impression on me.'

He looked at me gravely for a moment.

'That might be an explanation,' he answered de-
liberately, 'but frankly, if I were asked, I should give
a very different one.'

'And that would be?' came, sharp and compelling,
the voice of Madonna.

He turned to her, shrugged his shoulders and
laughed. 'Why, since you ask me,' he said, 'I should
hazard the opinion that Lazzaro, here, was of considerable assistance to the Lord Giovanni in the
penning of those verses with which he delighted us
all — and you, Madonna, I believe, particularly.'

Madonna Paola crimsoned, and her eyes fell. The
others looked at us with inquiring glances — at her,
at Filippo and at me. With a fresh laugh Filippo
turned to me.

'Confess, now, am I not right?' he asked good-
humouredly.

'Magnificent,' I murmured in tones of protest,
'ask yourself the question. Was it a likely thing that
the Lord Giovanni would enlist the services of his
jester in such a task?'

'Give me a straightforward answer,' he insisted.
'Am I right or wrong?'

'I am giving you more than a straightforward
answer, my lord,' I still evaded him, and more boldly

now. 'I am setting you on the highroad to solve the
matter for yourself by an appeal to your own good
sense and reason. Was it in the least likely, I repeat,
that the Lord Giovanni would seek the services of
his Fool to aid him write the verses in honour of the
lady of his heart?'

With a burst of mocking laughter, Filippo smote
the table a blow of his clenched hand.

'Your prevarications answer me,' he cried. 'You
will not say that I am wrong.'

'But I do say that you are wrong!' I exclaimed,
suddenly inspired. 'I did not assist the Lord Giovanni with his verses. I swear it.'

His laughter faded, and his eyes surveyed me with
a sudden solemnity.

'Then why did you evade my question?' he
demanded shrewdly. And then his countenance
changed as swiftly again. It was illumined by the
light of sudden understanding. 'I have it!' he cried.
'The answer is plain. You did not *assist* the Lord
Giovanni to write them. Why? Because you wrote
them yourself, and you gave them to him that he
might pass them off as his own.'

It was a merciful thing for me that the whole company fell into a burst of laughter and applauded
Filippo's quick discernment, which they never
doubted. All talked at once, and a hundred proofs
were advanced in support of Filippo's opinion. The
Lord Giovanni's celebrated dullness of mind, amounting almost to stupidity, was cited, and they reminded
one another of the profound astonishment with which
they had listened to the compositions that had suddenly burst from him.

Filippo turned to his sister, on whose pale face I

saw it written that she was as convinced as any there, and my feelings were those of a dastard who has broken faith with the man who trusted him.

'Do you appreciate now, Madonna,' he murmured, 'the deceits and wiles by which that craven crept like a snake into your esteem?'

I guessed at once that by that thrust he sought to incline her more to the union he had in view for her.

'At least he was no craven,' answered she. 'His burning desire to please me may have betrayed him into this foolish duplicity. But he still must live in my memory as a brave and gallant gentleman; or have you forgotten, Filippo, that noble combat with the forces of Ramiro del' Orca?'

To such a question Filippo had no answer, and presently his mood sobered a little. For myself, I was glad when the time came to withdraw from that company that twitted and pestered me and played upon my sense of shame at the imprudence I had committed.

Now that I look back, I can scarce conceive why it should have so wrought upon me; for, in truth, the little love I bore the Lord Giovanni might rather have led me to rejoice that his imposture should be laid bare to the eyes of all the world. I think that really there was an element of fear in my feelings — fear that, upon reflection, Madonna Paola might ask herself how came that burning sincerity into the love-songs written in her honour which it was now disclosed that I had penned. The answer she might find to such a question was one that might arouse her pride and so outrage it as to lead her to cast me out of her friendship and never again suffer me to approach her.

Such a conclusion, however, she fortunately did not arrive at. Haply she accounted the fervour of those lines assumed, for when on the morrow she met me, she did no more than gently chide me for the deceit that I had had a hand in practising upon her. She accepted my explanation that my share in that affair had been wrung from me with threats of torture, and putting it from her mind she returned to the matter of the approaching alliance she sought to elude, renewing her prayers that I should aid her.

'I have,' she told me then, 'one other friend who might assist us, and who has the power, perhaps, if he but has the will. He is the Governor of Cesena, and for all that he holds service under Cesare Borgia, yet he seems much devoted to me, and I do not doubt that to further my interests he would even consent to pit his wits against those of the family he serves.'

'In which case, Madonna,' answered I, spurred to it, perhaps, by an insensate pang of jealousy at the thought that there should be another beside myself to have her confidence, 'he would be a traitor. And it is ever an ill thing to trust a traitor. Who once betrays may betray again.'

That she manifested no resentment, but, on the contrary, readily agreed with me, showed me how idle had been that jealousy of mine, and made me ashamed of it.

'Why, yes,' she mused, 'it is the very thought that had occurred to me, and caused me to spurn the aid he proffered when last he was here.'

'Ah!' I cried. 'What aid was that?'

'You must know, Lazzaro,' said she, 'that he comes often to Pesaro from Cesena, being a man in whom the Duke places great trust, and on whom he has bestowed considerable powers. He never fails to lie at the Palace when he comes, and he seems to — to have conceived a regard for me. He is a man of twice my years,' she added hurriedly, 'and haply looks upon me as he might upon a daughter.'

I sniffed the air. I had heard of such men.

'A week ago, when last he came, I was cast down and grieved by the affair of this marriage, which Filippo had that day disclosed to me. The Governor of Cesena, observing my sadness, sought my confidence with a kindliness of which you would scarce believe him capable; for he is a fierce and blustering man of war. In the fullness of my heart there was nothing that seemed so desirable as a friendly ear into which I might pour the tale of my affliction. He heard me gravely, and when I had done he placed himself at my disposal, assuring me that if I would but trust myself to him, he would defeat the ends of the House of Borgia. Not until then did I seem to bethink me that he was the servant of that house, and his readiness to betray the hand that paid him sowed mistrust and a certain loathing of him in my mind. I let him see it, perhaps, which was unwise, and, may be, even ungrateful. He seemed deeply wounded, and the subject was abandoned. But I have since thought that perhaps I acted with a rashness that was —'

'With a rashness that was eminently justifiable,' I interrupted her. 'You could not have been better advised than to have mistrusted such a man.'

But touching this same Governor of Cesena, there was a fine surprise in store for me. At dusk some two days later there was a sudden commotion in the courtyard of the Palace, and when I inquired of a groom into its cause, I was informed that His Excellency the Governor of Cesena had arrived.

Curious to see this man whose willingness to betray the house he served, where Madonna was concerned, was by no means difficult to probe, I descended to the banqueting-hall at supper-time.

They were not yet at table when I entered, and a group was gathered in the centre of the room about a huge man, at sight of whose red head and crimson, brutal face I would have turned and sought again the refuge of my own quarters but that his wolf's eye had already fastened on me.

'Body of God!' he swore, and that was all. But his eyes were on me in a marvellous stare, as were now — impelled by that oath of his — the eyes of all the company. We looked at each other for a moment, then a great laugh burst from him, shaking his vast bulk and wrinkling his hideous face. He thrust the intervening men aside as if they had been a growth of sedges he would penetrate, and he advanced towards me; the Lord Filippo and his sister looking on with all the rest in interested surprise.

In front of me he halted, and setting his hands on his hips he regarded me with a brutal mirth.

'What may your trade be now?' he asked at last contemptuously.

I had taken rapid stock of him in the seconds that were sped, and from the surpassing richness of his apparel, his gold-broidered doublet and crimson, fur-edged surcoat, I knew that Messer Ramiro del' Orca was grown to the high estate of Governor of Cesena.

'A new trade even as yours,' I answered him.

'Nay, that is no answer,' he cried, overlooking my offensiveness. 'Do you still follow the trade of arms?'

'I think,' Filippo interposed, 'that Your Excellency is in some error. This gentleman is Lazzaro Biancomonte, a poet of whom Italy will one day be proud, despite the fact that for a time he acted as the Lord Giovanni Sforza's Fool.'

Ramiro looked at his interlocutor, as the mastiff may look at the lapdog. He grunted, and blew out his cheeks.

'There is yet another part he played,' said he, 'as I have good cause to remember — for he is the only man that can boast of having unhorsed Ramiro del' Orca. He was for a brief season the Lord Giovanni Sforza himself.'

'How?' asked the profoundly amazed Filippo, whilst all present pressed closer to miss nothing of the disclosure that seemed to impend. Myself, I groaned. There was naught that I could say to stem the tide of revelation that was coming.

'Do you then keep this paladin here arrayed like a clerk?' quoth Ramiro in his sardonic way. 'And can it be that the secret of his feat of arms has been guarded so well that you are still in ignorance of it?'

Filippo's wits worked swiftly, and swiftly they pieced together the hints that Ramiro had let fall.

'You will tell us,' said he, 'that the fight in the streets of Pesaro, in which Your Excellency's party suffered defeat, was led by Biancomonte in the armour of Giovanni Sforza?'

Ramiro looked at him with that displeasure with which the jester visits the man who by anticipation robs his story of its points.

'It was known to you?' growled he.

'Not so. I have but learnt it from you. But it nowise astonishes me.'

And he looked at his sister, whose eyes devoured me, as if they would read in my soul whether this thing were indeed true. Under her eyes I dropped my glance like a man ashamed at hearing a disgraceful act of his paraded.

'Had it indeed been the Lord Giovanni, he had been dead that day,' laughed Ramiro grimly. 'Indeed it was nothing but my astonishment at sight of the face I was about to stab, after having broken the fastenings of his visor, that stayed my hand for long enough to give him the advantage. But I bear you no grudge for that,' he ended, turning on me with a ferocious smile, 'nor yet for that other trick by which — as Boccadoro the Fool — you bested me. I am not a sweet man when thwarted, yet I can admire wit and respect courage. But see to it,' he ended, with a sudden and most unreasonable ferocity, his visage empurpling if possible still more, 'see to it that you pit neither that courage nor that wit against me again. I have heard the story of how you came to be Fool of the Court of Pesaro. Cesena is a dull place, and we might enliven it by the presence of a jester of such nimble wits as yours.'

He turned without awaiting my reply, and strode away to take his place at table, whilst I walked slowly to my accustomed seat, and took little part in the conversation that ensued, which, as you may imagine, had me and that exploit of mine for scope.

Anon an elephantine trumpeting of laughter seemed to set the air aquivering. Ramiro was lying back in his chair a prey to such a passion of mirth that it swelled the veins of his throat and brow until I thought that they must burst — and, from my soul, I hoped they would. Adown his rugged cheeks two tears were slowly trickling. The Lord Filippo, as presently transpired, had been telling him of the epic I had written in praise of the Lord Giovanni's prowess. Naught would now satisfy that ogre but he must have the epic read, and Filippo, who had retained a copy of it, went in quest of it, and himself read it aloud for the delight of all assembled and the torture of myself who saw in Madonna Paola's eyes that she accounted the deception I had practised on her a thing beyond pardon.

Filippo had a taste for letters, as I think I have made clear, and he read those lines with the same fire and fervour that I, myself, had breathed into them two years ago. But instead of the rapt and breathless attention with which my reading had been attended, the present company listened with a smile, whilst ever and anon a short laugh or a quiet chuckle would mark how well they understood to-night the subtle ironies which had originally escaped them.

I crept away, sick at heart, while they were still making sport over my work, cursing the Lord Giovanni, who had forced me to these things, and my own mad mood that had permitted me in an evil hour to be so forced. Yet my grief and bitterness were little things that night compared with what Madonna was to make them on the morrow.

She sent for me betimes, and I went in fear and trembling of her wrath and scorn. How shall I speak of that interview? How shall I describe the immeasurable contempt with which she visited me, and which I felt was perhaps no more than I deserved?

'Messer Biancomonte,' said she coldly, 'I have ever accounted you my friend, and disinterested the motives that inspired a heart seemingly noble to do

service to a forlorn and helpless lady. It seems that I
was wrong. That the indulging of a warped and malignant spirit was the inspiration you had to appear to
befriend me.'

'Madonna, you are over-cruel,' I cried out,
wounded to the very soul of me.

'Am I so?' she asked, with a cold smile upon her
ivory face. 'Is it not rather you who were cruel?
Was it a fine thing to do to trick a lady into giving
her affection to a man for gifts which he did not possess? You know in what manner of regard I held the
Lord Giovanni Sforza so long as I saw him with the
eyes of reason and in the light of truth. And you,
who were my one professed friend, the one man who
spoke so loudly of dying in my service, you falsified
my vision, you masked him — either at his own and
at my brother's bidding, or else out of the malignancy
of your nature — in a garb that should render him
agreeable in my eyes. Do you realise what you have
done? Does not your conscience tell you? You have
contrived that I have plighted my troth to a man
such as I believed the Lord Giovanni to be. Mother
of Mercy!' she ended, with a scorn ineffable, 'when
I dwell upon it now, it almost seems that it was to
you I gave my heart, for yours were the deeds that
earned my regard — not his.'

Such was the very argument that I had hugged to
my starving soul, at the time the things she spoke of
had befallen, and it had consoled me as naught in life
could have consoled me. Yet now that she employed
it with such a scornful emphasis as to make me realise
how far beneath her I really was, how immeasurably
beyond my reach was she, it was as much consolation
to me as confession without absolution may be to the

perishing sinner. I answered nothing. I could not trust myself to speak. Besides, what was there that I could say?

'I summoned you back to Pesaro,' she continued pitilessly, 'trusting in your fine words and deeming honest the offer of services you made me. Now that I know you, you are free to depart from Pesaro when you will.'

Despite my shame, I dared, at last, to raise my eyes. But her face was averted, and she saw nothing of the entreaty, nothing of the grief that might have told her how false were her conclusions. One thing alone there was might have explained my actions, might have revealed them in a new light; but that one thing I could not speak of.

I turned in silence, and in silence I quitted the room; for that, I thought, was, after all, the wisest answer I could make.

CHAPTER XIII

POISON

DESPITE Madonna Paola's dismissal, I remained in Pesaro. Indeed, had I attempted to leave, it is probable that the Lord Filippo would have deterred me, for I was much grown in his esteem since the disclosures that had earned me the disfavour of Madonna. But I had no thought of going. I hoped against hope that anon she might melt to a kinder mood, or else that by yet aiding her, despite herself, to elude the Borgia alliance, I might earn her forgiveness for those matters in which she held that I had so gravely sinned against her.

The epithalamium, meanwhile, was forgotten utterly, and I spent my days in conceiving wild plans to save her from the Lord Ignacio, only to abandon them when in more sober moments their impracticable quality was borne in upon me.

In this fashion some six weeks went by, and during the time she never once addressed me. We saw much during those days of the Governor of Cesena. Indeed his time seemed mainly spent in coming and going 'twixt Cesena and Pesaro, and it needed no keen penetration to discern the attraction that brought him. He was ever all attention to Madonna, and there were times when I feared that perhaps she had been drawn into accepting the aid that once before he had proffered. But these fears were short-lived, for, as time sped, Madonna's aversion to the man grew plain for all to see. Yet he persisted until the very eve, almost, of her betrothal to Ignacio.

One evening in early December I chanced, through the purest accident, to overhear her sharp repulsion of the suit that he had evidently been pressing.

'Madonna,' I heard him answer, with a snarl, 'I may yet prove to you that you have been unwise so to use Ramiro del' Orca.'

'If you so much as venture to address me again upon the subject,' she returned in the very chilliest accents, 'I will lay this matter of your odious suit before your master Cesare Borgia.'

They must have caught the sound of my footsteps in the gallery in which they stood, and Ramiro moved away, his purple face pale for once, and his eyes malevolent as Satan's.

I reflected with pleasure that perhaps we had now seen the last of him, and that before that threat of Madonna's he would see fit to ride home to Cesena and remain there. But I was wrong. With incredible effrontery and daring he lingered. The morrow was a Sunday, and, on the Tuesday or Wednesday following, Cesare Borgia and his cousin Ignacio were expected. Filippo was in the best of moods, and paid no more heed to the Governor of Cesena's presence at Pesaro than he did to mine. It may be that he imagined Ramiro del' Orca to be acting under Cesare's instructions.

That Sunday night we supped together, and we were all tolerably gay, the topic of our talk being the coming of the bridegroom. Madonna's was the only downcast face at the board. She was pale and worn, and there were dark circles round her eyes that did much to mar the beauty of her angel face, and inspired me with a deep and sorrowing pity.

Ramiro announced his intention of leaving Pesaro

on the morrow, and ere he went he begged leave to pledge the beautiful Lady of Santafior, who was so soon to become the bride of the valiant and mighty Ignacio Borgia. It was a toast that was eagerly received, so eager and uproariously that even that poor lady herself was forced to smile, for all that I saw it in her eyes that her heart was on the point of breaking.

I remember how, when we had drunk, she raised her goblet — a beautiful chaste cup of solid gold — and drank, herself, in acknowledgment; and I remember, too, how, chancing to move my head, I caught a most singular, ill-omened smile upon the coarse lips of Messer Ramiro.

At the time I thought of it no more, but in the morning when the horrible news that spread through the Palace gained my ears, that smile of Ramiro del' Orca's recurred to me at once.

It was from the seneschal of the Palace that I first heard that tragic news. I had but risen, and I was descending from my quarters, when I came upon him, his old face white as death, a palsy in his limbs.

'Have you heard the news, Ser Lazzaro?' he cried in a quavering voice.

'The news of what?' I asked, struck by the horror in his face.

'Madonna Paola is dead,' he told me, with a sob.

I stared at him in speechless consternation, and for a moment I seemed forlorn of sense and understanding.

'Dead?' I remember whispering. 'What is it you say?' And I leaned forward towards him, peering into his face. 'What is it you say?'

'Well may you doubt your ears,' he groaned. 'But, Vergine Santissima! it is the truth. Madonna Paola, that sweet angel of God, lies cold and stiff. They found her so this morning.'

'God of Heaven!' I cried out, and leaving him abruptly I dashed down the steps.

Scarce knowing what I did, acting upon an impulsive instinct that was as irresistible as it was unreasoning, I made for the apartments of Madonna Paola. In the ante-chamber I found a crowd assembled, and on every face was pallid consternation written. Of my own countenance I had a glimpse in a mirror as I passed; it was ashen, and my hollow eyes were wild as a madman's.

Someone caught me by the arm. I turned. It was the Lord Filippo, pale as the rest, his affectations all fallen from him, and the man himself revealed by the hand of an overwhelming sorrow. With him was a grave, white-bearded gentleman, whose sober robe proclaimed the physician.

'This is a black and monstrous affair, my friend,' he murmured.

'Is it true, is it really true, my lord?' I cried in such a voice that all eyes were turned upon me.

'Your grief is a welcome homage to my own,' he said. 'Alas, Dio Santo! it is most hideously true. She lies there cold and white as marble, I have just seen her. Come hither, Lazzaro.' He drew me aside, away from the crowd and out of that ante-chamber, into a closet that had been Madonna's oratory. With us came the physician.

'This worthy doctor tells me that he suspects she has been poisoned, Lazzaro.'

'Poisoned?' I echoed. 'Body of God! but by whom? We all loved her. There was not in Pesaro a man worthy of the name but would have laid down his life in her service. Who was there, then, to poison that dear saint?'

It was then that the memory of Ramiro del' Orca, and the look that in his eyes I had surprised whilst Madonna drank, flashed back into my mind.

'Where is the Governor of Cesena?' I cried suddenly.

Filippo looked at me with quick surprise.

'He departed betimes this morning for his castle. Why do you ask?'

I told him why I asked; I told him what I knew of Ramiro's attentions to Madonna, of the rejection they had suffered, and of the vengeance he had seemed to threaten. Filippo heard me patiently, but when I had done he shook his head.

'Why, all being as you say, should he work so wanton a destruction?' he asked stupidly, as if jealousy were not cause enough to drive an evil man to destroy that which he may not possess. 'Nay, nay, your wits are disordered. You remember that he looked at Madonna whilst she drank, and you construe that into a proof that he had poisoned the cup she drank from. But then it is probable that we all looked at her in that same moment.'

'But not with such eyes as his,' I insisted.

'Could he have administered the poison with his own hands?' asked the doctor gravely.

'No,' said I, 'that were a difficult matter. But he might have bribed a servant to drop a powder in her wine.'

'Why, then,' said he, 'it should be an easy thing to find the servant. Do you chance to remember who served the wine?'

'I remember,' answered Filippo readily.

'Let the man be questioned; let him be racked if necessary. Thus shall you probably arrive at a true knowledge; thus discover under whose directions he was working.'

It was the only thing to do, and Filippo sent me about it there and then, telling me the servant in question was a Venetian of the name of Zabatello. If confirmation had been needed that this fellow had been the tool of the poisoner — there was no reason to suppose that he would have done the thing to have served any ends of his own — that confirmation I had upon discovering that Zabatello was fled from Pesaro, leaving no trace behind him.

Men were sent out by the Lord Filippo in every direction to endeavour to find the rogue and bring him back. Whether they caught him or not seemed, after all, a little thing to me. She was dead; that was the one all-absorbing, all-effacing fact that took possession of my mind, blotting out all minor matters that might be concerned with it. Even the now assured fact that she had been poisoned was a thing that found little room in my consideration on that day of my burning grief.

She was dead, dead, dead! The hideous phrase boomed again and again through my distracted mind. Compared with that overwhelming catastrophe, what signified to me the how or why or when she had died. She was dead, and the world was empty.

For hours I sat on the rocks, alone by the sea, on that stormy day of December, and I indulged my grief where no prying eyes could witness it, amid the solitude of wild and angry Nature. And the moan and thud with which the great waves hurled themselves against the base of the black rock on which I was perched afforded but a feeble echo of the storm that raged and beat within my desolated soul.

She was dead, dead, dead! The waves seemed to shout it as they leapt up and spattered me with brine; the wind now moaned it piteously, now shrieked it fiercely as it scudded by, wrapping its invisible coils about me, and seeming intent on tearing me from my resting-place.

Towards evening, at last, I rose, and skirting the Castle, I entered the town, dishevelled and bedraggled, yet caring nothing what spectacle I might afford. And presently a grim procession overtook me, and at sight of the black, cowled and visored figures that advanced in the lurid light of their wax torches, I fell on my knees there in the street, and so remained, my knees deep in the mud, my head bowed, until her sainted body had been borne past. None heeded me. They bore her to San Domenico, and thither I followed presently, and in the shadow of one of the pillars of the aisle I crouched whilst the monks chanted their funereal psalms.

The singing ended, the friars departed, and presently those of the Court and the sight-seers from the streets began to leave the church. In an hour I was alone — alone with the beloved dead, and there, on my knees, I stayed, and whether I prayed or blasphemed during that horrid hour, my memory will not let me say.

It may have been towards the third hour of night when at last I staggered up — stiff and cramped from my long kneeling on the cold stone. Slowly, in a half-dazed condition, I moved down the aisle and gained the door of the church. I essayed to open it. It re-

sisted my efforts, and then I realised that it was
locked for the night.

The appreciation of my position afforded me not
the slightest dismay. On the contrary, I think my
feelings were rather of relief. I had not known
whither I should repair — so distraught was my
mood — and now chance had settled the matter for
me by decreeing that I should remain.

I turned and slowly I paced back until I stood beside the great black catafalque, at each corner of
which a tall wax taper was burning. My footsteps
rang with a hollow sound through the vast, gloomy
spaces of that cold, empty church; my very breathing
seemed to find an echo in it. But these were not
things to occupy my mind in such a season, no more
than was the icy cold by which I was half-numbed —
yet of which I seemed to remain unconscious in the
absorbing anguish that possessed me.

Near the foot of the bier there was a bench, and
there I sat me down, and resting my elbows on my
knees I took my dishevelled head between my frozen
hands. My thoughts were all of her whose poor mur-
dered clay was there encased above me. I reviewed, I
think, each scene of my life where it had touched on
hers; I evoked every word she had addressed to me
since first I had met her on the road to Cagli.

And anon my mood changed, and, from cold and
frozen that it had been by grief, it grew ablaze with
the fire of anger and the lust to wreak vengeance upon
him that had brought her to this condition. Let
Filippo fear to move without proofs, let him doubt
such proofs as I had set before him and deem them
overslender to warrant action. Such scruples should
not serve to restrain me. I was no lukewarm brother.

Here in Pesaro I would remain until her poor body was delivered to the earth, and then I would set out upon a last emprise. Messer Ramiro del' Orca should account to me for this vile deed.

There in the House of Peace I sat gnawing my hands and maturing my bloody plans whilst the night wore on. Later a still more frenzied mood obsessed me — a burning desire to look again upon the sweet face of her I had loved, the sainted visage of Madonna Paola. What was there to deter me? Who was there to gainsay me?

I stood up and uttered that challenge aloud in my madness. My voice echoed mournfully up the aisles, and the sound of the echo chilled me, yet my purpose gathered strength.

I advanced, and after a moment's pause, with the silver-broidered hem of the pall in my hands, I suddenly swept off that mantle of black cloth, setting up such a gust of wind as all but quenched the tapers. I caught up the bench on which I had been sitting, and, dragging it forward, I mounted it and stood now with my breast on a level with the coffin-lid. I laid hands on it and found it unfastened. Without thought or care of how I went about the thing, I raised it and let it crash over to the ground. It fell on the stone flags with a noise like that of thunder, which boomed and reverberated along the gloomy vault above.

A figure, all in purest white, lay there under my eyes, the face covered by a veil. With deepest reverence, and a prayer to her sainted soul to forgive the desecration of my loving hands, I tremblingly drew that veil aside. How beautiful she was in the calm peace of death! She lay there like one gently sleeping, the faintest smile upon her lips, and as I looked it seemed hard to believe that she was truly dead. Why, her lips had lost nothing of their colour; they were as rosy red — or nearly so — as ever I had seen them in life. How could this be? The lips of the dead are wont to put on a livid hue. I stared a moment, my reverence and grief almost effaced by the intensity of my wonder. This face, so ivory pale, wore not the ashen aspect of one that would never wake again. There was a warmth about that pallor. And then I caught my nether lip in my teeth until it bled, and it is a miracle that I did not scream, seeing how over-wrought was my condition.

For it had seemed to me that the draperies on her bosom had slightly moved, a gentle, almost imper-ceptible heave as if she breathed. I looked, and there it came again.

God! into what madness was I come that my eyes could so deceive me? It was the draught that stirred the air about the church and blew great shrouds of wax adown the taper's yellow sides. I manned myself to a more sober mood, and looked again.

And now my doubts were all dispelled. I knew that I had mastered any errant fancy, and that my eyes were grown wise and discriminating, and I knew, too, that she lived. Her bosom slowly rose and fell; the colour of her lips, the hue of her cheeks confirmed the assurance that she breathed. The poison had failed in its work.

I paused a second yet to ponder. That morning her appearance had been such that the physician had been deceived by it, and had pronounced her cold. Yet now there were these signs of life. What could it portend but that the effects of the poison were passing off and that she was recovering?

In the wild madness of joy that sent the blood
drumming and beating through my brain, my first
impulse was to run for help. Then I bethought me of
the closed doors, and I realised that no matter how I
shouted none would hear me. I must succour her myself as best I could, and meanwhile she must be protected from the chill air of that December night in
that church that was colder than the tomb. I had my
cloak, a heavy, serviceable garment; and if more were
needed, there was the pall which I had removed, and
which lay in a heap about the legs of my bench.

I leaned forward, and passing my hand under her
head, I gently raised it. Then slipping it downwards,
I thrust my arm after it until I had her round the
waist in a firm grip. Thus I raised her from the
coffin, and the warmth of her body on my arm, the
ready, supple bending of her limbs, were so many
added proofs that she was not dead.

Gently and reverently I lifted her in my arms, an
intoxication of holy joy pervading me, and the prayers falling faster from my lips than ever they had done
since as a lad I had recited them at my mother's knee.
A moment I laid her on the bench, whilst I divested
myself of my cloak. Then suddenly I paused, and
stood listening, holding my breath.

Steps were advancing towards the door.

My first impulse was to rush forward and call to
those who came, shouting my news and imploring
their help. Then a sudden, an almost instinctive suspicion caught and chilled me. Who was it came at
such an hour? What could any man seek in the
Church of San Domenico at dead of night? Was the
church indeed their goal, or were they but passers-by?

That last question went not long unanswered. The

steps came nearer, whilst I stood appalled, my skin roughening like a dog's. They halted at the door. Something heavy hurtled against it.

A voice, the voice of Ramiro del' Orca — I knew it upon the instant — reached my ears which concentration had rendered superacute.

'It is locked, Baldassare. Get out those tools of yours and force it.'

My wits were working now at fever-pace. It may be that I am swift of thought beyond the ordinary man, or it may be that what then came to me was either a flash of inspiration or the conclusion to which I leapt by instinct. But in that moment the whole plot of Madonna's poisoning was revealed to me. Poisoned she had been — aye, but by some drug that did but produce for a little while the outward appearance of death so truly simulated as to deceive the most experienced of doctors. I had heard of such poisons, and here, in very truth, was one of them at work. His vengeance on her for her indifference to his suit was not so clumsy and primitive as that of simply slaying her. He had, by his infernal artifice, intended, secretly, to bear her off. To-morrow when men found a broken church-door and a violated bier, they would set the sacrilege down to some wizard who had need of the body for his dark practices of magic.

I cursed myself in that hour that I had not earlier been moved to peer into her coffin whilst yet there might have been time to have saved her. Now? The sweat stood out in beads upon my brow. At that door there were, to judge by the sound of footsteps and of voices, some three or four men besides Messer Ramiro. For only weapon I had my dagger. What could I do with that to defend her? Ramiro's plan

would suffer no frustration through my discovery;
when to-morrow the sacrilege was discovered the
cold body of Lazzaro Biancomonte lying beside the
desecrated bier would be but an item in the work of
profanation they would find — an item that nowise
would modify the conclusion to which I anticipated
they would come.

CHAPTER XIV

REQUIESCAT!

A STRANGE and mysterious thing is the working of terror on the human mind. Some it renders incapable of thought or action, paralysing their limbs and stagnating the blood in their veins; such creatures die in anticipating death. Others under the stress of that grim passion have their wits preternaturally sharpened. The instinct of self-preservation assumes command of all their senses, and urges them to swift and feverish action.

I thank God with a full heart that to this latter class do I belong. After one gelid moment, spent with eyes and mouth agape, my hands fallen limp beside me and my hair bristling with affright, I became myself again and never calmer than in that dread moment. I went to work with superhuman swiftness. My cheeks may have been livid, my very lips bloodless; but my hands were steady and my wits under full control.

Concealment — concealment for myself and her — was the thing that now imported; and no sooner was the thought conceived than the means were devised. Slender means were they, yet Heaven knows I was in no case to be exacting, and since they were the best the place afforded I must trust to them without demurring, and pray God that Messer Ramiro might lack the wit to search. And with that fresh hope it came to me that I must find a way so to dispose as to make him believe that to search would be a futile waste of energy.

The odds against me lay in the little time at my disposal. Yet a little time there was. The door was stout, and Messer Ramiro might take no violent means of bursting it, lest the noise should arouse the street — and I well could guess how little he would relish having lights to shine upon this deed of night of his.

With what tools his *sbirro* was at work I could not say; but surely they must be such as would leave me a few moments. Already the fellow had begun. I could make out a soft crunching sound, as of steel biting into wood. To act, then!

With movements swift as a cat's, and as silent, I went to work. Like a ghost I glided round the coffin to the other side, where the lid was lying. I took it up, and when for a moment I had deposited Madonna Paola on the ground, I mounted the bench and gently but quickly set back that lid as it had been. Next I gathered up the cumbrous pall, and mounting the bench once more I spread it across the coffin. This way and that I pulled it, straightening it into the shape that it had worn when first I had entered, and casting its folds into regular lines that would lend it the appearance of having remained undisturbed.

And what time I toiled, the half of my mind intent upon my task, the other half was as intent upon the progress of the worker at the door.

At last it was done. I set the bench where first it had been, at the foot of the catafalque, and gathering up Madonna in my arms, as though her weight had been an infant's, I bore her swiftly out of the circle of light of those four tapers into the black, impenetrable gloom beyond. On I sped towards the high altar, flying now as men fly in evil dreams, with the sensation

of an enemy upon them and their progress a mere
standing-still.

Thus I gained the chancel, hurtling against the
railing as I passed, and pausing for an instant, wondering whether those without could have heard the
noise which in my clumsiness I had made. But
the grinding sound continued uninterrupted, and I
breathed more freely. I mounted the altar steps, the
distant light behind me still feebly guiding me; I ran
round to the right, and heaved a great sigh of relief
to find my hopes verified, and that the altar of San
Domenico was as the altar of other churches I had
known. It stood a pace or so from the wall, and behind it there was just such narrow hiding-room as I
had looked to find.

I paused at the mouth of that black opening, and
even as I paused, something hard that gave out a
metallic sound fell at the far end of the church. Instinct told me it was the lock which those miscreants
had cut from the door. I waited for no more, but like
a beast scudding to cover I plunged into that black
space.

Madonna, wrapped in my cloak as she was, I set
down upon the ground, and then I crept forward on
hands and knees and thrust out my head, trusting to
the darkness to envelop me.

I waited thus for some seconds, my heart beating
now against my ribs as if it would hurl itself out of
my bosom, my head and face on fire with the fever of
reaction that succeeded my late cold pallor.

From where I watched it was impossible to see the
door hidden in the black gloom. Away in the centre
of the church, an island of light in that vast sea of
blackness, stood the catafalque with its four wax

torches. Something creaked, and almost immediately
I saw the flames of those tapers bend towards me,
beaten over by the gust that smote them from the
door. Thus I surmised that Ramiro and his men had
entered. The soft fall of their feet, for they were
treading lightly now, succeeded, and at last they came
into view, shadowy at first, then sharply outlined as
they approached the light.

A moment they stood in half-whispered conversation, their voices a mere boom of sound in which no
word was to be distinguished. Then I saw Ramiro
suddenly step forward — I knew him by his great
height — and drag away, even as I had done, the pall
that hid the coffin. Next he seized the bench and gave
a brisk order to his men in a less cautious voice, so
that I caught his words.

'Spread a cloak,' said he, and, in obedience, the
four that were with him took a cloak among them,
each holding one of its corners. It was thus that he
meant to bear her with him.

He mounted now the bench, and I could imagine
with what elation of mind he put out his hands to
remove the coffin-lid. As well as if his soul had been
transformed into a book conceived for my amusement
did I surmise the exultant mood that then possessed
him. He had tricked Filippo; he had outwitted us all
— Madonna herself, included — and he was leaving
no trace behind him that should warrant any so
much as to dare to think that this vile deed was the
work of Messer Ramiro del' Orca, Governor of Cesena.

But Fate, that arch-humourist, that jester of the
gods, delights in mighty contrasts, and has a trick of
exalting us by false hopes and hollow lures on the very
eve of working our discomfiture. From the soul that

but a moment back had been aglow with evil satisfaction there burst a sudden blasphemous cry of rage that disregarded utterly the sanctity of that consecrated place.

'By the Death of Christ! the coffin is empty!'

It was the roar of a beast enraged, and it was succeeded by a heavy crash as he let fall the coffin-lid; a second later a still louder sound awoke the night echoes of that silent place. In a burst of maniacal frenzy he had caught the coffin itself a buffet of his mighty fist, and hurled it from its trestles.

Then he leapt down from the bench, and flung all caution to the winds in the excitement that possessed him.

'It is a trick of that smooth-faced knave Filippo,' he cried. 'They have laid a trap for us, animals, and you never informed yourselves.'

I could imagine the foam about the corners of his mouth, the swelling veins in his brow, and the mad bulging of his hideous eyes, for terror spoke in his words, and the Governor of Cesena, overbearing bully though he was, could on occasion, too, become a coward.

'Out of this!' he growled at them. 'See that your swords hang ready. Away!'

One of them murmured something that I could not catch. Mother in Heaven! If it should be a suggestion of what actually had taken place, a suggestion that the church should be searched ere they abandoned it! But Ramiro's answer speedily relieved my fears.

'I'll take no risks,' he barked. 'Come! Let us go separately. I first, and do you follow me and get clear of Pesaro as best you can.' His voice grew lower, and from what else he said I but caught the words, 'Cesena' and 'to-morrow night,' from which I gathered that he was appointing that as their next meeting-place.

Ramiro went, and scarce had the echoes of his foot-steps died away ere the others followed in a rush, fearful of being caught in some trap that was here laid for them, and but restrained from flying on the instant by their still greater fear of that harsh master, Ramiro.

Thanking Heaven for this miraculous deliverance, and for the wit it had lent me so to prepare a scene that should thoroughly mislead those ravishers, I turned me now to Madonna Paola. Her breathing was grown more heavy and more regular, so that in all respects she was as one sleeping healthily. Soon I hoped that she might awaken, for to seek to bear her thence and to the Palace in my arms would have been a madness. And now it occurred to me that I should have restoratives at hand against the time of her re-gaining consciousness. Inspiration suggested to me the wine that should be stored in the sacristy for al-tar purposes. It was unconsecrated, and there could be no sacrilege in using it.

I crept round to the front of the altar. At the angle a candle-branch protruded, standing no higher than my head. It held some three or four tapers, and was so placed to enable the priest to read his missal at early Mass on dark winter mornings. I plucked one of the candles from its socket, and hastening down the church, I lighted it from one of the burning tapers of the bier. Screening it with my hand, I retraced my steps and regained the chancel. Then, turning to the left, I made for a door that I knew should give access to the sacristy. It yielded to my touch, and I passed down a short stone-flagged passage, and entered the spacious chamber beyond.

An oak settle was placed against one wall, and above it hung an enormous, rudely carved crucifix. Facing it against the other wall loomed a huge piece of furniture, half-cupboard, half-buffet. On a bench in a corner stood a basin and ewer of metal, whilst a few vestments hanging beside these completed the furniture of this austere and whitewashed chamber. Setting my candle on the buffet, I opened one of the drawers. It was full of garments of different kinds, among which I noticed several monks' habits. I rummaged to the bottom only to find some odd pairs of sandals.

Disappointed, I closed the drawer, and tried another, with no better fortune. Here were undervestments of fine linen, newly washed and fragrant with rosemary. I abandoned the drawer and gave my attention to the cupboard above. It was locked, but the key was there. It opened, and my candle reflected a blaze on gold and silver vessels, consecrated chalices, a dazzling monstre, and several richly carved ciboria of solid gold, set with precious stones. But in a corner I espied a dark-brown, gourd-shaped object. It was a skin of wine, and, with a half-suppressed cry of joy, I seized it. In that instant a piercing scream rang through the stillness of the church, and startled me so that I stood there for some seconds, frozen in horror, a hundred wild conjectures leaping to my mind.

Had Ramiro remained hidden, and was he returned? Did the scream mean that Madonna Paola had been awakened by his rough hands?

A second time it came, and now it seemed to break

the hideous spell that its first utterance had cast over
me. Dropping the leather bottle, I sped back, down
the stone passage to the door that abutted on the
chancel.

There, by the high altar, I saw a form that seemed
at first luminous and ghostly, but in which presently
I recognised Madonna Paola, the dim rays of the distant tapers finding out the white robe with which her
limbs were hung. She was alone, and I knew then
that it was but the very natural fear consequent upon
awakening in such a place that had provoked the cry
I had heard.

'Madonna,' I called, advancing swiftly towards
her. 'Madonna Paola!' There was a gasp, a moment's stillness, then —

'Lazzaro?' she cried questioningly. 'What has
happened? Why am I here?'

I was beside her now, and found her trembling like
an aspen.

'Something horrible has happened, Madonna,' I answered. 'But it is over now, and the evil is averted.'

'But how come I here?'

'That you shall learn.' I stooped to gather up the
cloak which had slipped from her shoulders as she
advanced. 'Do you wrap this about you,' I urged her,
and with my own hands I assisted to enfold her in
that mantle. 'Are you faint, Madonna?' I asked.

'I scarce know,' she answered in a frightened voice.
'There is a black horror upon me. Tell me,' she implored again, 'what does it mean?'

I drew her away now, promising to satisfy her in
the fullest manner once she were out of these forbidding surroundings. I led her to the sacristy and
seating her upon the settle I produced that wineskin

once again. At first she babbled like a child of not being thirsty; but I was insistent.

'It is no matter of quenching thirst, Madonna,' I told her. 'The wine will warm and revive you. Come, Madonna mia, drink.'

She obeyed me now, and having got the first gulp down her throat she drank a lusty draught that was not long in bringing a healthier colour to replace the ashen pallor of her cheeks.

'I am so cold, Lazzaro,' she complained.

I turned to the drawer in which I had espied the rough monks' habits, and pulling one out I held it for her to don. She sat there now, in that garment of coarse black cloth, the cowl flung back upon her shoulder, the fairest postulate that ever entered upon a novitiate.

'You are good to me, Lazzaro,' she murmured plaintively, 'and I have used you very ill.' She paused a second, passing her hand across her brow. Then — 'What is the hour?' she asked.

It was a question that I left unheeded. I bade her brace herself and have courage for the tale I was to tell. I assured her that the horror of it all was passed and that she had naught to fear. So soon as her natural curiosity should be satisfied it should be hers to return to her brother at the Palace.

'But how came I thence?' she cried. 'I must have lain in a swoon, for I remember nothing.' And then her swift mind, leaping to a reasonable conclusion, and assisted, perhaps, by the memory of the shattered catafalque which she had seen — 'Did they account me dead, Lazzaro?' she asked of a sudden, her eyes dilating with a curious affright as they were turned upon my own.

'Yes, Madonna,' answered I, 'you were accounted dead.' And, with that, I told her the entire story of what had befallen, saving only that I left my own part unmentioned, nor sought to explain my opportune presence in the church. When I spoke of the coming of Ramiro and his knaves she shuddered and closed her eyes in very awe. At length, when I had done, she opened them again, and again she turned them full upon me. Their brightness seemed to increase a moment, and then I saw that she was quietly weeping.

'And you were there to save me, Lazzaro?' she murmured brokenly. 'Lazzaro mio, it seems that you are ever at hand when I have need of you. You are indeed my one true friend — the one true friend that never fails me.'

'Are you feeling stronger, Madonna?' I asked abruptly, roughly almost.

'Yes, I am stronger.' She stood up as if to test her strength. 'Indeed, little ails me saving the horror of this thing. The thought of it seems to turn me sick and dizzy.'

'Sit then and rest,' said I. 'Presently, when you are more recovered, we will set out.'

'Whither shall we go?' she asked.

'Why, to the Palace, to your brother.'

'Why, yes,' she answered, as though it were the last suggestion that she had been expecting. 'And to-morrow — it will be to-morrow, will it not? — comes the Lord Ignacio to claim his bride. He will owe you no mean thanks, Lazzaro.'

There was a pause. I paced the chamber, a hundred thoughts crowding my mind, but overriding them all the conjecture of how far it might be from

matins, and how soon we might be discovered by the
monks. Presently she spoke again.

'Lazzaro,' she inquired very gently, 'what was it
brought you to the church?'

'I came with the others, Madonna, to the burial
service,' answered I, and fearing such questions as
might follow — questions that I had been dreading
ever since I had brought her to the sacristy — 'If
you are recovered we had best be going,' I told her
gruffly.

'Nay, I am not yet enough recovered,' answered
she. 'And before we go, there are some points in this
strange adventure that I would have you make clear
to me. Meanwhile, we are very well here. If the good
fathers come upon us, what shall it signify?'

I groaned inwardly, and I grew, I think, more afraid
than when Ramiro and his men had broken into the
church an hour ago.

'What kept you here after all were gone?'

'I remained to pray, Madonna,' I answered
brusquely. 'Is aught else to be done in a church?'

'To pray for me, Lazzaro?' she asked.

'Assuredly, Madonna.'

'Faithful heart,' she murmured. 'And I had used
you so cruelly for the deception you practised. But
you merited my cruelty, did you not, Lazzaro? Say
that you did, else must I perish of remorse.'

'Perhaps I deserved it, Madonna. But perhaps
not so much as you bestowed, had you but understood my motives,' I said unguardedly.

'If I had understood your motives?' she mused.
'Aye, there is much I do not understand. Even in
this night's transactions there are not wanting things
that remain mysterious despite the explanations you

have supplied me. Tell me, Lazzaro, what was it led
you to suppose that I still lived?'

'I did not suppose it,' I blundered like a fool, never
seeing whither her question led.

'You did not?' she cried, in deep surprise; and now,
when it was too late, I understood. 'What was it,
then, induced you to lift the coffin-lid?'

'You ask me more than I can tell you,' I answered,
almost roughly. 'Do you thank God, Madonna, that
it was so, and never plague your mind to learn the
"why" of it.'

She looked at me with eyes that were singularly
luminous.

'But I must know,' she insisted. 'Have I not
the right? Tell me now: Was it that you wished to
see my face again before they gave me over to the
grave?'

'Perhaps it was that, Madonna,' I answered in
confusion, avoiding her glance. Then — 'Shall we be
going?' I suggested fiercely. But she never heeded
that suggestion.

She spoke as if she had not heard, and the words
she uttered seemed to turn me into stone.

'Did you love me then so much, dear Lazzaro?'

I swung round to face her now, and I know that
my face was white — whiter than hers had been
when I had beheld her in her coffin. My eyes seemed
to burn in their sockets as they met hers. A madness
overtook me and whelmed my better judgment. I
had undergone so much that day through grief, and
that night through a hundred emotions, that I was no
longer fully master of myself. Her words robbed me,
I think, of my last lingering shred of reason.

'Love you, Madonna?' I echoed, in a voice that

was as unlike my own as was the mood that then possessed me. 'You are the air I breathe, the sun that lights my miserable world. You are dearer to me than honour, sweeter than life. You are the guardian angel of my existence, the saint to whom I have turned morning and evening in my prayers for grace. Do I love you, Madonna — ?'

And there I paused. The thought of what I did and what the consequences must be rushed suddenly upon me. I shivered as a man shivers in awaking. I dropped on my knees before her, bowing my head and flinging wide my arms.

'Forgive, Madonna,' I cried entreatingly. 'Forgive and forget. Never again will I offend.'

'Neither forgive nor forget will I,' came her voice, charged with an ineffable sweetness, and her hands descended on my bowed head, as if she would bless and soothe me. 'I am conscious of no offence that craves forgiveness, and what you have said I would not forget if I could. Whence springs this fear of yours, dear Lazzaro? Am I more than woman, or you less than man that you should tremble for the confession that in a wild moment I have dragged from you? For that wild moment I shall be thankful to my life's end; for your words have been the sweetest ever my poor ears listened to. Once I thought that I loved the Lord Giovanni Sforza. But it was you I loved; for the deeds that earned him my affection were deeds of yours and not of his. Once I told you so in scorn. Yet since then I have come soberly to ponder it. I account you, Lazzaro, the noblest friend, the bravest gentleman and the truest lover that the world has known. Need it surprise you, then, that I love you, and that mine would be a happy life if

I might spend it in growing worthy of this noble love
of yours?'

There was a knot in my throat and tears in my
eyes — a matter at which I take no shame. Air
seemed to fail me for a moment, and I almost thought
that I should swoon, so overcome was I. Transport
the blackest soul from among the damned of hell,
wash it white of its sins and seat it on one of the glori-
ous thrones of Heaven, then ponder its emotions,
and you may learn something of what I felt. At last,
when I had mastered the exquisite torture of my
joy —

'Madonna mia,' I cried, 'bethink you of what you
say. You are the noble lady of Santafior, and I —'

'No more of this,' she interrupted me. 'You are
Lazzaro Biancomonte, of patrician birth, no matter
to what odd shifts a cruel fortune may have driven
you. Will you take me?'

She had my face between her palms, and she forced
my glance to meet her own saintly eyes.

'Will you take me, Lazzaro?' she repeated.

'Holy Flower of the Quince!' was all that I could
murmur, whereat she gently smiled. 'Santo Fior di
Cotogno!'

And then a great sadness overwhelmed me. A
tide that neaped the frail bark of happiness high and
dry upon the shores of black despair.

'To-morrow, Madonna, comes the Lord Ignacio
Borgia,' I groaned.

'I know, I know,' said she. 'But I have thought
of that. Paola Sforza di Santafior is dead. *Requies-
cat!* We must dispose that they will let her rest in
peace.'

CHAPTER XV

AN ILL ENCOUNTER

SPEECHLESS I stared at her a moment, so taken was I with the immensity of the thing that she suggested. Fear, amazement, and joy jostled one another for the possession of my mind.

'Why do you look so, Lazzaro?' she exclaimed at last. 'What is it daunts you?'

'How is the thing possible?' quoth I.

'What difficulty does it present?' she questioned back. 'The Governor of Cesena has rendered very possible what I propose. We may look on him to-morrow as our best friend.'

'But Ramiro knows,' I reminded her.

'True, but do you think that he will dare to tell the world what he knows? He might be asked to say how he comes by his knowledge, and that should prove a difficult question to answer. Tell me, Lazzaro,' she continued, 'if he had succeeded in carrying me away, what think you would have been said in Pesaro to-morrow when the coffin was found empty?'

'They would assume that your body had been stolen by some wizard or some daring student of anatomy.'

'Ah! And if we were quietly to quit the church and be clear of Pesaro before morning, would not the same be said?'

'Probably,' answered I.

'Then why hesitate? Is it that you do not love me enough, Lazzaro?'

I smiled, and my eyes must have told her more than any protestation could. Then I sighed. 'I hesitate, Madonna, because I would not have you do now what you might come, hereafter, bitterly to repent. I would not let you be misled by the impulse of a moment into an act whose consequences must endure as long as life itself.'

'Is that the reasoning of a lover?' she asked me, very quietly. 'Is this cold argument, this weighing of issues, consistent with the stormy passion you professed so lately?'

'It is,' I answered stoutly. 'It is because I love you more than I love myself that I would have you reflect ere you adventure your life upon such a broken raft as mine. You are Paola Sforza di Santafior, and I —'

'Enough of that,' she interrupted me, rising. She swept towards me, and before I knew it her hands were on my shoulders, her face upturned, and her blue eyes on mine, depriving me of all will and all resistance. 'Lazzaro,' said she, and there was an intensity almost fierce in her low tones, 'moments are flying and you stand here reasoning with me, and bidding me weigh what is already weighed for all time. Will you wait until escape is rendered impossible, until we are discovered, before you will decide to save me, and to grasp with both hands this happiness of ours that is not twice offered in a lifetime?'

She was so close to me that I could almost feel the beating of her heart. Some subtle perfume reaching me and combining with the dominion that her eyes seemed to have established over me completed my subjugation. I was as warm wax in her hands. Forgotten were all considerations of rank and station.

We were just a man and a woman whose fates were linked irrevocably by love. I stooped suddenly, under the sway of an impulse I could not resist, and kissed her upturned face, turning almost dizzy in the act. Then I broke from her clasp, and bracing myself for the task to which we stood committed by that kiss—

'Paola,' said I, 'we must devise the means to get away. I will bear you to my mother's home near Biancomonte, that you may dwell there at least until we are wed. But the thing that exercises my mind is how to make our unobserved escape from Pesaro.'

'I have thought of it already,' she informed me quietly.

'You have thought of it?' I cried. 'And of what have you thought?'

For answer she stepped back a pace, and drew the cowl of the monk's habit over her head until her features were lost in the shadows of it. She stood before me now, a diminutive Dominican brother. Her meaning was clear to me at once. With a cry of gladness I turned to the drawer whence I had taken the habit in which she was arrayed, and selecting another one I hastily donned it above the garments that I wore.

No sooner was it done than I caught her by the arm.

'Come, Madonna,' I bade her in an urgent voice.

At the first step she stumbled. The habit was so long that it cumbered her feet. But that was a difficulty soon conquered. With my dagger I cut a piece from the skirt of it, enough to leave her freedom of movement; and, that accomplished, we set out.

We crossed the church swiftly and silently, and a moment I left her in the porch whilst I surveyed the street. All was quiet. Pesaro still slept, and it must have wanted some two hours or more to the dawn.

A fine rain was falling as we sallied out, and there was a sting in the December wind which made us draw our cowls the tighter about our faces. Abandoning the main street, I led her down some narrow alleys, deserted like all the rest of the city, and not so much as a stray cat abroad in that foul weather. It was very dark, and a hundred times we stumbled, whilst in some places I almost carried her bodily to avoid the filth of the quarter we were traversing. At length we gained the space in front of the gates that open on to the northern road, known as Porta Venezia, and I would have blundered on and roused the guard to let us out, using the Borgia ring once more — that talisman whose power had grown during these years, so that it would now open me almost any door in Italy. But Paola stayed me. Wisely she counselled that we should do nothing that might draw too much attention upon ourselves, and she urged me to wait until the dawn, when the guard would be astir and the gates opened.

So we fled to the shelter of a porch, and there we waited, huddling ourselves out of the reach of the icy rain. We talked little during the time we spent there. For my own part I had overmuch food for thought, and a very natural anxiety racked me. Soon the monks would be descending to the church, and they would discover the havoc there, and spread the alarm.

Who could say but that they might even discover the abstraction of the two habits from the sacristy, and the hue and cry for two men in the sackcloth of Dominicans would be afoot — for they would infer

that two men so disguised had made off with the body
of Madonna Paola. The thought stirred me like a
goad. I stood up. The night was growing thinner,
and, suddenly, even as I rose, a light gleamed from
one of the windows of the guard-house.

'God be thanked for that fellow's early rising,' I
cried out. 'Come, Madonna, let us be moving.'

And I added my newly conceived reasons for quitting the place without further delay.

Cursing us for being so early abroad — a curse to
which I responded with a sonorous '*Pax Domini sit
tecum*' — the still somnolent sentinel opened the
postern and let us pass. I was glad in the end that
we had waited and thus avoided the necessity of showing my ring, for should inquiries be made concerning
two monks, that ring of mine might have betrayed
the identity of one of them.

I gave thanks to Heaven that I knew the country
well. A quarter of a league or so from Pesaro we
quitted the highroad and took to the by-paths with
which I was well acquainted.

Day came, grey and forbidding at first, but presently the rain ceased and the sun flashed out a thousand diamonds from the drenched hedge-rows.

We plodded on, and at length, towards noon, when
we had gained the neighbourhood of the village of
Cattolica, we halted at the hut of a peasant on a
small campagna. I had divested myself of my monk's
habit, and cut away the cowl from Madonna's. She
had thereafter fashioned it by means that were mysterious to my dull man's mind into a more feminine-
looking garb.

Thus we now presented ourselves to the old man
who was the sole tenant of that lonely and squalid

house. A ducat opened his door as wide as it would go, and gave us free access to every cranny of his dwelling. Food he procured us — rough black bread, some pieces of roasted goat, and some goat's milk — and on this we regaled ourselves as though it had been a ducal banquet, for hunger had set us in the mood to account anything delicious. And when we had eaten we fell to talking, the old man having left us to go about such peasant duties as claimed his attention, and our talk concerned ourselves, our future first, and later on our past. I remember that Madonna returned to the matter of the deception that I had practised, seeking to learn what reasons had impelled me, and I answered her in all truth.

'Madonna mia, I think it must have been to win your love. When Giovanni Sforza bade me, with many a threat, to write those verses, I undertook the task with ready gladness, for in its performance I was to pour out the tale of the passion that was consuming my poor heart. It occurred to me that if those verses were worthy, you might come to love their author for their beauty, and so I strove to render them beautiful. It was the same spirit urged me to don the Lord Giovanni's armour and fight in that splendid if futile skirmish. Even as you had come to love the author for his verses, so might you come to love the warrior for his valour. That you should account the one and the other the work of Giovanni Sforza was to me a little thing, since I was well content to think that you but loved him because you accounted his the things that I had performed. Therefore was I the one you truly loved, although you did not know it. Could you but conceive what consolation that reflection was to me, you would deal lightly with me for my deceit.'

'I can conceive it,' she answered, very gently, her eyes downcast; 'and now that I know the motives that impelled you, I almost love you for that deceit itself, for it seems to me that it holds some quality well worthy of devotion.'

Such was our talk, all of a nature to help us to a better understanding of each other, and all seeming to endear us more and more by showing us how close the past had already drawn us.

Later I rose and announced my intention of adventuring into Cattolica, there to procure her garments more seemly than those she wore, in which she might journey on and come into the presence of my mother. Also, there was in Cattolica a man I knew, of whom I hoped for the loan of enough money to enable me to purchase mules, to the end that we might journey in more dignity and comfort. It was then about the twentieth hour, and I hoped to return by nightfall. I took my leave of Madonna, enjoining her to rest and to seek sleep whilst I was absent; and with that I set out.

Cattolica was no more than a half-league distant, and I looked to reach it in a half-hour or so. I fell into thought as I trudged along, and I was building plans for the sunlit future that was to be ours. I was a man transformed that day, and I could have sung in spite of the chill December wind that buffeted me, so full of joy and gladness was my heart.

At Biancomonte I was likely to spend my days as little better than a peasant, but surely a peasant's estate with such a companion as was to be mine was preferable to an emperor's throne without her.

The bleak landscape seemed to me invested with a beauty that at no other time I should have noticed. God was good. I swore a thousand times the world was a good world — so good that Heaven could scarce be better.

I had come, perhaps, the better half of the distance I had to travel, and I was giving full rein to my joyous fancy, when suddenly I espied ahead a company of horsemen. They were approaching me at a brisk pace but I took no thought of them, accounting myself secure from any molestation. If it so happened that it was a search party from Pesaro, seeking two men disguised as monks who had ravished the coffin of Madonna Paola di Santafior, what should they want of Lazzaro Biancomonte? And so, in my confidence, I advanced even as they trotted quickly towards me.

Not until they were within a matter of a hundred paces did I raise my eyes to take their measure; and then I halted on my step, smitten of a sudden by an unreasoning and unreasonable fear, as to see at their head the bulky form of the Governor of Cesena. He saw me, too, and, what was worse, he recognised me on the instant, for he clapped spurs to his horse and came at me as if he would ride me down. Within three paces of me he drew up his steed. Whether the memory of the other two occasions on which I had thwarted him arose now in his mind and made him wonder had not some fatality brought me across his path again to send awry his pretty schemes concerning Madonna Paola, I cannot say for certain; yet some suspicion of it occurred to me and filled me with apprehension.

'Body of Bacchus!' he roared. 'Is it truly you, Boccadoro?'

'They call me Biancomonte now, Magnificent,' I answered him. But my tone was respectful, for it could profit me nothing to incense him.

'A fig for what they call you,' he snapped contemptuously. 'Whence are you?'

'From Pesaro,' I answered truthfully.

'From Pesaro? But you are travelling towards it.'

'True. I was making for Cattolica, but I missed my way in seeking to shorten it. I am now returning by the highroad.'

The explanation satisfied him on that point, and being satisfied, he asked me when I had left Pesaro. A moment I hesitated.

'Late last night,' said I at last. He looked at me, my foolish hesitation having perhaps unslipped a suspicion that was straining at its leash.

'In that case,' said he, 'you can scarcely have heard the strange story that is being told there?'

I looked at him, as if puzzled, for a second. 'If you mean the story of Madonna Paola's end, I heard it yesterday.'

'Why, what story was that?' quoth he in some surprise, his beetling brows coming together in one broad line of fur.

I shrugged my shoulders. 'Men said that she had been poisoned.'

'Oh, that,' he cried indifferently. 'But men say to-day that her body was stolen from the Church of San Domenico where it lay. An odd happening, is it not?' And his eyes covered me in a fierce scrutiny that again suggested to me those suspicions of his that I might be the man who had anticipated him. I was soon to learn that he had more grounds than at first I thought for those same suspicions.

'Odd, indeed,' I answered calmly, for all that I felt my pulses quickening with apprehension. 'But is it true?' I added.

He shrugged his shoulders. 'Rumour's habit is to lie,' he answered. 'Yet for such a lie as that, so monstrous an imagination would be needed that, rather, am I inclined to account it truth. There are no more poets in Pesaro since you left. But at what hour was it that you quitted the city?'

To hesitate again were to betray myself; it were to suggest that I was seeking an answer that should sort well with the rest of my story. Besides, what could the hour signify?

'It would be about the first hour of night,' I said.

He looked at me with increasing strangeness.

'You must indeed have wandered from your road to have got no farther than this in all that time. Perhaps you were hampered by some heavy burden?' He leered evilly, and I turned cold.

'I was burdened with nothing heavier than this body of mine and a rather uneasy conscience.'

'Where, then, have you tarried?'

At this I thought it time to rebel. Were I too meekly to submit to this examination, my very meekness might afford him fresh grounds for doubts.

'Once have I told you,' I answered wearily, 'that I lost my way. And, however much it may flatter me to have Your Excellency evincing such an interest in my concerns, I am at a loss to find a reason for it.'

He leered prodigiously once more, and his eyebrows shot up to the level of his cap.

'I will tell you, brute beast,' he answered me. 'I question you because I suspect that you are hiding something from me.'

'What should I hide from Your Excellency?'

He dared not enlighten me on that point, for should his suspicions prove unfounded he would have uselessly betrayed himself.

'If you are honest, why do you lie?'

'I?' I ejaculated. 'In what have I lied?'

'In that you have told me that you left Pesaro at the first hour of night. At the third hour you were still in the Church of San Domenico, whither you followed Madonna Paola's bier.'

It was my turn to knit my brows. 'Was I indeed?' quoth I. 'Why, yes, it may well be. But what of that? Is the hour in which I quitted Pesaro a matter of such moment as to be worth lying over? If I said that I left about the first hour, it is because I was under the impression that it was so. But I was so distraught by grief at Madonna's death that I may have been careless in my account of time.'

'More lies,' he blazed with sudden passion. 'It may have been the third hour, you say. Fool, the gates of Pesaro close at the second hour of night. Where are your wits?'

Outwardly calm, but inwardly in a panic — more for Madonna's sake than for my own — I promptly held out the hand on which I wore the Borgia ring. In a flash of inspiration did that counter suggest itself to me.

'There is a key that will open any gate in Romagna at any hour.'

He looked at the ring, and of what passed in his mind I can but offer a surmise. He may have remembered that once before I had fooled him with the help of that gold circlet; or he may have thought that I was secretly in the service of the Borgias, and that, acting in their interests, I had carried off Madonna Paola. Be that as it may, the sight of the ring threw him into a fury. He turned on his horse.

'Lucagnolo!' he called, and a man of officer's rank detached himself from the score of men-at-arms and rode forward. 'Let six men escort me home to Cesena. Take you the remainder and beat up the country for three leagues about this spot. Do not leave a house outside Cattolica unsearched. You know what we are seeking?'

The man inclined his head.

'If it is within the circle you have appointed, we will find it,' he answered confidently.

'Set about it,' was the surly command, and Ramiro turned again to me. 'You have gone a little pale, good Messer Boccadoro,' he sneered. 'We shall soon learn whether you have sought to fool me. Woe betide you, should it be so. We bear a name for swift justice at Cesena.'

'So be it then,' I answered as calmly as I might. 'Meanwhile, perhaps you will now suffer me to go my ways.'

'The readier since your way must lie with ours.'

'Not so, Magnificent, I am for Cattolica.'

'Not so, animal,' he mimicked me with elephantine grace, 'you are for Cesena, and you had best go with a good will. Our manner of constraining men is reputed rude.' He turned again. 'Ercole, take you this man behind you. Assist him, Stefano.'

And so it was done, and a few minutes later I was riding, strapped to the steel-clad Ercole, away from Paola at every stride. Thus at every stride the anguish that possessed me increased, as the fear that they must find her rose ever higher.

CHAPTER XVI

IN THE CITADEL OF CESENA

I WILL not harass you at any further length with the feelings that were mine as we sped northward towards Cesena. If you are a person of some imagination and not destitute of human sympathy, you will be able to surmise them; if you are not — why, then, my tale is not for you, and it is more than probable that you will have wearied of it and flung it aside long before you reach this page.

We rode so hard that by sunset Cesena was in sight, and ere night had fallen we were within the walls of the citadel. It was when we had dismounted and I stood in the courtyard between Ercole and another of the soldiers that Ramiro again addressed me.

'Animal,' said he, 'they tell me that I bear a name for harsh measures and rough ways. You shall be a witness hereafter of how deeply I am maligned. For instead of putting you to the question and loosening your lying tongue with the rack, I am content to keep you a prisoner until my men return with that which I suspect you to be hiding from me. But if I then discover that you have sought to fool me, you shall flutter from Ramiro del' Orca's flagstaff.'

He pointed up to the tower of the Castle, from which a beam protruded, laden at that moment with a ghastly burden just discernible in the thickening gloom. He named it well when he called it his 'flagstaff,' and the miserable banner of carrion that hung

from it was a fitting pennon for the ruthless Governor
of Cesena. Worthy was he to have worn the silver
hauberk of Werner von Urslingen with its motto,
'The enemy of God, of pity, and of mercy.'

Forbidding, black-browed men caught me with
rough hands and dragged me off to a dank, unlighted
prison, as empty of furniture as it was full of noisome
smells. And there they left me to my ugly thoughts
and my deeply despondent mood what time the
Governor of Cesena supped with his officers in the
hall of the Castle.

Ramiro drank deep that night as was his habit, and
being overladen with wine it entered his mind that in
one of his dungeons lay Lazzaro Biancomonte, who,
at one time, had been known as Boccadoro, the
merriest Fool in Italy. In his drunkenness he grew
merry, and when Ramiro del' Orca grew merry men
crossed themselves and betook them to their prayers.
He would fain be amused, and to serve that end he
summoned one of his *sbirri* and bade the fellow drag
Boccadoro from his dungeon and fetch him into his
presence.

When they came for me I turned cold with fear that
Madonna was already taken, and, by contrast with
such a fear as that, the reflection that he might carry
out his threat to hang me from that black beam of his,
faded into insignificant proportions.

They ushered me into a great hall, not ill-furnished,
the floor strewed plentifully with rushes, and warmed
by an enormous fire of blazing oak. By the door stood
two pikemen in armour, like a pair of statues; in the
centre of the floor was a heavy oaken board, laden
now with flagons and beakers, at which sat Ramiro
with a pair of gossips so villainous to look at, that the

sight of them reminded me of the adage, 'God makes a man and then accompanies him.'

The Governor made a hideous noise at sight of me, which I was constrained to accept as an expression of horrid glee.

'Boccadoro,' said he, 'do you recall that when last I had the honour of being entertained by your pert tongue, I promised you that did you ever cross my path again I would raise you to the dignity of Fool of my Court of Cesena?'

Into what magniloquence does vanity betray us! His Court of Cesena! As well you might describe a pig-sty as a bower of roses.

But his words, despite the unsavoury thing of which they seemed to hold a promise, fell sweetly on my ear, inasmuch as for the time they relieved my fears touching Madonna. It was not to advise me of her capture that he had had me haled into his odious presence. I gathered courage.

'Have you not fools enough already at Cesena?' I asked him.

A moment he looked as if he were inclining to anger. Then he burst into a coarse laugh, and turned to one of his gossips.

'Did I not tell you, Lampugnani, that his wit was quick and penetrating? Hear him, rogue. Already has he discerned your quality.' He laughed consumedly at his own jest, and turning to me he pointed to a crimson bundle on a chair beside me. 'Take those garments,' he roughly bade me. 'Go dress yourself in them, then come you back and entertain us.'

Without answering him, and already anticipating the nature of the clothes he bade me don, I lifted one of the garments from the heap. It was a foliated jester's

cap, with a bell hanging from every point, which gave
out a tinkling sound as I picked it up. I let it fall again
as though it had scorched me, the memory of what
stood between Madonna Paola and me rising like a
warning spectre in my mind. I would not again defile
myself by the garb of folly; not again would I incur
the shame of playing the Fool for the amusement of
others.

.'May it please Your Excellency to excuse me,' I
answered in a firm tone. 'I have made a vow never
again to put on motley.'

He eyed me sardonically for a moment, as if enjoy-
ing in anticipation the pleasure of compelling me
against my will. He sat back in his chair and threw
one heavily booted leg across the other.

'In the Citadel of Cesena,' said he, 'we fear neither
God nor Devil, and vows are as water to us — things
we cannot stomach. It does not please me to excuse
you.'

I may have paled a little before the sinister smile
with which he accompanied his words, but I stood
my ground boldly.

'It is not,' said I, 'a question of what a vow may
be to you and yours, but of what a vow is to me. It is
a thing I cannot break.'

'Sangue di Cristo!' he snarled, 'we will break it
for you, then — that or your bones. Resolve yourself, beast, the motley or the rack — or yet, if you
prefer it, there is the cord yonder.' And he pointed to
the far end of the chamber where some ropes were
hanging from a pulley, the implements of the ghastly
torture of the cord. Of such a nature was this monster that he made a torture-chamber of his dining-
hall.

'Let the rogue make acquaintance with it,' laughed Lampugnani, showing a mouthful of yellow teeth behind his black beard that bushed his lips. 'I'll swear his dancing would afford us more amusement than his quips. Swing him up, Illustrious.'

But the Illustrious seemed to ponder the matter.

'You shall have five minutes in which to decide,' he informed me presently. 'They say that I am cruel. Behold how patient is my clemency. Five minutes shall you have where many another would hang you out of hand for bearding him as you have done me.'

'You may begin at once,' said I. 'Neither five minutes nor five years will alter my determination.'

His brow grew black with anger. 'We shall see,' was all he said.

There was a silence now in which we waited, a storm of thoughts battling in my mind. Presently Ramiro caught up one of the flagons and applied it to his cup. It proved empty, and in a gust of passion he hurled it against the wall where it burst into a thousand pieces. Clearly he was very angry, and it taxed my wits to account for the little measure of patience he was showing me.

'Beppo!' he called. A page lounging by the buffet sprang to attention. He was a slender, rather delicate lad, fair of hair and blue of eyes, not more than twelve years of age. An elderly man who stood beside him — one Mariani, the seneschal of Cesena — stepped forward also, solicitude in his glance.

'Bring me wine,' bawled the ogre. 'Must I tell you what I need? If you do not put those eyes of yours to better service, I'll have them plucked from your empty head. Bestir, animal.'

The old man caught up a beaker from the buffet and handed it to the boy.

'Here, my son,' said he. 'Hasten to His Excellency.'

The lad took the beaker from his father's hands, and trembling in his fear of Ramiro's anger, he sprang forward to serve him. In his haste the poor youth slipped in some grease that had clung to the rushes. In seeking to recover himself he tripped over the feet of one of the halberdiers that guarded me, and measured his length upon the floor at Ramiro's feet, flooding the Governor's legs with the wine he carried.

How shall I tell you of the horror that was the sequel?

For just one instant Ramiro looked down at the sprawling lad, his eyes glowing like a madman's. Then suddenly he rose, stooped, and set one hand to the boy's belt, the other to the collar of his jerkin. Feeling himself lifted, and knowing whose were the dread hands that held him, poor Beppo uttered a single scream of terror. Then Ramiro swung him round with an ease that displayed the man's prodigious strength. For just a second he seemed to hesitate how to dispose of the human bundle that he held. Then, as if suddenly taking his resolve, that devil hurled the lad across the little intervening space, straight into the heart of the blazing fire.

Beppo hurtled against the logs with a sickening crash, and a thousand sparks leapt up and vanished in the cavern of the chimney. Ramiro wheeled sharply about, and snatching the pike from the hands of one of my guards, he pinned down the poor body of the boy to make sure of his victim's entire destruction.

Away by the buffet old Mariani looked on with a
face as grey as ashes, his eyes protruding in horror at
the thing they witnessed. One glimpse I had of him,
and I scarce know which was the sight that sickened
me more, the father's anguish or the twitching limbs
of the burning child. Two legs and two arms protruded from the blaze and writhed and wriggled horribly what time the flames peeled the garments from
them and licked the flesh from the bones. At length
they fell still and sank down into the white heat of the
logs, a hideous, pungent odour spreading through the
chamber. From the old man by the buffet, who had
stood spellbound during this ghastly scene, there
broke at last an anguished cry.

'Mercy, my lord, mercy!'

The Governor of Cesena straightened himself
from his task, pulled the pike from the flames, and
restored it to the man-at-arms. Then turning to
Mariani: 'Fetch me wine,' he bade him curtly, as he
seated himself once more upon the chair from which
he had risen to perform that deed of ghastly ruthlessness.

A torch spluttered suddenly in its scone, and the
fierce hissing of the fire — like some monster licking
its chops over a bloody meal — were the only sounds
that disturbed the stillness that ensued.

Every man there, including Ramiro's table companions, was white to the lips; for accustomed though
they might be to horrors in that brigand's nest, this
was a horror that surpassed anything they had ever
witnessed. The silence irked Messer Ramiro. He
looked round from under his shaggy brows, and he
spluttered out an oath.

'Will you bring me this wine, pig?' he growled at

the almost senseless Mariani, and in his air and voice there was a promise of such terrific things that the old man put aside his horror to make room for his fears, and mechanically seizing another flagon he hurried forward to minister to the wants of his fearful lord.

Ramiro eyed him with cynical amusement.

'Your hand shakes, Mariani,' he derided him. 'Are you cold? Go warm yourself,' he added, with a brutal laugh and a jerk of his thumb towards the fire.

My eyes have looked upon some gruesome sights and I have heard such tales of ruthless cruelty as you would deem almost passing possibility. I have read of the awful doings of the Lord Bernabo Visconti at Milan in the olden time, but I believe that compared with this monster of Cesena that same Bernabo was no worse than a sucking dove. How it befell that men permitted him to live, how it was that none bethought him to put poison in his wine or a knife in his back, is something that I shall never wholly understand. Could it be that these robbers of whom he made a hedge for his protection were no better than himself, or was it that the man's terrific brutality was on such a scale that it filled them with an almost supernatural awe of him? To men better versed than am I in the mysterious ways of human nature do I leave the answering of these questions.

The ogre turned his bloodshot eyes upon me, as with his hand he caressed his tawny beard. He seemed to have cooled a little now, and to have regained some mastery of his drunken self. Old Mariani tottered back to his buffet, and stood leaning against it, his eyes wandering, with the look of a man demented,

to the fire that had devoured his child. There, indeed,
if he escaped the madness with which the poignancy
of his grief was threatening him, was a tool that might
turn its edge against this inhuman monster, this
devil, this bloody carnifex of a Governor.

'Chance,' said Ramiro, 'has designed that you
should see something of how we deal with clumsy
knaves at Cesena, Boccadoro. To disobedient ones I
can assure you that we are not half so merciful. There
is no such short shrift for them. You have had more
than the time I promised you for reflection. The
garments await you yonder. Let us know —'

The door opened suddenly, and a servant entered.

'A courier from the Lord Vitellozzo Vitelli, Tyrant
of Città di Castello,' he announced, unwittingly
breaking in upon Ramiro's words, 'with urgent messages for the High and Mighty Governor of Cesena.'

On the instant Ramiro rose, the expression of his
face changing from cynical amusement to sober concern, the task upon which he was engaged forgotten.

'Admit him instantly,' he commanded. And
whilst he waited he paced the chamber in long strides,
his chin thrust slightly forward, suggestive of deep
thought. And during that pause, I, too, was thinking.
Not indeed of him, nor vainly speculating upon such
matters as might be involved in the message, the an-
nouncement of which seemed so deeply to engage his
mind, but chiefly of my own and Madonna Paola's
concerns.

It was not fear of what I had seen that now sent my
thoughts into a new channel and inspired me with the
wisdom of obeying Ramiro del' Orca's behest that I
should don the hateful motley and play the Fool for
his diversion. It was not that I feared death; it was

that I feared what the consequences of my death might be to Paola di Santafior.

However desperate a position may seem, unlooked-for loopholes oft present themselves, and so long as we live and have sound limbs to aid us to seize such opportunities as may offer, it is a weak thing utterly to abandon hope.

Was it, then, not better to submit to the shame of the motley once again for a little time, when by so doing I might perhaps live to work my own salvation, and Madonna's should she suffer capture, rather than stubbornly to invite him to put me to death out of a feeling of false pride?

The very resolve seemed to lend me strength and to revive the hope that lay moribund in my breast. And then, scarce was it taken, when the door again opened, and a man, who was splashed from head to foot with mud, in earnest of how hard he had ridden, was ushered in.

He advanced to Messer Ramiro, bowed and presented a package. Ramiro broke the seal, and standing with his back to the fire, immediately in the light shed by one of the wax torches, he read the letter. Then his eyes wandered to the man who had brought it, and to me it seemed that they dwelt particularly upon the hat the courier was holding in his hand.

'Take this good fellow to the kitchen,' he bade the servant that had introduced him, 'let him be fed and rested.' Then, turning to the man, himself, 'I shall require you to set out at daybreak with my answer,' he said; and so, with a wave of the hand, he dismissed him. As the messenger departed Ramiro returned to the table, filled himself a cup of wine and drank.

'What says the Lord Vitelli?' Lampugnani ventured to ask him.

'If he knew you,' answered Ramiro, with a scowl, 'he would counsel me to strangle some of the over-inquisitive rascals that surround me.'

'"Over-inquisitive?"' echoed Lampugnani boldly. 'Body of God! It were enough to wake the curiosity of an ecstatic hermit to have a mud-splashed courier from Città di Castello at Cesena three times within one little week.'

Ramiro looked at him, and by his glance it was plain to see that the words had jarred his temper. Whatever it was that Vitelli wrote to Ramiro, this gentleman was not minded to divulge it.

'If you have supped, Lampugnani,' said the Governor slowly, his eyes upon his offending officer, 'perhaps you will find some duty to perform ere you seek your bed.'

Lampugnani turned crimson, and for a moment seemed to hesitate. Then he rose. He was a man of choleric aspect, and that he served under Ramiro del' Orca was as much a danger to the Governor as to himself. He had not the air of one whom it was wise to threaten in however veiled a manner.

'Shall I fetch you this fellow's hat ere I sleep?' he inquired, with contemptuous insolence.

Not a word did Ramiro answer him, but his glance fastened upon Lampugnani with an expression before which that impudent ruffian lowered his own bold eyes. Thus for a moment; then with an awkward laugh to cover the intimidation that he felt, Lampugnani walked heavily from the room and banged the door after him.

There was about it all a strangeness that set

my wits to work in a mighty busy fashion. That
work suffered interruption by the harsh voice of
Ramiro.

'Are you resolved, Boccadoro?' he growled at me.
'Have you decided for the motley or the cord?'

Instantly I fell into the part I was to play.

'Did I choose the latter,' said I, with an assumption
of sudden airiness and such a grimace as was part
and parcel of my old-time trade, 'then were I truly
worthy of the former, for I should have proved myself, indeed, a fool. Yet if I choose the former, I pray
that you'll not follow the same course of reasoning,
and hold me worthy of the latter.'

When he had understood its subtleties, for his wits
were of a quality that would have disgraced a calf, he
roared at the conceit, and, seemingly thrown into a
better humour by the promise of more such entertainment, he bade my guards release me, and urged
me to assume the motley without more delay.

What time I was obeying him my mind was returning to that matter of Lampugnani's words, and
it is not difficult to understand how I should arrive at
the only possible conclusion they suggested. The hats
of the other messengers from Vitelli, that the officer
had mentioned, had been brought to Ramiro. The
reason for this that at once arose in my mind was that
within the messenger's hat there was a second and
more secret communication for the Governor.

This secrecy and Ramiro's display of anger at seeing a hint of it betrayed by Lampugnani struck me,
not unnaturally, as suspicious. What were these
hidden communications that passed between Vitellozzo Vitelli and the Governor of Cesena? It was a
matter of which I could not pretend to offer a solu-

tion, but, nevertheless, it was one, I thought, that promised to repay investigation.

Ramiro grew impatient, and my reflections suffered interruption by his rough command that I should hasten. One of the men-at-arms helped me to truss my points, and when that was done I stepped forward — Boccadoro the Fool once more.

CHAPTER XVII

THE SENESCHAL

FOR an hour or so that night I played the Fool for Messer Ramiro's entertainment in a manner which did high justice to the fame that at Pesaro I had earned for the name of Boccadoro.

Beginning with quip and jest and paradox, aimed now at him, now at the officer who had remained to keep him company in his cups, now at the servants who ministered to him, now at the guards standing at attention, I passed on later to play the part of narrator, and I delighted his foul and prurient mind with the story of Andreuccio da Perugia and another of the more licentious tales of Messer Giovanni Boccaccio. I crimson now with shame at the manner in which I set myself to pander to his mood that with my wit I might defend my life and limbs, and preserve them for the service of my Holy Flower of the Quince in the hour of her need.

One man alone of all those present did I spare my banter. This was the old seneschal, Mariani. He stood at his post by the buffet, and ever and anon he would come forward to replenish Messer Ramiro's cup in obedience to the monster's imperious orders.

What fortitude was it, I wondered, that kept the old man outwardly so calm? His face was as the face of one who is dead, its features set and rigid, its colour ashen. But his step was tolerably firm, and his hand seemed to have lost the trembling that had assailed it under the first shock of the horror he had witnessed.

As I watched him furtively I thought that were I
Ramiro I should beware of him. That frozen calm
argued to me some terrible labour of the mind beneath that livid mask. But the Governor of Cesena
appeared insensible, or else he was contemptuous of
danger from that quarter. It may even have delighted his outrageous nature to behold a man whose
son he had done to death with such brutality continue obedient and submissive to his will, for it may
have flattered his vanity by the concession that bearing seemed to make to his grim power.

An hour went by, my second tale was done, and I
was now entrancing Messer Ramiro with some im-
promptu verses upon the divorce of Giovanni Sforza,
a theme set me by himself, when I was interrupted by
the arrival of a soldier, who entered unannounced.

I paled and turned cold at the cry with which
Ramiro rose to greet him, and the words he dropped,
which told me that here was one of the riders of the
party that, under Lucagnolo, had been ordered to
search the country about Cattolica. Had they found
Madonna?

'Messer Lucagnolo,' the fellow announced, 'has
sent me to report to you the failure of his search to
the west and north of Cattolica. He has beaten the
country thoroughly for three leagues of the town
on those two sides, as you desired him, but unfor-
tunately without result. He is now spreading his
search to the south, and not a house is being left un-
visited. By morning he hopes to report again to Your
Excellency.'

A wild wave of joy swept through my soul. They
had ransacked the country west and north of Cattolica without result. Why, then, assuredly, they had

missed the peasant's hut that sheltered her, and where she waited yet for my return. Their search to the south I knew would prove equally futile. I could have fallen on my knees in a prayer of thanksgiving had my surroundings been other than they were.

Ramiro's eye wandered round to me and settled on me in a lowering glance. By his face it was plain that the message disappointed him.

'I wonder,' said he, 'whether we could make you talk?' And from me his eyes roamed on to the instrument of torture at the end of that long chamber. I grew sick with fear, for if he were to do this thing, and maim me by it, how should I avail myself or her hereafter?

'Excellency,' I cried, 'since you met me you have hinted at something that I am hiding from you, at something touching which I could give you information did I choose. What it may be passes all thought of mine. But this I do assure you: no torture could make me tell you what I do not know, nor is any torture needed to extract from me such information as I may be possessed of. I do but beg that you will frankly question me upon this matter, whatever it may be, and Your Excellency shall be answered to the best of my knowledge.'

He looked at me as if taken aback a little by my assurance and the seemingly transparent candour of my speech, and in his face I saw that he believed me. A moment he hesitated yet; then —

'I am seeking knowledge concerning Madonna Paola di Santafior,' he said presently, resuming, as he spoke, his seat at table. 'As I told you, the body, which was believed to be dead, was stolen in the night from San Domenico. Know you aught of this?'

It may be an ignoble thing to lie, but with what
other weapon was I to fight this brigand? Surely if
an exception can be made to the rule, and a lie become
a meritorious thing, such an occasion as this would
surely justify such an exception.

'I know nothing,' I answered boldly, unhesitat-
ingly, and even with a ring of truth and sincerity
that was calculated to convince, 'nor can I even believe this rumour. It is a wild story. That the body
has been stolen may be true enough. Such things
occur; though he was a bold man who laid hands
upon the body of a person of such importance. But
that she lives — Gesù! that is an old wife's tale. I
had, myself, the word of the Lord Filippo's physician
that she was dead.'

'Nevertheless, this old wife's tale, as you dub it,
is one of which I have had confirmation. Lend me
your wits, Boccadoro, and you shall not regret it.
Exercise them now, and conjecture me who could
have abstracted the body from the church. In seeking this information I am acting in the interests of the
noble House of Borgia which I serve and to which she
was to have been allied, as you well know.'

I could have laughed to see how the apparent sincerity of my denial had convinced him to such an ex-
tent that he even sought my help to discover the true
thief, and to account for his interest in the matter he
lied to me of his service to the House of Borgia.

'I will gladly lend you these wits,' said I, 'to dis-
prove to you the rumour of which you say that you
have confirmation. Let us accept the statement that
the body has been stolen. That much, no doubt, is
true, for even rumours require some slight founda-
tion. But who in all this world could say that when

the body was taken it was not dead? Clearly but one man — he that administered the poison. And, I ask Your Excellency, would he be likely to tell the world what he had done?'

He might have answered me: 'I am that man.' But he did not. Instead, he hung his head, as if pondering the words of wisdom I had uttered — words meant to convince him of my own innocence in the matter; and this they achieved, at least in part. He flashed me a look of sudden suspicion, it is true; but it faded almost as soon as it shone from his brooding eye.

'Maybe I am a fool that I do not string you up and test the truth of what you say,' he grumbled. 'But I incline to believe you, and you are a merry rogue. You shall remain and have peace and comfort so long as you amuse me. But tremble if I discover that you have sought to deceive me. You shall have the cord first and other things after, and your death shall be the thing you'll pray for long before it takes you from my vengeance. If you know aught, speak now and you shall find me merciful. Your life and liberty shall be the recompense of your honesty towards me.'

'I repeat, Excellency,' I answered, without changing colour, 'that all that I know have I already told you.'

He was convinced, I think, for the time being.

'Get you gone, then,' he bade me. 'I have other business to deal with ere I sleep. Mariani, see that Boccadoro is well lodged.'

The old man bowed, and lifting a torch from its socket, he silently motioned me to go with him. I made Messer Ramiro a profound obeisance, and withdrew in the wake of the seneschal.

He led me up a flight of stairs that rose from the hall and along a gallery that ran half round it, then plunging down a corridor he halted presently, and, opening a door, ushered me into a tolerably furnished room.

A servant followed bringing the clothes that I had worn when I arrived.

The old man lingered a moment after the servant had withdrawn, and his hollow eyes rested on me for a second. I thought that he was on the point of saying something, and I waited returning his glance with one that quailed before the anguish of his own. I feared to speak, to offer any expression of the sympathy that filled my heart; for in that strange place I could not tell how far a man was to be trusted — even a man so wronged as this one. On his own part it may be that a like doubt beset him concerning me, for in the end he departed as he had come, no word having passed his ashen lips.

Left alone, I surveyed my surroundings by the light of the taper he had left in the iron sconce on the wall. The single window overlooked the courtyard, so that even had I been disposed and able to cut through the iron that barred it, I should but succeed in falling into the hands of the guards who abounded in that nest of infamy.

So that, for the night at least, the notion of flight must be abandoned. What the morrow would bring forth we must wait and see. Perhaps some way of escape would offer itself. Then my thoughts returned to Paola, and I was tortured by surmises as to her fate, and chiefly as to how she could have eluded the search that must have been made for her in the hut where I had left her. Had the peasant befriended her,

I wondered; and what did she think of my protracted absence? I sat on the edge of the bed and gave rein to my conjectures. The noises in the castle had all ceased, and still I sat on, unconscious of time, my taper burning low.

It may have been midnight when I was startled by the sound of a stealthy step in the corridor near my door. A heavy footfall I should have left unheeded, but this soft tread aroused me on the instant, and I sat listening.

It halted at my door, and was succeeded by a soft, scratching sound. Noiselessly I rose, and with ready hands I waited, prepared, in the instinct of self-preservation, to fall upon the intruder, however futile the act might be. But the door did not open as I expected. Instead, the scratching sound continued, growing slightly louder. Then it occurred to me, at last, that whoever came might be a friend craving admittance, and proceeding stealthily that others in the castle might not overhear him.

Swiftly I crossed to the door, and opened. On the threshold a dark figure straightened itself from a stooping posture, and the light of the taper behind me fell on a face of a pallor that seemed to glisten in its intensity. It was the face of Mariani, the seneschal of the Castle of Cesena.

One glance we exchanged, and intuitively I seemed to apprehend the motive of this midnight visit. He came either to bring me aid or to seek mine, with vengeance for his guerdon. I stood aside, and silently he entered my room and closed the door.

'Quench your taper,' he bade me in a husky whisper.

Without hesitation I obeyed him, a strange excitement thrilling me. For a second we stood in the dark, then another light gleamed as he plucked away the cloak that masked a lanthorn which he had brought with him. He set the lanthorn on the floor, and held the cloak in his hand, ready at a moment's notice to conceal the light in its folds. Then pulling me down beside him on the bed, where he had perched himself:

'My friend,' said he, 'it may be that I bring you assistance.'

'Speak, then,' I bade him. 'You shall not find me slow to act if there is the need or the way.'

'So I had surmised,' he said. 'Are you not that same Boccadoro, Fool of the Court of Pesaro, who donned the Lord Giovanni's armour and rode out to do battle in his stead?'

I answered him that I was that man.

'I have heard the tale,' said he. 'Indeed, all Italy has heard it, and knows you for a man of steel, as strong and audacious as you are cunning and resourceful. I know against what desperate odds you fought that day, and how you overcame this terrible Ramiro. This it is that leads me to hope that in the service of your own ends you may become the instrument of my vengeance.'

'Unfold your project, man,' I muttered, fiercely almost, in my burning eagerness. 'Let me hear what you would have me do.'

He did not answer me until a sob had shaken his old frame.

'That boy,' he muttered brokenly, 'that golden-haired angel sent me for the consolation of my decaying years, that lad whom Ramiro destroyed so foully and wantonly, was my son. Futile though the attempt had proved, I had certainly set my hands at the tyrant's neck, but that I founded hopes on you of a surer and more terrible revenge. That thought has manned me and upheld me when anguish was near to slaying me outright. To see the boy burn so under my very eyes! God of mercy and pity! That I should have lived so long!'

'Your child burned but a moment, suffered but an instant; for the deed, Ramiro will burn in hell through countless generations, through interminable ages.'

It was a paltry consolation, perhaps, but it was the best that then occurred to me.

'Meanwhile,' I begged him, 'do you tell me what you would have me do.'

I urged him to it that he might, thereby, suffer his mind to rest a moment from pondering that ghastly thing that he had witnessed, that scene that would live before his eyes until they closed in their last sleep.

'You heard Lampugnani quip Ramiro with the fact that three messengers have ridden desperately within the week from Città di Castello to Cesena, and you heard, perhaps, his obscure reference to the hat?'

'I heard both, and both I weighed,' said I. The old man looked at me as if surprised.

'And what,' he asked, 'was the conclusion you arrived at?'

'Why, simply this: that whilst the messenger bore some letter from Vitelli to Ramiro that should serve to lull the suspicions of any who, wondering at so much traffic between these two, should be moved to take a peep into those missives, the true letter with which the courier rides is concealed within the lining of his hat — probably unknown even to himself.'

He stared at me as though I had been a wizard.

'Messer Boccadoro —' he began.

'My name,' I corrected him, 'is Biancomonte —
Lazzaro Biancomonte.'

'Whatever be your name,' he returned, 'of the
quality of your wits there can be no question. You
have guessed for yourself the half of what I was come
to tell you. Has your shrewdness borne you any
further? Have you concluded aught concerning the
nature of those letters?'

'I have concluded that it might repay some trouble
to discover what is contained in letters that are sent
with so much secrecy. I can conceive nothing that
might lie between the Lord of Città di Castello and
this ruffian of Cesena, and yet — treason lurks often
where least it is expected, and treason makes stranger
bedfellows than misfortune.'

'Lampugnani was no fool, and yet a great fool,' the
old man murmured. 'He surmised what you have
surmised. With each of the messengers Ramiro has
dealt in the same manner. He has sent each to be fed
and refreshed whilst waiting to return with the answer
he was penning. For their refreshment he has ordered
a very full, stout wine — not drugged, for that they
might discover upon awaking; but a wine that of itself
would do the work of setting them to sleep very
soundly. Then, when all slept, and only he remained
at table, like the drunkard that he is, it has been his
habit to descend himself to the kitchen and possess
himself of the messenger's hat. With this he has
returned to the hall, opened the lining and withdrawn
a letter.

'Then, as I suppose, he has penned his answer,
thrust it into the lining, where the other one had been,
and secured it, as it was before, with his own hands.
He has returned the hat to the place from whence he

took it, and when the courier awakens in the morning
there is another letter put into his hand, and he is
bidden to bear it to Vitelli.'

He paused a moment; then continued: 'Lampugnani must have suspected something and watched
Ramiro to make sure that his suspicions were well
founded. In that he was wise, but he was a fool to
allow Ramiro to see what he had discovered. Already
he has paid the penalty. He is lying with a dagger in
his throat, for an hour ago Ramiro stabbed him while
he slept.'

I shuddered. What a place of blood was this!
Could it be that Cesare Borgia had no knowledge of
what things were being performed by his Governor of
Cesena?

'Poor Lampugnani!' I sighed. 'God rest his soul.'

'I doubt but he is in hell,' answered Mariani, without emotion. 'He was as great a villain as his master,
and he has gone to answer for his villainy even as this
ugly monster of a Ramiro shall. But let Lampugnani
be. I am not come to talk of him.

'Returning from his bloody act, Ramiro ordered me
to bed. I went, and as I passed Lampugnani's room I
saw the door standing wide. It was thus that I learnt
what had befallen. I remembered his words concerning the hat and I remembered old suspicions of my
own aroused by the thought of the potent wine which
Ramiro had ordered me to see given to the couriers. I
sped back to the gallery that overlooks the hall.
Ramiro was absent, and I surmised at once that he
was gone to the kitchen. Then was it that I thought
of you and of what service you might render if things
were indeed as I now more than suspected. Like an
inspiration it came to me how I might prepare your

way. I ran down to the hall, sweating in my terror
that he should return ere I had performed the task I
went on. From the buffet I drew a flagon of that same
stout wine that Ramiro used upon his messengers. I
ripped away the seal and crimson cord by which it is
distinguished, and placing it on the table I removed
the flagon I had set for him before I had first departed.

'Then I fled back to the gallery, and from the
shadows I watched for his return. Soon he came,
bearing a hat in his hand; and from that hat he took a
letter, all as you have surmised. He read it, and I
saw his face lighten with a fierce excitement. Then he
helped himself freely to wine, and drank thirstily, for
all that he was overladen with it. One of the qualities
of this wine is that in quenching thirst it produces
yet a greater. Ramiro drank again, then sat with the
letter before him in the light of the single taper I had
left burning. Presently he grew sleepy. He shook himself and drank again. Then again he sat conning his
epistle, and thus I left him and came hither in quest
of you.'

There followed a pause.

'Well?' I asked at length. 'What is it you would
have me do? Stab him as he sleeps?'

He shook his head. 'That were too sweet and
sudden a death for him. If it had been no more than
a matter of that, my old arms would have lent me
strength enough. But think you it would repay me
for having seen my boy pinned by that monster's pike
to the burning logs?'

'What is it, then, you ask of me?'

'If that letter were indeed the treasonable docu-
ment we account it; if its treason should be aimed at
Cesare Borgia — it could scarce be aimed at another

— would it not be a sweet thing to obtain possession of it?'

'Aye, but when he wakes to-morrow and finds it gone — what then? You know this Governor of Cesena well enough to be assured that he would ransack the castle, torture, rack, burn and flay us all until the missive were forthcoming.'

'That,' he groaned, 'is what deterred me. If I had the means of getting the letter sent to Cesare Borgia, or of escaping with it myself from Cesena, I should not have hesitated. Cesare Borgia is lying at Faenza, and I could ride there in a day. But it would be impossible for me to leave the place before morning. I have duties to perform in the town, and I might get away whilst I am about them, but before then the letter will have been missed, and no one will be allowed to leave the citadel.'

'Why, then,' said I, 'the only hope lies in abstracting that letter in such a manner that he shall not suspect the loss; and that seems a very desperate hope.'

We sat in silence for some moments, during which I thought intently to little purpose.

'Does he sleep yet, think you?' I asked presently.

'Assuredly he must.'

'And if I were to go to the gallery, is there any fear that I should be discovered by others?'

'None. All at Cesena are asleep by now.'

'Then,' said I, rising, 'let us take a look at him. Who knows what may suggest itself? Come.' I moved towards the door, and he took up his lanthorn and followed me, enjoining me to tread lightly.

CHAPTER XVIII

THE LETTER

ON tiptoe I crept down that corridor to the gallery above the banqueting-hall, secure from sight in the enveloping darkness, and intent upon allowing no sound to betray my presence, lest Ramiro should have awakened. Behind me, treading as lightly, came Messer Mariani.

Thus we gained the gallery. I leaned against the stout oaken balustrade, and looked down into the black pit of the hall, broken in the center by the circle of light from the two tapers that burnt upon the table. The other torches had all been quenched.

At the table sat Messer Ramiro, his head fallen forward and sideways upon his right arm which was outstretched and limp along the board. Before him lay a paper which I inferred to be the letter whose possession might mean so much.

I could hear the old man breathing heavily beside me as I leaned there in the dark, and sought to devise a means by which that paper might be obtained. No doubt it would be the easiest thing in the world to snatch it away without disturbing him. But there was always to be considered that when he waked and missed the letter we should have to reckon with his measures to regain possession of it.

It became necessary, therefore, to go about it in a manner that should leave him unsuspicious of the theft. A little while I pondered this, deeming the thing desperate at first. Then an idea came to me on a sudden, and turning to Mariani I asked him could he find me a sheet of paper of about the size of that letter held by Ramiro. He answered me that he could, and bade me wait there until he should return.

I waited, watching the sleeper below, my excitement waxing with every second of the delay. Ramiro was snoring now — a loud, sonorous snore that rang like a trumpet-blast through that vast empty hall.

At last Mariani returned, bringing the sheet of paper I had asked for, and he was full of questions of what I intended. But neither the place nor the time was one in which to stand unfolding plans. Every moment wasted increased the uncertainty of the success of my design. Someone might come, or Ramiro might awaken despite the potency of the wine he had been given — for on so well-seasoned a toper the most potent of wines could have but a transient effect.

So I left Mariani, and moved swiftly and silently to the head of the staircase.

I had gone down two steps, when, in the dark, I missed the third, the bells in my cap jangling at the shock. I brought my teeth together and stood breathless in apprehension, fearing that the noise might awaken him, and cursing myself for a careless fool to have forgotten those infernal bells. Above me I heard a warning hiss from old Mariani, which, if anything, increased my dread. But Ramiro snored on, and I was reassured.

A moment I stood debating whether I should go on, or first return to divest myself of that cap of mine. In the end I decided to pursue the latter course. The need for swift and sudden movement might come ere I was done with this adventure, and those bells might easily be the undoing of me. So back I went to the surprise and infinite dismay of Mariani until I had whispered in his ear the reason. We retreated together to the corridor, and there, with his help, I removed my jangling headgear, which I left him to restore to my chamber.

Whilst he went upon that errand I returned once more on mine, and this time I gained the foot of the stairs without mishap, and stood in the hall. Ramiro's back was towards me. On my right stood the tall buffet from which the boy had fetched him wine that evening; this I marked out as the cover to which I must fly in case of need.

A second I stood hesitating, still considering my course; then I went softly forward, my feet making no sound in the rushes of the floor. I had covered half the distance, and, growing bolder, I was advancing more swiftly and with less caution, when suddenly my knee came in contact with a three-legged stool that had been carelessly left where none would have suspected it. The blow may have hurt me; afterwards, indeed, I was conscious of a soreness at the knee; but at the moment I had no thought or care for physical pain. The bench went over with a crash, and for all that the rushes may have deadened in part the sound of its fall, to my nervous ear it boomed like the report of a cannon through the stillness of the place.

I turned cold as ice, and sweat of fear sprang out to moisten me from head to foot. Instantly I dropped on all fours, lest Ramiro, awaking suddenly, should turn; and I waited for the least sign that should render advisable my seeking the cover of the buffet. In the gallery above I could picture old Mariani clenching his teeth at the noise, his knees knocking together, and his face white with horror; for Ramiro's snoring had abruptly ceased. It came to an end with a choking catch of the breath, and I looked to see him raise his head and start up to ascertain what it was that had aroused him. But he never stirred, and for all that he no longer snored, his breathing continued heavy and regular, so that I was cheered by the assurance that I had but disturbed his slumber, not dispelled it.

Yet, since I had disturbed and lightened it, a greater precaution was now necessary, and I waited there for some ten minutes maybe, a period that must have proved a very eternity to the old man upstairs. At last I had the reward of hearing the snoring recommence; lightly at first, but soon with all its former fullness.

I rose and proceeded now with a caution that must guard me from any more unlooked-for obstacles. Moreover, as I approached, the darkness was dispelled more and more at every stride in the direction of the light. At last I reached the table, and stood silent as a spectre at Ramiro's side, looking down upon the features of the sleeping man.

His face was flushed, and his tawny hair tumbled about his damp brow; his lips quivered as he breathed. For a moment, as I stood gazing on him, there was murder in my mind. His dagger hung temptingly in his girdle. To have drawn it and rid the world of this monster might have been a worthy deed, acceptable in the eyes of Heaven. But how should it profit me? Rather must it prove my destruction at the hands of his followers, and to be destroyed just then, with Paola depending upon me, and life full of promise once I regained my liberty, was something I had no mind to risk.

My eyes wandered to the letter lying on the table. If this were of the nature we suspected, it should prove a safer tool for his destruction.

To read it as it lay was an easy matter, and it came to me then that ere I decided upon my course it might be well that I should do so. If by chance it were innocent of treason, why, then, I might resort to the risk of that other and more desperate weapon — his own dagger.

At the foot of the short flight of steps that led from the hall to the courtyard I could hear the slow pacing of the sentry placed there by Ramiro. But unless he were summoned, it was extremely unlikely that the fellow would leave his post, so that, I concluded, I had little to fear from that quarter. I drew back and taking up a position behind Ramiro's chair — a position more favourable to escape in the untoward event of his awaking — I craned forward to read the letter over his shoulder. I thanked God in that hour for two things: that my sight was keen, and that Vitellozzo Vitelli wrote a large, bold hand.

Scarcely breathing, and distracted the while by the mad racing of my pulses, I read; and this, as nearly as I can remember, is what the letter contained:

ILLUSTRIOUS RAMIRO — Your answer to my last letter reached me safely, and it rejoiced me to learn that you had found a man for our undertaking. See that you have him in readiness, for the hour of action is at hand. Cesare goes south on the second or third day of the New Year, and he has announced to me his intention of passing through Cesena on his way, there to investigate certain charges of maladministration which have been preferred against you. These concern, in particular, certain misappropriation of grain and stores, and an excessive severity of rule, of which complaints have reached him. From this you will gather that out of a spirit of self-defence, if not to earn the reward which we have bound ourselves to pay you, it is expedient that you should not fail us. The occasion of the Duke's visit to Cesena will be, of all, the most propitious for our purpose. Have your arbalister posed, and may God strengthen his arm and render true his aim to the end that Italy may be rid of a tyrant. I commend myself to your Excellency, and I shall anxiously await your news.

VITELLOZZO VITELLI

Here indeed were my hopes realised. A plot there was, and it aimed at nothing less than the Duca Valentino's life. Let that letter be borne to Cesare Borgia at Faenza, and I would warrant that within a dozen hours of his receipt of it he would so dispose that all who had suffered by the cruel tyranny of Ramiro del' Orca would be avenged, and those who were still suffering would be relieved. In this letter lay my own freedom and the salvation of Madonna Paola, and of this letter it behoved me at once to become possessed. It was a far safer alternative than that dagger of his.

A moment I stood pondering the matter for the last time, then stepping sideways and forward, so that I was again beside him, I put out my hand and swiftly whipped the letter from the table. Then standing very still, to prevent the slightest rustle, I remained a second or two observing him. He snored on, undisturbed by my light-fingered action.

I drew away a pace or two, as lightly as I might, and folding the letter I thrust it into my girdle. Then from my open doublet I drew the sheet that Mariani had supplied me, and, advancing again, I placed it on the table in a position almost identical with that which the original had occupied, saving that it was removed a half-finger's breadth from his hand, for I feared to allow it actually to touch him lest it should arouse him.

Holding my breath, for now was I come to the most desperate part of my undertaking, I caught up one of the tapers and set fire to a corner of the sheet. That done, I left the candle lying on its side against the paper, so as to convey the impression to him, when presently he awakened, that it had fallen from its sconce. Then, without waiting for more, I backed swiftly away, watching the progress of the flames as they devoured the paper and presently reached his hand and scorched it.

At that I dropped again on all fours, and having gained the corner of the buffet, I crouched there, even as with a sudden scream of pain he woke and sprang upright, shaking his blistered hand. As a matter of instinct he looked about to see what it was had hurt him. Then his eyes fell upon the charred paper on the table, and the fallen candle, which was still burning across one end of it, and even to the dull wits of Ramiro del' Orca the only possible conclusion was suggested. He stared at it a moment, then swept that flimsy sheet of ashes from the table with an oath, and sank back once more into his great leathern chair.

'Body of God!' he swore aloud, 'it is well that I had read it a dozen times. Better that it should have been burnt than that someone should have read it whilst I slept.'

The idea of such a possibility seemed to arouse him to fresh action, for seizing the fallen candle and re-placing it in its socket, he rose once more, and holding it high above his head he looked about the hall.

The light it shed may have been feeble, and the

shadows about my buffet thick; but, as I have said, my doublet was open, and some ray of that weak candlelight must have found out the white shirt that was showing at my breast, for with a sudden cry he pushed back his chair and took a step towards me, no doubt intent upon investigating that white something that he saw gleaming there.

I waited for no more. I had no fancy to be caught in that corner, utterly at his mercy. I stood up suddenly.

'Magnificent, it is I,' I announced with a calm and boundless effrontery.

The boldness of it may have staggered him a little, for he paused, although his eyes were glowing horribly with the frenzy that possessed him, the half of which was drunkenness, the other fear and wrath lest I should have seen his treacherous communication from Vitelli.

'What make you here?' he questioned threateningly.

'I thirsted, Excellency,' I answered glibly. 'I thirsted, and I bethought me of this buffet where you keep your wine.'

He continued to eye me, some six paces off, his half-drunken wits no doubt weighing the plausibility of my answer. At last —

'If that be all, what cause had you to hide?' he asked me shrewdly.

'One of your candles fell over and awakened you,' said I. 'I feared you might resent my presence, and so I hid.'

'You came not near the table?' he inquired. 'You saw nothing of the paper that I held? Nay, by the Host! I'll take no risks. You were born 'neath an un-

lucky star, fool; for be your reason for your presence
here no more than you assert, you have come in a
season that must be fatal to you.'

He set the candle on the table, then carrying his
hand to his girdle he withdrew it sharply, and I
caught the gleam of a dagger.

In that instant I thought of Mariani waiting above,
and like a flash it came to me that if I could outpace
this drunken brigand, and, gaining the gallery well
ahead of him, transfer that letter to the old man's
hands, I should not die in vain. Cesare Borgia would
avenge me, and Madonna Paola, at least, would be
safe from this villain. If Mariani could reach Valentino
at Faenza, I could answer for it that within four-and-
twenty hours Messer Ramiro del' Orca would be the
banner on that ghastly beam that he facetiously
dubbed his flagstaff; and he would be the blackest,
dirtiest banner that ever yet had fluttered there.

The thought conceived in the twinkling of an eye,
I acted upon without a second's hesitation. Ere
Ramiro had taken his first step towards me, I had
sprung to the stairs and I was leaping up them with
the frantic speed of one upon whose heels death is
treading closely.

A singular, fierce joy was blent with my measure of
fear; a joy at the thought that even now, in this
extremity, I was outwitting him, for never a doubt
had he that the burnt paper he had found on the
table was all that was left of Vitelli's letter. His fears
were that I might have read it, but never a suspicion
crossed his mind of such a trick as I had played upon
him.

So I sped on, the gigantic Ramiro blundering after
me, panting and blaspheming, for although powerful,

his bulk and the wine he had taken left him no
nimbleness. The distance between us widened, and
if only Mariani would have the presence of mind to
wait for me at the mouth of the passage, all would
be as I could wish it before his dagger found my
heart.

I was assuring myself of this when in the dark I
stumbled, and striking my legs against a stair I
hurtled forward. I recovered almost immediately,
but, in my frenzy of haste to make up for the instant
lost, I stumbled a second time ere I was well upon my
feet.

With a roar Ramiro must have hurled himself forward, for I felt my ankle caught in a grip from which
there was no escaping, and I was roughly and brutally
dragged back and down those stairs; now my head, now
my breast beating against the steps as I descended
them one by one.

But even in that hour the letter was my first
thought, and I found a way to thrust it farther under
my girdle so that it should not be seen.

At last I reached the hall, half-stunned, and with
all the misery of defeat and the certainty of the
futility of my death to further torture my last
moments. Over me stood Ramiro, his dagger upheld,
ready to strike.

'Dog!' he taunted me, 'your sands are run.'

'Mercy, Magnificent,' I gasped. 'I have done
nothing to deserve your poniard.'

He laughed brutally, delaying his stroke that he
might prolong my agony for his drunken entertainment.

'Address your prayers to Heaven,' he mocked me,
'and let them concern your soul.'

And then, like a flash of inspiration came the words that should delay his hand.

'Spare me,' I cried, 'for I am in mortal sin.'

Impious, abandoned villain though he was, he said too much when he boasted that he feared neither God nor Devil. He was prone to forget his God, and the lessons that as a babe he had learnt at his mother's knee — for I take it that even Ramiro del' Orca had once been a babe — but deep down in his soul there had remained the fear of hell and an almost instinctive obedience to the laws of Mother Church. He could perform such ruthless cruelties as that of hurling a page into the fire to punish his clumsiness; he could rack and stab and hang men without the least shadow of compunction or twinge of conscience, but to slay a man who professed himself to be in mortal sin was a deed too appalling even for this ruthless butcher.

He hesitated a second, then he lowered his hand, his face telling me clearly how deeply he grudged me the respite which, yet, he dared not do other than accord me.

'Where shall I find me a priest?' he grumbled. 'Think you the Citadel of Cesena is a monastery? I will wait while you make an act of contrition for your sins. It is all the shrift I can afford you. And get it done, for it is time I was abed. You shall have five minutes in which to clear your soul.'

By this it seemed to me — as it may well seem to you — that matters were but little mended, and instead of employing the respite he accorded me in the pious collecting of thoughts which he enjoined, I sat up — very sore from my descent of the stairs — and employed those precious moments in putting forward arguments to turn him from his murderous purpose.

'I have lived too ungodly a life,' I protested, 'to be able to squeeze into Paradise through so narrow a gate. As you would hope for your own ultimate salvation, Excellency, I do beseech you not to imperil mine.'

This disposed him, at least, to listen to me, and I proceeded to assure him of the harmless nature of my visit to the hall in quest of wine to quench my thirst. I was running the grave risk of dying with lies on my lips, but I was too desperate to give the matter thought just then. His mood seemed to relent; the delay, perhaps, had calmed his first access of passion, and he was grown more reasonable. But when Ramiro cooled he was, perhaps, more malignant than ever, for it meant a return to his natural condition, and Ramiro's natural condition was one of cruelty unsurpassed.

'It may be as you say,' he answered me at last, sheathing his dagger, 'and at least you have my word that I will not slay you without first assuring myself that you have lied. For to-night you shall remain in durance. To-morrow we will apply the question to you.'

The hope that had been reviving in my breast fell dead once more, and I turned cold at that threat. And yet, between now and to-morrow, much might betide, and I had cause for thankfulness, perhaps, for this respite. Thus I sought to cheer myself. But I fear I failed. To-morrow he would torture me, not so much to ascertain whether I had spoken truly, but because to his diseased mind it afforded diversion to witness a man's anguish. No doubt it was that had urged him now to spare my life and accord me this merciless piece of mercy.

In a loud voice he called the sentry who was pacing below, and in a moment the man appeared in answer to that summons.

'You will take this knave to the chamber set apart for him up there, and you will leave him secure under lock and bar, bringing me the key of his door.'

The fellow informed himself which was the chamber, then turning to me he curtly bade me go with him. Thus was I haled back to my room, with the promise of horrors on the morrow, but with the night before me in which to scheme and pray for some miracle that might yet save me. But the days of miracles were long past. I lay on my bed and deplored with many a sigh that bitter fact. And if aught had been wanting to increase the weight of fear and anguish on my already overburdened mind, and to aid in what almost seemed an infernal plot to utterly distract me, I had it in fresh, wild conjectures touching Madonna Paola. Where, indeed, could she be that Ramiro's men had failed to find her for all that they had scoured that part of the country in which I had left her to wait for my return? What if, by now, worse had befallen her than the capture with which Ramiro's lieutenant was charged?

With such doubts as these to haunt me, fretted as I was by my utter inability to take a step in her service, I lay there for an hour or so in such agony of mind as is begotten only of suspense. In my girdle still reposed the treasonable letter from Vitelli to Ramiro, a mighty weapon with which to accomplish the butcher's overthrow. But how was I to wield it, imprisoned here?

I wondered why Mariani had not returned, only to remember that the soldier who had locked me in had carried the key of my prison-chamber to Ramiro.

Suddenly the stillness was disturbed by a faint tap at my door. My instincts and my reason told me it must be Mariani at last. In an instant I had leapt from the bed and whispered through the keyhole:

'Who is there?'

'It is I — Mariani — the seneschal,' came the old man's voice, very softly, but nevertheless distinctly. 'They have taken the key.'

I groaned, then in a gust of passion I fell to cursing Ramiro for that precaution.

'You have the letter?' came Mariani's voice again.

'Aye, I have it still,' I answered.

'Have you seen what it contains?'

'A plot to assassinate the Duke — no less. Enough to get this bloody Ramiro broken on the wheel.'

I was answered by a sound that was as a gasp of malicious joy. Then the old man's voice added:

'Can you pass it under the door? There is a sufficient gap.'

I felt, and found that he was right; I could pass the half of my hand underneath. I took the letter and thrust it through. His hands fastened on it instantly, almost snatching it from my fingers before they were ready to release it.

'Have courage,' he bade me. 'Listen. I shall endeavour to leave Cesena in the morning, and I shall ride straight for Faenza. If I find the Duke there when I arrive, he should be here within some twelve or fourteen hours of my departure. Fence with Ramiro, temporise if you can till then, and all will be well with you.'

'I will do what I can,' I answered him. 'But if he slays me in the meantime, at least I shall have the

satisfaction of knowing that he will not be long in
following me.'

'May God shield you,' he said fervently.

'May God speed you,' I answered him, with a still
greater fervour.

That night, as you may well conceive, I slept but
little, and that little ill. The morning, instead of reliev-
ing the fears that in the darkness had been with me,
seemed to increase them. For now was the time for
Mariani to act, and I was fearful as to how he might
succeed. I was full of doubts lest some obstacle should
have arisen to prevent his departure from Cesena,
and I spent my morning in wearisome speculation.

I took an almost childish satisfaction in the thought
that since, being a prisoner, I could no longer count
myself the Fool of the Court of Cesena, I was free to
strip the motley and assume the more sober garments
in which I had been taken, and which — as you may
recall — had been placed in my chamber on the
previous evening. It was the very plainest raiment.
For doublet I wore a buff brigandine, quilted and
daggerproof, and caught at the waist by a girdle of
hammered steel; my wine-coloured hose were stout
and serviceable, as were my long boots of untanned
leather. Yet prouder was I of this sober apparel than
ever king of his ermine.

It may have been an hour or so past noon when, at
last, my solitude was invaded by a soldier who came
to order me into the presence of the Governor. I had
been sitting at the window, leaning against the bars
and looking out at the desolate white landscape, for
there had been a heavy fall of snow in the night, which
reminded me — as snow ever did — of my first meeting with Madonna Paola.

I rose upon the instant, and my fears rose with me. But I kept a bold front as I went down into the hall, where Ramiro and the blackguards of his Court were sitting, with three or four men-at-arms at attention by the door. Close to the pulleys appertaining to the torture of the cord stood two leather-clad ruffians — Ramiro's executioners.

At the head of the board, which was still strewn with fragments of food — for they had but dined — sat Ramiro del' Orca. With him were half a dozen of his officers, whose villainous appearance pronounced them worthy of their brutal leader. The air was heavy with the pungent odour of viands. I looked round for Mariani, and I took some comfort from the fact that he was absent. Might Heaven please that he was even then on his way to Faenza.

. Ramiro watched my advance with a smile in which mockery was blent with satisfaction, for all that of the resumption of my proper raiment he seemed to take no heed. No doubt he had dined well, and he was now disposing himself to be amused.

'Messer Boccadoro,' said he, when I had come to a standstill, 'there was last night a matter that was not cleared up between us and concerning which I expressed my intention of questioning you to-day. I should proceed to do so at once, were it not that there is yet another matter on which I am, if possible, still more desirous you should tell us all you know. Once already have you evaded my questions with answers which at the time I half believed. Even now I do not say that I utterly disbelieve them, but I wish to assure myself that you told the truth; for if you lied, why then we may still be assisted by such information as the cord shall squeeze from you. I am referring to the mysterious disappearance of Madonna Paola di Santafior — a disappearance of which you have assured me that you knew nothing, being even in ignorance of the fact that the lady was not really dead. I had confidently expected that the party searching for Madonna Paola would have succeeded ere this in finding her. But this morning my hopes suffered disappointment. My men have returned empty-handed once more.'

'For which mercy may Heaven be praised!' I burst out.

He scowled at me; then he laughed evilly.

'My men have returned — all save three. Captain Lucagnolo, with two of his followers, has undertaken to go beyond the area I appointed for the search, and to proceed to the village of Cattolica. While he is pursuing his inquiries there, I have resolved to pursue my own here. I now call upon you, Boccadoro, to tell us what you know of Madonna Paola's whereabouts.'

'I know nothing,' I answered stoutly. 'I am prepared to take oath that I know nothing of her whereabouts.'

'Tell me, then, at least,' said he, 'where you bestowed her.'

I shook my head, pressing my lips tight.

'Do you think that I would tell you if I had the knowledge?' was the scornful question with which I answered him. 'You may pursue your inquiries as you will and where you will, but I pray God they may all prove as futile as must those that you would pursue here and upon my own person.'

This was how I fenced with him, this was the manner in which I followed Mariani's sound advice that I should temporise! Oh! I know that my words were

the words of a fool, yet no fear that Ramiro would
inspire me could have restrained them.

There was a murmur at the table, and his fellows
turned their eyes on Ramiro to see how he would
receive this bearding. He smiled quietly, and raising
his hand he made a sign to the executioners. Rude
hands seized me from behind, and the doublet was
torn from my back by fingers that never paused to
untruss my points.

They turned me about, and hurried me along until
I stood under the pulleys of the torture, and one of
the men held me securely whilst the other passed the
cords about my wrists. Then both the executioners
stepped back, to be ready to hoist me at the Governor's signal.

He delayed it, much as an epicure delays the con-
sumption of a delectable morsel, heightening by suspense the keen desire of his palate. He watched me
closely, and had my lips quivered or my eyelids
fluttered, he would have hailed with joy such signs of
weakness. But I take pride in truthfully writing that
I stood bold and impassively before him, and if I was
pale I thank Heaven that pallor was the habit of my
countenance, so that from that he could gather no
satisfaction. And standing there, I gave him back
look for look, and waited.

'For the last time, Boccadoro,' he said slowly,
attempting by words to shake a demeanour that was
proof against the impending facts of the cord, 'I ask
you to remember what must be the consequences of
this stubbornness. If not at the first hoist, why then
at the second or the third, the torture will compel you
to disclose what you may know. Would you not be
better advised to speak at once, while your limbs are

soundly planted in their sockets, rather than let yourself be maimed, perhaps for life, ere you will do so?'

There was a stir of hoofs without. They thundered
on the planks of the drawbridge and clattered on the
stones of the courtyard. The thought of Cesare
Borgia rose to my mind. But never did drowning
man clutch at a more illusory straw. Cold reason
quenched my hope at once. If the greatest imaginable
success attended Mariani's journey, the Duke could
not reach Cesena before midnight, and to that it
wanted some ten hours at least. Moreover, the
company that came was small to judge by the sound
— a half-dozen horses at the most.

But Ramiro's attention had been diverted from me
by the noise. Half-turning in his chair, he called to
one of the men-at-arms to ascertain who came. Before the fellow could do his bidding, the door was
thrust open and Lucagnolo appeared on the threshold,
jaded and worn with hard riding.

A certain excitement arose in me at sight of him,
despite my confidence that he must be returning
empty-handed.

Ramiro rose, pushed back his chair and advanced
towards the new-comer.

'Well?' he demanded. 'What news?'

'Excellency, the girl is here.'

That answer seemed to turn me into stone, so great
was the shock of this sudden shattering of the confidence that had sustained me.

'My search in the country failing,' pursued the
captain, as he came forward, 'I made bold to exceed
your orders by pushing my inquiries as far as the
village of Cattolica. There I found her after some
little labour.'

Surely I dreamt. Surely, I told myself, this was not possible. There was some mistake. Lucagnolo had brought some wench whom he believed to be Madonna Paola.

But even as I was assuring myself of this, the door opened again, and between two men-at-arms, white as death, her garments stained with mud and all but reduced to rags, and her eyes wild with a great fear, came my beloved Paola.

With a sound that was a grunt of satisfaction, Ramiro strode forward to meet her. But her eyes travelled past him and rested upon me, standing there between the leather-clad executioners with the cords of the torture pinioning my wrists, and I saw the anguish deepen in their blue depths.

CHAPTER XIX

DOOMED

ACROSS the length of that hall our eyes met —
hers and mine — and held each other's glances.
To me the room and all within it formed an indistinct
and misty picture, from out of which there clearly
gleamed my Paola's sweet, white face.

All at the table had risen with Ramiro, and now,
copying their leader, they bared their heads in outward token of such respect as certainly would have
been felt by any men less abandoned than were they
before so much saintly beauty and distress.

Lucagnolo had stepped aside, and Ramiro was now
bowing low and ceremoniously before Madonna. His
face I could not see, since his back was towards me,
but his tones, as they floated across the hall to where
I stood, came laden with subservience.

'Madonna, I give praise and thanks to Heaven for
this,' said he. 'I was afflicted by the gravest mis-
givings for your safety, and I am more than thankful
to behold you safe and sound.'

There was a hypocritical flavour of courtliness
about his words, and a mincing of his tones that suggested the efforts of a bull-calf to imitate the war-
bling of a throstle.

Madonna paid him no heed; indeed, she appeared
not to have heard him, for her eyes continued to look
past him and at me. At last her lips parted, and although she scarcely seemed to raise her voice above
a whisper, the word uttered reached my ears across

the stillness of the great room, and the word was
'Lazzaro!'

At mention of my name, and at the tone in which
it was uttered — a tone that betrayed some measure
of what was in her heart — Ramiro wheeled sharply
in my direction, his brows wrinkling. A certain crafti-
ness he had, for all that I ever accounted him the
dullest-witted clod that ever rose to his degree of
honour. He must have realised how expedient it was
that in all he did he should present himself to Madonna in a favourite light.

'Release him,' he bade the executioners that held
me, and in an instant I was set free. The order given,
he turned again to Madonna.

'You have been torturing him,' she cried, and her
words were hard and fierce, her eyes blazing. 'You
shall repent it, Ser Ramiro. The Lord Cesare Borgia
shall hear of it.'

Her anger betrayed her more and more, and however hidden it may have been to her, to me it was
exceeding clear that she was encompassing my
destruction. Ramiro laughed easily.

'Madonna, you are at fault. We have not been
torturing him, though I confess that we were on the
point of putting him to the question. But your timely
arrival has saved his limbs, for the question we were
asking him concerned your whereabouts.'

I would have shouted to her to be wary how she
answered him, for some premonition of how he was
about to trick her entered my mind. But realising
the futility of such a course, I held my peace and
waited agonisedly.

'You had tortured him in vain then,' she answered
scornfully. 'For Lazzaro Biancomonte would never

have betrayed me. Nor could he have betrayed me if
he would, for after your men had searched the hut in
which I was hidden, I walked to Cattolica thinking
foolishly that I should be safer there.'

Lackaday! She had told him the very thing he had
sought to know. Yet to make doubly sure he pursued
the scent a little farther.

'Indeed, it seems to me that had I tortured him I
had given him no more than he deserved for having
abandoned you in that hut. Madonna, I tremble to
think of the harm that might have come to you
through that knave's desertion.' And he scowled
across at me, much as the Pharisee might have
scowled upon the publican.

'He is no knave,' she answered, and I could have
groaned to hear her working my undoing, though not
by so much as a sign might I inspire her with caution,
for that sign must have been seen by others. 'Nor did
he abandon me. He left me only to go in quest of the
necessaries for our journey. If harm has come to me
the blame of it must not rest on him.'

'Of what harm do you speak, Madonna?' he cried,
in a voice laden with concern.

'Of what harm?' she echoed, eyeing him with a
scorn that would have slain him had he any manhood
left. 'Of what harm? Mother of Mercy, defend me!
Do you ask the question? What greater harm could
have come to me than to have fallen into the hands
of Ramiro del' Orca and his brigands?'

He stood looking at her, and I doubt not that his
face was a very picture of simulated consternation.

'Surely, Madonna, you do not understand that we
are your friends, that you can so abuse us. But you
will be faint, Madonna,' he cried, with a fresh and

deep solicitude. 'A cup of wine.' And he waved his hand towards the table.

'It would poison me, I think,' she answered coldly.

'You are cruel, and — alas! — mistrustful,' said he. 'Can you guess nothing of the anxiety that has been mine these two days, of the fears that have haunted me as I thought of you and your wanderings?'

Her lip curled, and her face took on some slight vestige of colour. Her spirit was a thing for which I might then have come to love her had it not been that already I loved her to distraction.

'Yes,' said she, 'I can guess something of your dismay when you found your schemes frustrated; when you found that you had come too late to San Domenico.'

'Will you not forgive me that shift to which my adoration drove me?' he implored in a honeyed voice — and a more fearful thing than Ramiro the butcher was Ramiro the lover.

At that scarcely covert avowal of his passion she recoiled a step she might before a thing unclean. The little colour faded from her cheek, the scorn departed from her lip, and a sickly, deadly fear overspread her lovely face. God! that I should stand there and witness this insult to the woman I adored and worshipped with a fervour that the Church seeks to instil into us for those about the throne of Heaven. It might not be. A blind access of fury took me. Of the consequences I thought nothing. Reason left me utterly, and the slight hope that might lie in temporising was disregarded.

Before those about me could guess my purpose, or those others, too engrossed in the scene at the far end of the hall, could intervene, I had sprung from

between the executioners and dashed across the space
that separated me from the Governor of Cesena. One
well-aimed blow, and there should be an end to Messer
Ramiro. That was the only thought that found room
in my disordered mind.

One or two there were who cried out as I sped
past them, swift as the hound when it speeds after
the fleeing hare. But I was upon Ramiro ere any
could have sufficiently mastered his surprise to in-
terfere.

By the nape of his great neck I caught him from
behind, and setting my knee at his spine I wrenched
him backward, and so flung him over on the floor.
Down I went with him, my hand reaching for the
dagger at his jewelled girdle, and I had found and
drawn it in that swift action of mine ere he had bethought him of his hands. Up it flashed and down. I
sank it through the crimson velvet of his rich doublet,
straight at the spot where his heart should be — if he
were so human as to have a heart. The next instant I
turned cold and sick. My desperate effort had been
all for nothing. In my hand I was left with the bronze
hilt of his great poniard; the blade had broken off
against the mesh of steel the coward wore beneath his
finery.

There was a rush of feet about us, a piercing
scream from Madonna Paola, and it was to her that I
owed my life in that grim moment. A dozen blades
were naked and would have transfixed me as I lay,
but that she covered my body with her own and bade
them strike at me through her.

A moment later and the powerful hands of the
Governor of Cesena were at my throat. I was lifted
and tossed aside, as though I had been a hound and

he the bull I had beset. And as he swung me over and crushed me to the ground, he knelt above me and grinned horribly into my purpling face.

A second we stayed so, and I thought indeed that my hour was come, when suddenly I felt the blood in my head released once more. He had taken his hands from my throat. He seized me now by the collar and dragged me rudely to my feet.

'Take this knave and lock him in his chamber,' he bade a couple of his *bravi*. 'I may have need of him ere he dies.'

'Messer Ramiro,' came the interceding voice of Madonna Paola, 'what he did, he did for me. You will not let him die for it?'

There was a pause during which he looked at her, whilst the men were roughly dragging me across the hall.

'Who knows, Madonna?' he said, with a bow and an infernal smile. 'If you were to beg his life, it might even come to pass that I might spare it.'

He did not wait for her answer, but stepping after me, he called to the men that led me. In obedience they halted, and he came forward. We were now at the foot of the staircase.

'Boccadoro,' said he, planting himself before me, and eyeing me with eyes that were very full of malice, 'you will recall the punishment I promised you if I came to discover it was you had thwarted me in Pesaro. It is the second time you have fooled Ramiro del' Orca. There does not live the man who can boast that he did it thrice, nor will I risk it that you be that man. Make your peace with Heaven, for at sunset — in an hour's time — you hang. There is one little thing that might save you even yet, and if you find life sweet, you would do well to pray that that little thing may come to pass.'

I answered him nothing, but I bowed my head in token that I had heard, and he signed to the men to proceed with me, whilst turning on his heel he stepped down the hall again to where Madonna Paola, overcome with weakness, had sunk upon a stool.

As I was leaving the gallery I had a last glimpse of her, sitting there with drawn face and haggard eyes that followed me as I passed from her sight, whilst Ramiro del' Orca stood beside her murmuring words that did not reach me. His so-called courtiers and his men-at-arms were trooping out of the room, no doubt in obedience to his dismissal.

CHAPTER XX

THE SUNSET

I HAVE heard tell of the calm that comes upon brave men when hope is dead and their doom has been pronounced. Uncertainty may have tortured and made cowards of them; but once that uncertainty is dissolved and suspense is at an end, resignation enters their soul, and, possessing it, gives to their bearing a noble and dignified peace. By the mercy of Heaven they are made, maybe, to see how poor and evanescent a thing is life; and they come to realise that since to die is a necessity there is no avoiding, as well might it betide to-day as ten years hence.

Such a mood, however, came not to soothe that last hour of mine, and yet I account myself no coward. It was an hour of such torture and anguish as never before I had experienced — much though I had undergone — and the source of all my suffering lay in the fact that Madonna Paola was in the hands of the ogre of Cesena. Had it not been for that most untoward circumstance I almost believe that while I waited for the sun to set on that December afternoon, my mood had not only been calm but even in some measure joyous, for it must have comforted my last moments to reflect that for all that Messer Ramiro was about to hang me, yet had I sown the seeds of his own destruction ere he had brought me to this pass.

I did, indeed, reflect upon it, and it may even be that, in spite of all, I culled some grain of comfort from the reflection. But let that be. My narrative

would drag wearily were I to digress that I might tell
you at length the ugly course of my thoughts whilst
the sands of my last hour were running swiftly out.
For, after all, my concern and yours is with the story
of Lazzaro Biancomonte, sometime known as Boccadoro the Fool, and not with his philosophies —
philosophies so unprofitable that it can benefit no man
that I should set them down.

My windows faced west, and so I was able to watch
the fall of the sun, and measure by its shortening distance from the horizon the ebbing of my poor life. At
last the nether rim of that round, fiery orb was on
the point of touching the line of distant hills, and it
was casting a crimson glow along the white, snow-
sheeted landscape that was singularly suggestive of
a tide of blood — a very fitting tide to flow and ebb
about the walls of the Castle of Cesena.

One little thing there was might save me, Ramiro
had said. But I had shut the thought out of my mind
to keep me from utter distraction. The only little
thing in which I held that my salvation could lie
would be in the miraculous arrival of Cesare Borgia,
and of that not the faintest hope existed. If the
greatest luck attended Mariani's errand and the
greatest speed were made by the Duke once he
received the letter, he could not reach Cesena in less
than another eight hours. And another eight minutes,
to reckon by the swift sinking of the sun would see
the time appointed for my hanging. I thought of
Joshua in that grim hour, and in a mood that approached the whimsical I envied him his gift. If I
could have stayed the setting of the sun, and held it
where it was till midnight, all might yet be well if
Mariani had been diligent and Cesare swift.

The key grating in the lock put an end to my vague musings, and reminded me of the fact that I had neglected to employ that last hour as would have become a good son of Mother Church. For an instant I believe that my heart turned me to thoughts of God, and sent up a prayer for mercy for my poor sinful soul. Then the door swung wide. Two halberdiers and a carnifex in his odious leathern apron stood before me. Clearly Ramiro sought to be exact, and to have me hanging the instant the sun should vanish.

'It is time,' said one of the soldiers, whilst the executioner, stepping into my chamber, pinioned my wrists behind me, and retaining hold of the cord bade me march. He followed, holding that slender cord, and so, like a beast to the shambles, went I.

Once more they led me into the hall, where the shadows were lengthening in dark contrast to the splashes of sunlight that lingered on the floor, and whose blood-red hue was deepened by the gules of the windows through which it was filtered.

Ramiro was waiting for me, and six of his officers were in attendance. But, for once, there were no men-at-arms at hand. On a chair, the one usually occupied by Ramiro, himself, sat Madonna Paola, still in her torn and bedraggled raiment, her face white, her eyes wild as they had been when first she had been haled into Ramiro's presence, some two hours ago, and her features so rigidly composed that it told the tale of the awful self-control she must be exerting — a self-control that might end with a sudden snap that would plunge her into madness.

A wild rage possessed me at sight of her. Let Ramiro be ruthless and cruel where men were concerned; that was a thing for which forgiveness might be found him. But that he should submit a lady, delicately nurtured as was Madonna, to such horrors as she had undergone since she had awakened from his sleeping-potion in the Church of San Domenico, was something for which no hell could punish him condignly.

Ramiro met me with a countenance through the assumed gravity of which I could espy his wicked, infernal mockery peeping forth.

'I deplore your end, Lazzaro Biancomonte,' said he slowly, 'for you are a brave man, and brave men are rare. You were worthy of better things, but you chose to cross swords with Ramiro del' Orca, and you have got your death-blow. May God have mercy on your soul.'

'I am praying,' said I, 'for just so much mercy as you shall have justice. If my prayer is heard, I should be well content.'

He changed countenance a little. So, too, I thought, did Madonna Paola. My firmness may have yielded her some grain of comfort. Ramiro set his hands on his hips, and eyed me squarely.

'You are a dauntless rogue,' he confessed.

I laughed for answer, and in that moment it entered my mind that I might yet enjoy some measure of revenge in this life. More than that, I might benefit Madonna. For were the seed I was about to sow to take root in the craven heart of Ramiro del' Orca, it would so fully occupy his mind that he would have little time to bestow on Paola in the few hours that were left him. But before I could bethink me of words he was speaking again.

'I held out to you a slender hope,' said he. 'I told you that there was one little thing might save you.

That hope has borne no fruit; the little thing I spoke
of has not come to pass. It rested with Madonna
Paola, here. She had it in her hands to effect your
salvation; but she has refused. Your blood rests on
her head.'

She shuddered at the words, and a low moan
escaped her. She covered her face with her hands. A
moment I stood looking at her; then I shifted my
glance to Ramiro.

'Will it please you, Illustrious, to allow me a
few moments' conversation with Madonna Paola di
Santafior?'

I invested my tones with a weight of meaning that
did not escape him. His face suddenly lightened,
whilst one of his officers — a fellow very fitly named
Lupone — laughed outright.

'Your hero seems none so heroic after all,' he said
derisively to the Governor. 'The imminence of death
makes him amenable.'

Ramiro scowled on him for answer. Then, turning
to me —

'Do you think you could bend her stubbornness?'
quoth he.

'I might attempt it,' answered I.

His eyes flashed with evil hope; his lips parted in a
smile. He shot a glance at Madonna, who had withdrawn her hands from her face and was regarding me
now with a strange expression of horror and in-
credulity — marvelling, no doubt, to find me such a
craven as I must have seemed.

Ramiro looked at the diminishing sunlight on the
floor.

'In some five minutes the sun will have completely
set,' said he. 'Those five minutes you shall have to

seek to enlist Madonna's aid on your behalf. If you succeed — and she may tell you on what terms you are to have your life — you shall depart from Cesena to-night a free man.'

He paused a moment, and his eyes, lighted by an odious smile, rested once more on Madonna Paola. Then he bade all withdraw, and went with them into an adjoining chamber, fondly nurturing the hopes that were begotten of his belief that Lazzaro Biancomonte was a villain.

When we were alone, she and I, I stood a moment where they had left me, my hands pinioned behind me, and the cord which the executioner had held trailing the ground like a lambent tail. Then I went slowly forward until I stood close before her. Her eyes were on my face, still with that same look of unbelief.

'Madonna mia,' said I, 'do not for an instant think that it is my purpose to ask of you any sacrifice that might save my worthless life. Rather was my purpose in seeking these few moments with you, to strengthen and encourage you by such news as it is mine to bring.'

She looked now as if she scarcely understood.

'If I will wed him to-night, he has promised that you shall go free,' she said in a whisper. 'He says that he can bring a priest from the neighbourhood at a moment's notice.'

'Do not heed him,' I cried sternly.

'I do not heed him,' said she, more composedly. 'If he seeks to force me, I shall find a way of setting myself free. Dear Mother of Heaven! Death were a sweet and restful thing after all that I have suffered in these days.'

Then she fell suddenly to weeping.

'Think me not an utter coward, Lazzaro. Willingly

would I do this thing to save so noble a life as yours,
did I not think that you must hate me for it. I was
stout and firm in my refusal, confident that you would
have had me so. Was I not right, my poor, poor
Lazzaro?'

'Madonna, you were right,' I answered firmly and
calmly.

'And you are to die, amor mio,' she murmured
passionately. 'You are to die when the promise of
happiness seemed held out to us. And yet, were you
to live at the price at which life is offered you, would
your life be endurable? Tell me the truth, Lazzaro;
swear it to me. For if life is the dearer thing to you,
why, then, you shall have your life.'

'Need you ask me, Paola?' questioned I. 'Does
not your heart tell you how much easier is death than
would be such a life as I must lead hereafter, even if
we could trust Ramiro, which we cannot. Be brave,
Madonna, and help me to be brave and to bear myself
with a becoming fortitude. Now listen to what I have
to tell you. Ramiro del' Orca is a traitor who is
plotting the death of his overlord. Proofs of it are by
now in the hands of Cesare Borgia, and in some seven
or eight hours the Duke himself should be here to put
this monster to the question touching those matters.
I will say a word in his ear ere I depart that will fill
his mind with a very wholesome fear, and you will find
that during the few hours left him he will have little
leisure to think of you and afflict you with his odious
wooing. Be strong, then, for a little while, for Cesare
is coming to set you free.'

She looked at me now with eyes that were wide
open. Suddenly —

'Could we not gain time?' she cried, and in her

eagerness she rose and set her hands upon my shoulders. 'Could I not pretend to acquiesce to his wishes, and so delay your end?'

'I have thought of it,' I answered gloomily, 'but the thought has brought me no hope. Ramiro is not to be trusted. He might tell you that he sets me free, but he dare not do so; he fears that I may have knowledge of his dealings with Vitelli, and assuredly he would break faith with us. Again the coming of the Duke might be delayed. Alas!' I ended in despair, 'there is nothing to be done but to let things run their course.'

There was even more in my mind than I expressed. My mistrust of Ramiro went further than I had explained, and concerning Madonna more closely than it did me.

'Nay, Lazzaro mine,' she still protested, 'I will attempt it. It is, at least, well worth the risk.'

'You forget,' said I, 'that even when Cesare comes we cannot say how he will bear himself towards you. You were to have been betrothed to his cousin, Ignacio. It is a matter upon which he may insist.'

She looked at me for a moment with anguish in her eyes that turned my misery into torture.

'Lazzaro,' she moaned, 'was ever woman so beset? I think that Heaven must have laid some curse upon me.'

Her face was close to mine. I stooped forward and kissed her on her brow.

'May God have you in His keeping, Madonna mia,' I murmured. 'The sun is gone.'

'Lazzaro!' It was the cry of a breaking heart. Her arms went around my neck, and in a passion of grief her kisses burned on my lips.

Then the door of the anteroom opened — and I thanked God for the mercy of that interruption. I whispered a word to her, and in obedience she sprang back, and sank limp and broken on the chair once again.

Ramiro entered, his men behind him, his face alight with eagerness. There and then I swamped his hopes.

'The sun is gone, Magnificent,' said I. 'You had best get me hanged.'

His brow darkened, for there was a note of mockery and triumph in my voice.

'You have fooled me, animal,' he cried. His jaw set, and his eyes continued to regard me with an evil glow. Then he laughed terribly, shrugged his shoulders, and spoke again. 'After all, it shall avail you little.' He turned to the carnifex. 'Federigo, do your work,' said he, whereupon the fellow stepped behind me, and the halberdiers ranged themselves one on either side of me again.

'A word ere I go, Messer del' Orca,' I demanded insolently.

He tooked at me sharply, wondering, maybe, at the fresh tone I took.

'Say it and begone,' he sullenly permitted me.

I paused a moment to choose fitting words for that portentous death-song of mine. At length —

'You boasted to me a little while ago,' said I, smiling grimly, 'that the man did not live who had thrice fooled you. That man does live, for that man am I.'

'Bah!' he returned contemptuously, thinking, no doubt, that I referred to my interview with Madonna Paola. 'You may take what pride you will from such a thought. You are upon the threshold of death.'

'True, but the thought is one that affords me more comfort and joy than pride. As much comfort and joy as you shall take horror when I tell you in what manner I have fooled you.' I paused to heighten the sensation of my words.

'To such good purpose have I used my wits that ere another sun shall rise and set you will have followed me along the black road that I am now treading — the road whose bourne is the gallows. Bethink you of the charred paper that last night you brushed from this table when you awoke to find a candle fallen on the treacherous letter Vitellozzo Vitelli sent you in the lining of a hat.'

His jaw fell, his face flamed redder than ever for a second, then it went grey as ashes.

'Of what do you prate, fool?' he questioned huskily, seeking to bluster it before the startled glances of his officers.

'I speak,' said I, 'of that charred paper. It was I who laid the candle across it; but it was a virgin sheet I burned. Vitelli's letter I had first abstracted.'

'You lie!' he almost screamed.

'To prove that I do not, I will tell you what it contained. It held proof that bribed by the Tyrant of Città di Castello you had undertaken to pose an arbalister to slay the Duke on the occasion of his coming visit to Cesena.'

He glared at me a moment in furious amazement. Then he turned to his officers.

'Do not heed him,' he bade them. 'The dog lies to sow doubts in your minds ere he goes out to hang. It is a puerile revenge.'

I laughed with amused confidence. There was one among them had heard Lampugnani's words touching the messenger's hat — words that had cost the fellow his life. But my concern was little with the effect my words might produce upon his followers.

'By to-morrow you will know whether I have lied or not. Nay, before then shall you know it, for by midnight Cesare Borgia should be at Cesena. Vitellozzo Vitelli's letter is in his hands by now.'

At that Ramiro burst into a laugh. So convinced was he of the impossibility of my having got the letter to the Duke, even if what I had said of its abstraction were true, that he gathered assurance from what seemed to him so monstrous an exaggeration.

'By your own words are you confounded,' said he. 'Out of your own mouth have you proven your lies. Assuming that all you say were true, how could you, who since last night have been a prisoner, have got a messenger to bear anything from you to Cesare Borgia?'

I looked at him with a contemptuous amusement that daunted him.

'Where is Mariani?' I asked quietly. 'Where is the father of the lad you so brutally and wantonly slew yesternight? Seek him throughout Cesena, and when you find him not, perhaps you will realise that one who had seen his own son suffer such an outrageous and cruel death at your brigand's hands would be a willing and ready instrument in an act that should avenge him.'

Vergine santa! What a consternation was his. He must have missed Mariani early in the day, for he took no measure, asked no questions that might confirm or refute the thing I announced. His face grew livid, and his knees loosened. He sank on to a chair and mopped the cold sweat from his brow with his

great brown hand. No thought had he now for the
eyes of his officers or their opinions. Fear, icy and
horrid, such fear as in his time he had inspired in a
thousand hearts was now possessed of his. Sweet
indeed was the flavour of my vengeance.

His officers instinctively drew away from him before the guilt so clearly written on his face, and their
eyes were full of doubt as to how they should proceed
and of some fear — for it must have been passing
through their minds that they stood, themselves, in
danger of being involved with him in the Duke's
punishment of his disloyalty.

This was more than had ever entered into my calculations or found room in my hopes. By a brisk appeal
to them, it almost seemed that I might work my
salvation in this eleventh hour.

Madonna watched the scene with eyes that suggested to me that the same hope had arisen in her own
mind. My halberdiers and the carnifex alone stood
stolidly indifferent. Ramiro was to them the man that
hired them; with his intriguing they had no concern.

For a moment or two there was a silence, and
Ramiro sat staring before him, his white face glistening with the sweat of fear. A very coward at heart
was this overbearing ogre of Cesena, who for years
had been the terror and scourge of the countryside.
At last he mastered his emotion and sprang to his
feet.

'You have had the laugh of me,' he snarled, fury
now ringing in his voice. 'But ere you die you may
regret it that you mocked me.'

He turned to the executioner.

'Strip him,' he commanded fiercely. 'He shall
not hang as I intended — at least not before we have

torn every bone of his body from its socket. To the
cord with him!' And he pointed to the torture at the
end of the hall.

The executioner made shift to obey him when
suddenly Madonna Paola leapt to her feet, her cheeks
flushed and her eyes bright with a new excitement.

'Is there none here,' she cried, appealing to Ramiro's
officers, 'that will draw his sword in the service of his
overlord, the Duca Valentino? There stands a traitor,
and there one who has proven his loyalty to Cesare
Borgia. The Duke is likely to demand a heavy price
for the life of that faithful one to whose warning he
owes his escape of assassination. Will none of you side
now with the right that anon you may stand well with
Cesare Borgia when he comes? Or, by idly allowing
this traitor to have his way, will you participate in the
punishment that must be his?'

It was the very spur they needed. And scarce was
that final question of hers flung at those knaves, when
the answer came from one of them. It was that same
sturdy Lupone.

'I, for one, am for the Duke,' said he, and his
sword leapt from its scabbard. 'I draw my iron for
Valentino. Let every loyal man do likewise, and seize
this traitor.' And with his sword he pointed at
Ramiro.

In an instant three others bared their weapons and
ranged themselves beside him. The remaining two —
of whom was Lucagnolo — folded their hands, mani-
festing by that impassivity that they were minded to
take neither one side nor the other.

The carnifex paused in his labours of undressing
me, and the affair promised to grow interesting. But
Ramiro did not stand his ground. Fury swelling his

veins and crimsoning his huge face, he sprang to the door and bellowed to his guards. Six men trooped in almost at once, and reinforced by the halberdiers that had been guarding me, they made short work of the resistance of those four officers. In as little time as it takes me to record it, they were disarmed and ranged against the wall behind those guards and others that had come to their support — to be dealt with by Ramiro after he had dealt with me.

His fear of Cesare's coming was put by for the moment in his fierce lust to be avenged upon me who had betrayed him and the officers who had turned against him. Madonna sank back once more in her despair. The little spark that she had so bravely fanned to life had been quenched almost as soon as it had shown itself.

'Now, Federigo,' said Ramiro grimly, 'I am waiting.'

The executioner resumed his work, and in an instant I stood stripped of my brigandine. As the fellow led me, unresisting, to the torture — for what resistance could have availed me now? — I tried to pray for strength to endure what was to come. I was done with life; for some portion of an hour I must go through the cruellest of agonies; and then, when it pleased God in His mercy that I should swoon, it would be to wake no more in this world. For they would bear out my unconscious body, and hang it by the neck from that black beam they called Ramiro del' Orca's flagstaff.

I cast a last glance at Madonna. She had fallen on her knees, and with folded hands was praying intently, none heeding her.

Federigo halted me beneath the pulleys, and his

horrid hands grew busy adjusting the ropes to my wrists.

And then, when the last ray of hope had faded, but before the executioner had completed his hideous task, a trumpet blast, winding a challenge to the gates of the Castle of Cesena, suddenly rang out upon the evening air, and startled us all by its sudden and imperious note.

CHAPTER XXI

AVE CÆSAR!

FOR just an instant I allowed myself to be tortured by the hope that a miracle had happened, and here was Cesare Borgia come a good eight hours before it was possible for Mariani to have fetched him from Faenza. The same doubt may have crossed Ramiro's mind, for he changed colour and sprang to the door to bawl an order forbidding his men to lower the bridge.

But he was too late. Before he was answered by his followers, we heard the creaking of the hinges and the rattle of the running chains, ending in a thud that told us the drawbridge had dropped across the moat. Then came the loud continuous thunder of many hoofs upon its timbers. Paralysed by fear Ramiro stood where he had halted, turning his eyes wildly in this direction and in that, but never moving one way or the other.

It must be Cesare, I swore to myself. Who else could ride to Cesena with such numbers? But then, if it was Cesare, it could not be that he had seen Mariani, for he could not have ridden from Faenza. Madonna had risen too, and with a white face and straining eyes she was looking towards the door.

And then our doubts were at last ended. There was a jangle of spurs and the fall of feet, and through the open door stepped a straight, martial figure in a doublet of deep crimson velvet, trimmed with costly lynx furs and slashed with satin in the sleeves and

shoulder puffs; jewels gleamed in the massive chain
across his breast and at the marroquin girdle that
carried his bronze-hilted sword; his hose was of red
silk, and his great black boots were armed with golden
spurs. But to crown all this very regal splendour was
the beautiful, pale, cold face of Cesare Borgia, from
out of which two black eyes flashed and played like
sword-points on the company.

Behind him surged a press of mercenaries, in steel,
their weapons naked in their hands, so that no doubt
was left of the character of this visit.

Collecting himself, and bethinking him that, after
all, he had best dissemble a good countenance,
Ramiro advanced respectfully to meet his overlord.
But ere he had taken three steps the Duke stayed
him.

'Stand where you are, traitor,' was the imperious
command. 'I'll trust you no nearer to my person.'
And to emphasise his words he raised his gloved left
hand, which had been resting on his sword-hilt, and
in which I now observed that he held a paper.

Whether Ramiro recognised it, or whether it was
that the mere sight of a paper reminded him of the
letter which on my testimony should be in Cesare's
keeping, or whether again the word 'traitor' with
which Cesare branded him drove the iron deeper into
his soul, I cannot say; but to this I can testify; that he
turned a livid green, and stood there before his for-
midable master in an attitude so stricken as to have
aroused pity for any man less a villain than was he.

And now Cesare's eye, travelling round, alighted
on Madonna Paola, standing back in the shadows to
which she had instinctively withdrawn at his coming.
At sight of her he recoiled a pace, deeming, no doubt,

that it was an apparition stood before him. Then he looked again, and being a man whose mind was above puerile superstitions, he assured himself that by whatever miracle the thing was wrought, the figure before him was the living body of Madonna Paola Sforza di Santafior. He swept the velvet cap with its jewelled plume from off his auburn locks, and bowed low before her.

'In God's name, Madonna, how are you come to life again, and how do I find you here of all places?' She made no ado about enlightening him.

'That villain,' said she, and her finger pointed straight and firmly at Ramiro, 'put a sleeping-potion in my wine on the last night he dined with us at Pesaro, and when all thought me dead he came to the Church of San Domenico with his men to carry off my sleeping body. He would have succeeded in his fell design but that Lazzaro Biancomonte there, whom you have stayed him in the act of torturing to death, was beforehand and saved me from his clutches for a time. This morning at Cattolica his searching *sbirri* discovered me and brought me hither, where I have been for the past three hours, and where, but for Your Excellency's timely arrival, I shudder to think of the indignities I might have suffered.'

'I thank you, Madonna, for this clear succinctness,' answered Cesare coldly, as was his habit. They say he was a passionate man, and such, indeed, I do believe him to have been; but even in the hottest frenzy of rage, outwardly he was ever the same — icily cold and tranquil. And this, no doubt, was the thing that made him terrible.

'Presently, Madonna,' he pursued, 'I shall ask you

to tell me how it chanced that, having saved you, Messer Biancomonte did not bear you to your brother's house. But first I have business with my Governor of Cesena — a score which is rendered, if possible, heavier than it already stood by this thing that you have told me.'

'My lord,' cried out Ramiro, finding his tongue at last, 'Madonna has misinformed you. I know nothing of who administered the sleeping-potion. Certainly it was not I. I heard a rumour that her body had been stolen, and I —'

'Silence!' Cesare commanded sternly. 'Did I question you, dog?'

His beautiful, terrible eyes fastened upon Ramiro in a glance that defied the man to answer him. Cowed, like a hound at sight of the whip, Ramiro whimpered into silence.

Cesare waved his hand in his direction, half-turning to the men-at-arms behind him.

'Take and disarm him,' was his passionless command. And while they were doing his bidding, he turned to me and ordered the executioner beside me to unbind my hands and set me at liberty.

'I owe you a heavy debt, Messer Biancomonte,' he said, without any warmth, even now that his voice was laden with a message of gratitude. 'It shall be discharged. It is thanks to your daring and resource that the seneschal Mariani was able to bring me this letter, this piece of culminating proof against Ramiro del' Orca. It is fortunate for you that Mariani was not put to it to ride to Faenza to find me, or else I am afraid we had not reached Cesena in time to save your life. I met him some leagues this side of Faenza, as I was on my way to Sinigaglia.'

He turned abruptly to Ramiro.

'In this letter which Vitelli wrote you,' said he, 'it is suggested that there are others in the conspiracy. Tell me now, who are those others? See that you answer me with truth, for I shall compel proofs from you of such accusations as you may make.'

Ramiro looked at him with eyes rendered dull by agony. He moistened his lips with his tongue, and turning his head towards his men —

'Wine,' he gasped, from very force of habit. 'A cup of wine!'

'Let it be supplied him,' said Cesare coldly, and we all stood waiting while a servant filled him a cup.

Ramiro gulped the wine avidly, never pausing until the goblet was empty.

'Now,' said Cesare, who had been watching him, 'will it please you to answer my question?'

'My lord,' said Ramiro, revived and perhaps strengthened in spirit by the draught, 'I must first ask Your Excellency to be a little plainer with me. To what conspiracy is it that you refer? I know of none. What is this letter which you say Vitelli wrote me? I take it you refer to the Lord of Città di Castello. But I can recall no letters passing between us. My acquaintance with him is of the slightest.'

Cesare looked at him a second.

'Approach,' he curtly bade him, and Ramiro came forward, one of the Borgia halberdiers on either side of him, each holding him by an arm. The Duke thrust the letter under his eyes. 'Have you never seen that before?'

Ramiro looked at it a moment, and his attempt at dissembling bewilderment was a ludicrous thing to witness.

'Never,' he said brazenly at last.

Cesare folded the letter and slipped it into the breast of his doublet. From his girdle he took a second paper. He turned from Ramiro.

'Don Miguel,' he called.

From behind his men-at-arms a tall man, all dressed in black, stood forward. It was Cesare's Spanish captain, one whose name was as well known and as well dreaded in Italy as Cesare's own. The Duke held out to him the paper that he had produced.

'You heard the question that I asked Messer del' Orca?' he inquired.

'I heard, Illustrious,' answered Miguel, with a bow.

'See that you obtain me an answer to it, as well as an account of the other matters that I have noted on this list — concerning the misappropriation of stores, the retention of taxes illicitly levied, and the wanton cruelty towards my good citizens of Cesena. Put him to the question without delay, and record me his replies. The implements are yonder.'

And with the same calm indifference which characterised his every word and action Cesare pointed to the torture, and turned to Madonna Paola, as though he gave the matter of Ramiro del' Orca and his misdeeds not another thought.

'Mercy, my lord,' rang now the voice of Ramiro, laden with horrid fear. 'I will speak.'

'Then do so — to Don Miguel. He will question you in my name.' Again he turned to Madonna. 'Madonna Paola, may I conduct you hence? Things may perhaps occur which it is not seemly your gentle eyes should witness. Messer Biancomonte, attend us.'

Now, in spite of all that Ramiro had made me suffer, I should have been loath to have remained and witnessed his examination. That they would torture him was now inevitable. His chance of answering freely was gone. Even if he returned meek replies to Don Miguel's questions, that gentleman would, no doubt, still submit him to the cord by way of assuring himself that such replies were true ones.

Gladly, then, did I turn to follow the Duke and Madonna Paola into the adjoining chamber to which Cesare led the way, even as Don Miguel's voice was raised to command his men to clear the hall, to the end that he might conduct his examination in private.

The three of us stood in the anteroom. A servant had lighted the tapers and closed the doors, and the Duke turned to me.

'First, Messer Biancomonte, to discharge my debt. You are, if I am not misinformed, the lord by right of birth to certain lands that bear your name, which suffered sequestration during the reign of the late Costanzo, Tyrant of Pesaro, whose son Giovanni upheld that confiscation. Am I right?'

'Your Excellency is very well informed. The Lord of Pesaro did make me tardy restitution — so tardy, indeed, that the lands which he restored to me had already virtually passed from his possession.'

Cesare smiled.

'In recompense for the service you have rendered me this day,' said he, and my heart thrilled at the words and at the thought of the joy which I was about to bear to my old mother, 'I reinvest you in your lands of Biancomonte for so long as you are content to recognise in me your overlord, and to be loyal, true, and faithful to my rule.'

I bowed, murmuring something of the joy I felt and the devotion I should entertain.

'Then that is done with. You shall have the deed from my hand by morning. And now, Madonna, will you grant me some explanation of your conduct in leaving Pesaro in this man's company, instead of repairing to your brother's house, when you awakened from the effects of the potion Ramiro gave you, or must I seek the explanation from Messer Biancomonte?'

Her eyes fell before the scrutiny of his, and when they were raised again it was to meet my glance, and if Cesare could not, for himself, read the message of those eyes, why, then, his penetration was by no means what the world accounted it.

'My lord,' I cried, 'let me explain. I love Madonna Paola. It was love of her that led me to the church and kept me there that night. It was love of her and the overmastering passion of my grief at her so sudden death that led me, in a madness, to desire once more to look upon her face ere they delivered it to earth's keeping. Thus was it that I came to discover that she lived; thus was it that I anticipated Ramiro del' Orca. He came upon us almost before I had raised her from the coffin, yet love lent me strength and craft to delude him. We hid awhile in the sacristy, and it was there, after Madonna had revived, that the pent-up passion of years burst the bonds with which reason had bidden me restrain it.'

'By the Host!' cried Cesare, his brows drawn down in a frown. 'You are a bold man to tell me this. And you, Madonna,' he cried, turning suddenly to her, 'what have you to say?'

'Only, my lord, that I have suffered more, I think, in these past few days than has ever fallen to the lifetime's share of another woman. I think, my lord, that

I have suffered enough to have earned me a little peace and a little happiness for the remainder of my days. All my life have men plagued me with marriages that were hateful to me, and this has culminated in the brutal act of Ramiro del' Orca. Do you not think that I have endured enough?'

He stared at her for a moment.

'Then you love this fellow?' he gasped. 'You, Madonna Paola Sforza di Santafior, one of the noblest ladies in all Italy, confess to love this lordling of a few barren acres?'

'I loved him, Illustrious, when he was less, much less, than that. I loved him when he was little better than the Fool of the Court of Pesaro, and not even the shame of the motley that disgraced him could stay the impulse of my affections.'

He laughed curiously.

'By my faith,' said he, 'I have gone through life complaining of the want of frankness in the men and women I have met. But you two seem to deal in it liberally enough to satisfy the most ardent seeker after truth. I would that Pontius Pilate could have known you.' Then he grew sterner. 'But what account of this evening's adventure am I to bear to my cousin Ignacio?'

She hung her head in silence, whilst my own spirit trembled. Then suddenly I spoke.

'My lord,' said I, 'if you take her back to Pesaro, you may keep the deed of Biancomonte. For unless Madonna Paola goes thither with me, your gift is a barren one, your reward of no account or value to me.'

'I would not have it so,' said he, his head on one side and his fingers toying with his auburn beard.

'You saved my life, and you must be rewarded fittingly.'

'Then, Illustrious, in payment for my preservation of your life, do you render happy mine, and we shall thus be quits.'

'My lord,' cried Paola, putting forth her hands in supplication, 'if you have ever loved, befriend us now.'

A shadow darkened his face for an instant, then it was gone, and his expression was as inscrutable as ever. Yet he took her hands in his and looked down into her eyes.

'They say that I am hard, bloodthirsty, and un-feeling,' he said in tones that were almost of complaint. 'But I am not proof against so much appeal. Ignacio must find him a bride in Spain; and if he is wise and would taste the sweets of life, he will see to it that he finds him a willing one.

'As for you two, Cesare Borgia shall stand your friend. He owes you no less. I will be godfather to your nuptials. Thus shall the blame and conse-quences rest on me. Paola Sforza di Santafior is dead, men think. We will leave them thinking it. Filippo must know the truth. But you can trust me to make your brother take a reasonable view of what has come to pass. After all, there may be a disparity in your ranks. But it is purely adventitious, for noble though you may be, Madonna Paola, you are wed-ding one who seems no less noble at heart, whatever the parts he may have played in life.' He smiled in-scrutably, as he added: 'I have in mind that you once sought service with me, Messer Biancomonte, and if a martial life allures you still, I'll make you lord of something better far than Biancomonte.'

I thanked him, and Madonna joined me in that
expression of gratitude — an expression that fell
very short of all that was in our hearts. But touching
that offer of his that I should follow his fortunes, I
begged him not to insist.

'The possession of Biancomonte has from my
cradle been the goal of all my hopes. It is patrimony
enough for me, and there, with Madonna Paola, I'll
take a long farewell of ambition, which is but the seed
of discontent.'

'Why, as you will,' he sighed. And then, before
more could be said, there came from the adjoining
room a piercing scream.

Cesare raised his head, and his lips parted in the
faintest vestige of a smile.

'They are exacting the truth from the Governor of
Cesena,' said he. 'I think, Madonna, that we had
better move a little farther off. Ramiro's voice makes
indifferent music for a lady's ear.'

She was white as death at the horrid noise and all
the things of which it may have reminded her, and
so we passed from the ante-chamber and sought the
more distant places of the castle.

Here let me pause. We were married on the morrow which was Christmas Eve, and in the grey dawn
of the Christmas morning we set out for Biancomonte
with the escort which Cesare Borgia placed at our
disposal.

As we rode out from the Citadel of Cesena, we saw
the last of Ramiro del' Orca. Beyond the gates, in
the centre of the public square, a block stood planted
in the snow. On the side nearer the castle there was a
dark mass over which a rich mantle had been thrown;

it was of purple colour, and in the uncertain light it was not easy to tell where the cloak ended, and the stain that embrued the snow began. On the other side of the block a decapitated head stood mounted on an upright pike, and the sightless eyes of Ramiro del' Orca looked from his grinning face upon the town of Cesena, which he so had wantonly misruled.

Madonna shuddered and turned her head aside as we rode past that dread emblem of the Borgia justice.

To efface from her mind the memory of such a thing on such a day, I talked to her, as we cantered out into the country, of the life to come, of the mother that waited to welcome us, and of the glad tidings with which we were to rejoice her on that Christmas Day.

There is no moral to my story. I may not end with one of those graceful admonitions beloved of Messer Boccaccio to whom in my jester's days I owed so much. Not mine is it to say with him, 'Wherefore, gentle ladies' — or 'noble sirs — beware of this, avoid that other thing.'

Mine is a plain tale, written in the belief that some account of those old happenings that befell me may offer you some measure of entertainment, and written, too, in the support of certain truths which my contemporaries have been shamefully inclined and simoniacally induced to suppress. Many chroniclers set forth how the Lord Vitellozzo Vitelli and his associates were barbarously strangled by Cesare's orders at Sinigaglia, and wilfully — for I cannot believe that it results from ignorance — are they silent touching the reason, leaving you to imagine that it was done in obedience to a ruthlessness of character beyond parallel, so that you may come to consider Cesare Borgia as black as they were paid to paint him.

To confute them do I set down these facts of which my knowledge cannot be called in question, and also that you may know the true story of Paola di Santafior — and more particularly that part of it which lies beyond the death she did not die!

The sun of that Christmas Day was setting as we drew near to Biancomonte and the humble dwelling of my old mother. We fell into talk of her once more.

Suddenly Paola turned in her saddle to confront me.

'Tell me, Lord of Biancomonte, will she love me a little, think you?' she asked, to plague me.

'Who would not love you, Lady of Biancomonte?' counter-questioned I.

THE END